PICTURE PERFECT

LIMELIGHT #2

ELISABETH
GRACE

Cover design and photo by Regina Wamba of www.MaeIDesign.com
Interior formatting by Author E.M.S.

Published by Elisabeth Grace
Elisabeth-Grace.com

ISBN-13: 978-0-9921068-3-6

Printed in the United States of America.

PICTURE
PERFECT

LIMELIGHT #2

Dedicated to my mother who taught me hard work, responsibility, and that a mother would go to any length to help her children.

prologue

I stared at his face, knowing with every fiber of my being that I had to leave him. I didn't know him anymore. I didn't recognize the person he'd become. Was it my fault? Had I brought something out in him that had caused Vic to turn into this manipulative, jealous monster?

"Did you hear what I said, Skye?" Vic's voice was low and full of venom.

The hairs on my arms stood on end. "I already told you I can't go with you. My dad needs my help that night."

"These are important clients. I need you by my side at dinner. How is it going to look if you don't show up after I told them you'd be there?"

Vic was all about proving himself in his father's investment firm these days. While I admired that, I was so sick of fighting with him—all the freaking time. His demands and jealousy were too much for me to handle. He wasn't the guy I started dating seven months ago.

I looked around the living room of his small condo, feeling like the walls were closing in. "I can't do this anymore." I stood up from the couch and grabbed my purse off the end table. Vic shot to his feet and stood in front of me, his dark eyebrows drawn together, a crease up the center of his forehead. "What is that supposed to mean?" he asked between clenched teeth.

"I'm done arguing with you. This..." I said, motioning between us with my hand, "is over." Having a dad in politics meant I'd been raised to act like a lady and always keep my cool. That was difficult to do, however, with months of jealous accusations and manipulations from him running through my head.

"This is only over when I say it's over, Skye, and not before."

"You're impossible!" I screamed, whirling around to head for the door.

"You're not going anywhere!" he yelled from behind me. I'd just reached the door when his hand fastened onto my upper arm. He spun me around and pushed me against the door. "Who the hell is he?"

"What are you talking about?" I tried unsuccessfully to pry his hand off my arm.

"Don't lie, Skye. It does nothing but make you look like more of a whore than you already are."

His words were like a bucket of ice water in the face. Adrenaline exploded from my chest and flowed into my limbs. I yanked my arm from his grip, bashing my elbow against the door in the process. But I felt no pain in the moment—only anger.

"You jerk! You've been accusing me of sleeping around for months and you know I'm not. You're being irrational and I'm sick of it! I can't take it anymore. It's too much. I'm done! I'm done!"

Rage contorted his face and he grabbed both of my arms and shook me violently. Pain seared where his fingertips dug into my skin and warm liquid trickled down the back of my neck where my head hit the back of the door.

I was stunned. And scared. I'd never had a man lay his hands on me in anger before. I didn't know what to do. My face must have displayed my shock because suddenly his hands dropped to his sides.

"Skye...I'm so sorry. I didn't mean to—"

"I don't ever want to see you again. Don't call me. Don't text me. Ever." I turned, opened the door, and ran down the hall to the elevator with tears streaming down my face. He didn't follow me. Thank God. I don't know what I would have done.

When I reached my car in the parking lot, I cried more tears. Tears because I didn't know where things had gone wrong. Tears because I'd let things get so bad between us that it'd landed us here. I felt somehow at fault for the entire drama that had unfolded, even though deep inside I knew I'd done nothing wrong. I grabbed some tissues from my console and pressed them to the cut at the back of my head. It was only a small cut by the feel of it, but you wouldn't know by the amount of bright red liquid on the tissues.

I started the car and began to make my way back home. The impulse to call my best friend, Ellie, was immense, but I couldn't tell her...or anyone else, for that matter. It was too embarrassing. Plus, Ellie had never been a fan of Vic, and I couldn't handle an 'I told you so' right now. I was ashamed that she'd been able to see something in him that I hadn't.

When I pulled into the driveway of my parents' formidable home, I heard my phone alert me to a text message. I grabbed the cell from my purse and saw that it was from Vic. Not caring what he had to say, I deleted the text without looking at it and headed into the house for what was sure to be a long, sleepless night.

chapter one

Skye

Katie tossed some articles of clothing beside where I lay on my parents' couch. "Get your ass up."

I sat up and held out the clothes to inspect them. It looked like a pair of pleather capris and some kind of halter top. "What is this?" I asked.

"This is what you're wearing out tonight."

"I'm not going out tonight."

"Oh yes, you most certainly are. You've been sulking around and feeling sorry for yourself for too long. It's been a month, Skye. It's time to get back in the game. Besides, you have a job offer and a new apartment to celebrate."

A month of first dealing with and now avoiding Vic's incessant phone calls. *No thank you.* "I don't want in the game."

"It doesn't matter whether you do or don't. You need a night of drowning your sorrows, complete with some male attention to get you out of this slump. That asshat you got rid of isn't worth moping around for. Now get up. Let's go."

She grabbed my wrist and tried pulling me up off the

couch but I resisted. "I don't want to go out. I just want to stay in."

Katie let go of my hand and crossed her arms over her chest, which wasn't an easy feat because Katie was well-endowed in that department. When she just stared at me and began tapping her foot, I knew there was no use arguing with her.

Begrudgingly, I got up off the couch and headed to my room to get ready for a night of fun. *Right.*

A few hours later I was in a crush of people on the dance floor at Fahrenheit on Granby Street in downtown Norfolk, wearing faux-leather capris and a white halter top that bared a strip of my belly. My outfit didn't match my mood but Katie had insisted, and one thing I knew about Katie was that she didn't back down. She'd been steadily feeding me drinks all night so I was grinding to the beat of the pulsing music, feeling happier and sexier than I had in weeks.

I leaned in to Katie who was dancing across from me and shouted over the music. "Thanks for forcing me out tonight. You were right...I needed this."

"Told you! You just needed to get out and have some fun."

"Yeah, I suppose so."

Katie gripped both my shoulders. "It's not all bad. You move into your apartment next week, you're starting a new job, and you're finally free of that dickhead."

I gave her a small smile. She was right—about all of it. I also realized that I hadn't been mourning the loss of Vic, so much as the loss of what I *thought* we had. In no way was I missing his endless interrogations or jealous rages. Not one bit.

Katie removed her hands and went back to dancing. A prickling sensation moved up my spine and I suddenly had the sensation of being watched. When I spotted *who* was looking at me, I sucked in a breath. Leaning against the bar with a beer dangling in one hand was a lean muscled guy with deep brown eyes. He wore a tailored black shirt that hugged his biceps, and his brown hair was kept short at the sides and longer on the top. He had a grin on his face as he looked at me, but it belied the intensity in his eyes.

I looked away quickly when I felt a flush heat my skin. I wasn't embarrassed; the alcohol had long ago taken away my inhibitions, but the way he looked at me had me more than a little turned on. Even though we hadn't spoken a word, I could tell from his expression that he was undressing me with his eyes and thinking of all the ways he could take me. I'd by lying if I said I didn't like the feeling.

I knocked back the rest of my drink and tossed the plastic cup on the ground, something a sober me never would have done. With my hands raised in the air, I started grinding my hips to the beat. The music and the crowd pulsed around me until I felt so in tune with it I just closed my eyes and escaped. I was living in the moment, young and free. It'd been too long since I'd felt this way.

I would give this guy a show he'd never forget. I ran my hands up and down my body and closed my eyes, picturing myself and the stranger alone, imagining it was his hands exploring me. When the DJ changed up the set, I opened my eyes to see Katie flirting with some guy across from me and my mystery man gone. I felt more disappointed than I should have. I guess he wasn't enjoying the show. I didn't want to interrupt Katie so I motioned to her that I was going to get another drink and headed to the bar.

While I stood there trying to get the bartender's attention, a very drunk, very obnoxious guy came up next to me. He reeked of beer and swayed on his feet beside me. I tried to ignore him but that proved impossible.

"Hey, sweet tits. What do you say we get out of here?"

Seriously? Normally my training to never cause a scene in public would have kicked in, but the alcohol must have stolen that, too. "Does that approach ever actually work?" I asked him.

"Ah, come on. Give a guy a break. You can't tell me you're not trying to attract an audience dressed like that. I'm just sayin'...job well done." I rolled my eyes and turned to face the bar again. "You don't have to be a bitch about it."

I ignored his jab but a minute later when we still hadn't been served, motor mouth spoke back up. "Hows about we do a shot together and then see if yah wanna get a piece of thiiss," he slurred.

I looked back to him again. "Never. Going. To. Happen."

"You fucking—"

"I believe the lady said she wasn't interested, buddy. Why don't you move on your way?" The voice had come from behind me, and without looking I knew it was my mystery man. The voice was low, smooth, authoritative, and made my nipples pebble—not a good thing when you had a shirt on that didn't allow you to wear a bra.

I turned to get a close-up look at the guy who could elicit such a reaction in me with just a few words. He was even better looking than my rum-filled brain had registered from across the bar. I opened my mouth to speak but stopped short when I felt something warm slither down the front of my chest and on to my exposed belly. Mystery man's face contorted in horror and he snapped his head in the direction of my unwanted admirer. I looked over in time to see the drunk guy wiping something off his chin with the back of his sleeve.

That was when the stench of vomit hit me. Oh my fucking God, the guy had just puked on me! My own gag reflex kicked in and I pushed past the two guys to run for the bathroom. I managed to keep the contents of my own stomach down and burst through the door. I raced over to the sink, kicking my shoes off when I got there. There were a couple of girls in the bathroom, but when they saw the reason for my panic, they fled. I couldn't blame them.

As I pushed my bottoms off, I could have kissed Katie for giving me pleather pants to wear. None of the vomit had seeped through so I'd easily be able to rinse them clean. My shirt was a different story. I untied the strings around my neck and shimmied it down my body, uncaring that I stood in a public bathroom with just a pair of panties on. Who gave a shit when you were covered in a stranger's vomit? *Priorities, people.*

I ran the water as hot as I could get it and shoved my clothes under the tap. I wet some paper towels to wipe the remnants off my chest and belly, soaped myself up, and then thoroughly rinsed. When I was satisfied there was no more vomit on either me or my outfit, I pulled the wet pants back up my legs—not an easy feat, let me tell you. I don't care what size you are, it's like trying to get ten pounds of sausage in a five-pound sack. I wrung out my shirt and then pulled it up to put it back in place. I may have given Katie props for picking the impenetrable pleather pants, but now I was cursing her for the white shirt. My breasts and my puckered nipples were clearly visible. It was definitely time to bail. I'd have to cross my arms over my chest while I went in search of Katie.

I opened the door and peeked out into the hallway. Not seeing anyone, I stepped out, whirling when I heard a voice behind me. "You okay?" Mystery man stepped forward from the end of the darkened hallway. I quickly crossed my hands over my chest and stepped out of the light and into the darkness with him. "When you didn't come right back out, I wanted to make sure you were okay. I told the bouncer what happened. That guy's already eating concrete." He walked toward me, stopping only inches away.

"You may want to back up. I've rinsed myself off head to toe, but I can't guarantee that I don't still smell like puke."

"I'll take my chances," he said. He gently took each of my wrists and unfolded them from my chest, leaving my arms hanging at my sides. His eyes widened and his nostrils flared as he took in the see-through shirt clinging to me. He stood at least a head taller than me and the scent of his expensive cologne further lulled me under his spell.

"What are you doing?" I almost whispered.

"Enjoying the view." He raised a hand and lightly thumbed one of my nipples through the thin fabric. As his thumb flicked back and forth, I struggled not to let out a moan. Then he slowly brought his hand up across my collarbone and slid it underneath my hair to cup the back of my neck. Our eyes caught for moment before he crushed his lips to mine.

I lost myself then. I wasn't thinking about the fact that I didn't know his name, that ten minutes earlier I'd been covered in vomit, or the fact that I probably looked like a drowned rat. His hands roamed my back, cupping my ass and squeezing tight. I could feel him hard against my belly and I rubbed myself wantonly against him. It fueled my fire even more and I moved my hand in between us and gripped his erection, rubbing up and down.

In the midst of our lust-induced make-out session someone walked out of the men's bathroom door. "Oh, um...sorry." Whoever it was left but I pulled away. I needed to think and I couldn't do that with his hands all over my body. I could barely do it with just his eyes on me.

What the hell was I doing? "I'm sorry. I have to go."

His hand settled on my wrist as I moved to leave. "No, wait."

"This isn't me. I don't do this kind of thing."

He adjusted himself and I swore I wouldn't look down, but it was like there was a tractor beam and it was futile to resist. *Damn.* Judging from that bulge, I was missing out. "Don't run off. You're not seriously going to leave me like *this,* are you?" He motioned in the direction of his junk.

"I didn't mean to lead you on...I just..." I didn't know what else to say. I know I probably seemed like the biggest tease in the world. Instead of trying to come up with an excuse, I ran down the hallway with my hands over my chest. I'd rather risk embarrassment than be confined in a small space with that man for another second.

I found Katie on the periphery of the dance floor—thank

God—and one look at me told her we had to be going. I ended up telling her what happened with the vomit but left out the part about the hottie. If she knew I'd never hear the end of it, and I didn't want any reminders of this night. As far as I was concerned, it was a one-off...I'd had a little too much to drink and acted completely out of character. It would *not* happen again.

Landon

I waited until my blue balls had subsided a bit before I made my way back down the hall and into the crush of people. No sense alerting everyone to the very agitated state that the hot blonde had left me in. And somehow I had a feeling that walking funny around a rock hard erection would have done just that.

I found an empty spot at the bar and claimed my piece of real estate. Thankfully, the female bartender who had been eye-fucking and flirting with me all night, headed right over.

"Hey, handsome. What can I get ya?" The way she leaned on the bar in front of me and pressed her tits together didn't escape my notice. On any other Saturday night, I'd be all over lining her up to accompany me home, but it just pissed me off tonight. Why? Because those weren't the set of tits I was interested in at the moment.

"Shot of whiskey." I didn't want to encourage her so I didn't turn on the usual charm.

"Make it two."

"Comin' right up, boys." She flashed me a sultry smile and then turned and sashayed her way to the other side of the bar to grab our drinks.

I turned to see that my friend Scottie had squeezed in beside me. His sandy brown hair was a little lopsided and his shirt was askew, sure signs that he'd either been on the dance floor or all up on some chick. Something I should be doing right now, but for some reason, I couldn't get that damn blonde out of my head.

"How's your night going?" I asked him.

"Oh man. You should see this chick I've been grinding with on the dance floor. Killer body."

"So, why aren't you out there then?" Even I could hear the irritation in my voice over the loud music.

"What's your problem?"

"Don't have one."

The bartender returned with our shots and I threw a bill down on the bar, not paying her any attention. I grabbed the shot glass and poured the liquid down my throat, liking the burning feeling the trail of it left behind. I slammed the glass down on the bar and Scottie did the same.

"Saw you talking to that chick. Nice piece of ass. How'd that go?"

"It didn't."

Scottie smacked me on the back a couple of times and started laughing. "Holy shit! Did the 'Man of Steele' finally get shot down?" He continued laughing until I nudged him in the ribs with my elbow. "Fuck, man. That hurt!" Okay, maybe it was more than a nudge.

"Why don't you go back out onto the dance floor and see if—for once in your life—you can close the deal."

"Damn. She really got your panties in a bunch, didn't she?" Without waiting for an answer, he pushed off the bar and disappeared into the mass of people.

What pissed me off the most was that he was right. Why was I so bothered, besides the fact that she'd left me in this state? What was it about her that made her different?

Whatever. I was sure I'd forget all about her by the time I got up tomorrow. I just wasn't used to being shot down. Nobody likes losing. That's all this was.

Throughout the remainder of the night, I ran this mantra

through my head, willing myself to believe it and it seemed to have worked. That is, until I woke the next morning with my head throbbing, and the first image that came to mind was a set of soul-piercing blue eyes.

chapter two

Skye

I sat at my desk, rearranging everything for probably the tenth time that morning. Mr. Steele would be in any minute and I was nervous to meet my new boss. I wanted everything to be perfect.

I'd finally gotten an offer for a good job and had started a few weeks ago as the personal assistant to Landon Steele, the owner of an up-and-coming PR firm. Mr. Steele had grown his company and its stellar reputation quickly, especially for someone only a few years older than me, and had been named one of Virginia's "entrepreneurs to watch" a couple of years back.

Of course, I only knew what I had heard about him at this point because Mr. Steele had been away on business my first week on the job and then on vacation the second. Regardless, I'd already grown comfortable in the office and with my co-workers. There weren't many of us. Between the account executives, the media relations manager, the event coordinator, and the various administrative personnel, there were fifteen in total.

The office as a whole had a young, contemporary vibe, complete with sleek furniture for clients in the reception area, dark wood desks, and private offices for the account executives. Each office was enclosed in glass so you could see in them, but I'd learned within my first few days that there were switches that did this cool James Bond thing to make the glass opaque for privacy.

The phone on my desk rang, jarring me from my thoughts. I lifted the receiver and in my most professional voice said, "Mr. Steele's office, this is Skye speaking. How may I help you?"

"Skye, this is Mr. Steele."

"Hello, Mr. Steele. How are you this morning?"

"Listen, I have an appointment with a client in an hour, but I have a problem I have to deal with first. If I'm late, entertain him until I get there."

"Yes, sir."

"Good. Oh, and welcome aboard."

"Thank you, Mr. Steele." I was talking to myself because he'd already hung up. As I put the phone down, Marci walked up to my desk. She'd been the one to hire me and was probably in her mid-forties with short red hair and a penchant for bright colors.

"Morning, Skye. Is Mr. Steele in yet?" she asked.

"That was him on the phone. Apparently, he's running late and won't be in for a bit. He asked me to entertain his client if he arrived first."

"Late? That doesn't sound like him at all. I wonder what came up."

"He didn't say...Marci, can I ask you a question?"

"Of course."

Marci had shown me the ropes and I felt comfortable asking her what I wanted to know. "Is he always so gruff?"

"He was gruff?"

"A little. Maybe he was just in a hurry or something."

"Hmm...that's not how I would describe him. He's direct,

that's for sure, and you certainly know what he expects of you," she said, smirking. "We have a little joke around the office about how his last name is the best descriptor of him."

"How so?"

"Because the man has nerves of steel. Wait until you see him going in to pitch for a client. No fear. No nerves. Solid steel, I tell you."

"I guess that's how he's managed to do so well for himself."

"Definitely. Skye, I know you're nervous but you really don't need to be. You've done great since you started and Mr. Steele is a wonderful man to work for. You'll be fine."

"Thanks, Marci. I needed that." She came around the desk and gave me a hug. I really liked her. She was like the mother hen of the office and our conversation had put me at ease.

"Well, I'll leave you to it. Could you let him know I need to talk to him after his meeting?"

"Sure thing."

A while later, the receptionist at the front desk let me know the client had arrived. Douglas Merrick was the owner of a chain of restaurants throughout the state. Because he was already a client, the meeting today was to review the previous year and discuss the PR strategy moving forward.

When I arrived in the reception area, I saw he was a man of about sixty with a round belly and grey hair—what little was left. I introduced myself and shook his hand. If there was one area I had experience, it was schmoozing. You didn't grow up with a politician for a dad and not learn *that* fine art.

"Pleasure to meet you, Skye."

"The pleasure is all mine. Mr. Steele was detained but will join us shortly. Can I offer you a beverage while you wait?"

"I'm all right. I just finished my morning coffee." He patted his oversized belly and smiled.

"Well, then why don't you follow me and I'll show you to Mr. Steele's office. We can wait for him there."

"Terrific."

When I had Mr. Merrick situated comfortably, I figured the best way to pass the time would be to stick around and talk to him. I'd done my research. I knew Merrick had built his empire from the ground up, starting forty years ago.

"You must be very proud of the business you've been able to build since that first one on Main Street."

He chuckled. "How do you know about that? I'd bet my last dollar you weren't even born then."

"I've made it a point to know all of our clients and their businesses."

"It's been a lot of hard work, but it's been worth it. I wouldn't change a thing."

We continued to chat for a while before I heard someone outside the office call out a 'good morning' to Mr. Steele. I thought I'd done a good job keeping Mr. Merrick occupied, but I was relieved he was here to take over. I couldn't wait to meet him and see what he thought of the job I'd done here today.

Landon

My first day back in the office was *not* going according to plan. Getting stuck in the pouring rain with car troubles was certainly not on the agenda for day. I'd found someone to give me a boost easily enough, but I'd been soaked through and had to go back to my condo to change, making me late for my meeting.

I didn't do late. Or at least I hadn't before today.

I took the elevator up to the top floor of the office tower where Steele & Associates was located and entered through the reception area. I briefly acknowledged my employees as I made my way to my office. Hopefully, the new girl they'd hired in my absence had been able to handle the first assignment I'd given her. As I drew closer, I heard laughter coming from my office. Well, it *sounded* like everyone was enjoying themselves.

I stepped through the doorway and stopped short. Standing in front of me in a clinging V-neck pink dress was the girl I'd made out with at Fahrenheit. Un-fucking-believable.

I tried not to appreciate her long blond hair, delicate features, or her crystal blue eyes, but they were nearly impossible not to notice—at least if you were male, heterosexual, and had a pulse.

Both occupants of my office looked over at me. The charming smile that had lit her face moments earlier was wiped clean. Her eyes widened in panic as realization dawned. Well, at least she remembered me. It would have been a massive blow to my ego if she hadn't.

"Mr. Steele." She didn't say it like it was a question, even though this was our first official meeting.

I schooled my expression and nodded in her direction. Then, without missing a beat, I smiled at Merrick and moved closer to shake his hand.

"Mr. Merrick. How have you been?"

He stood to accept my greeting with a large grin. "Things are well, thank you. I was just getting to know your new assistant here. I think you made a fine choice in acquiring this one, Landon."

I quickly glanced her way to see that she was still looking at me like I had two heads, her mouth agape. "We aim to please," I said and patted him on the back. As I made my way to my chair, I said, "Skye, why don't you hit the privacy switch and close the door behind you."

"Yes, sir." Like a good assistant, she did as I instructed. Like a good boss, I tried not to let my gaze linger too long on the curve of her ass in that dress she was wearing. No such luck.

The meeting went as expected and I secured Merrick's

business for another year. The man loved to talk and I was happy to listen, but I couldn't keep my thoughts from drifting back to Skye. What were the chances that she'd ended up being the one working for me? Karma was definitely a bitch with a fucked-up sense of humor.

One thing was for sure, I needed to get my attraction to her in check. She may be blond, innocent-looking, and stacked, but she was my assistant. I never dipped my pen in the company ink.

Mr. Merrick and I passed by her desk as I escorted him to the elevators. She must have made an impression on him because he stopped to say his goodbyes before we continued toward the reception area. Hell, she'd made an impression on me when we'd first met, but his reaction didn't include sporting a rock-hard erection.

I was making my way back through the office when Marci stopped me.

"Mr. Steele, have you had a chance to meet your new assistant yet?"

"Briefly."

"Good. I wanted to let you know she's done exceptionally well getting up to speed on everything while you were away. I think she's going to do nicely."

"That remains to be seen. Let's take it one day at a time now that I'm back."

"Of course, sir."

I'd been harsher than I normally was with Marci. The irritation I felt from the night in the bar was coming back, and I couldn't seem to help it. Marci had been with me from the start though and didn't deserve such treatment.

I placed my hand on her elbow. "Marci, thanks for training Skye while I was away. I'm sure you've done all you can to make sure she's prepared to do her job."

She smiled and nodded, seemingly satisfied, and returned to her desk.

I made my way back toward my office and found Skye at

her desk. We obviously had to discuss our prior meeting since it was the proverbial elephant in the room—only this elephant was bright pink and waving a neon flashing sign that said "AWKWARD." Thankfully, Skye saved me the trouble of having to figure out how to bring it up.

She stood from her chair as she saw me approach. "Mr. Steele, I have to say that I'm sorry about what happened the night we met. It's not like me to do something like that and I panicked, so I left you there and didn't come back to explain. I feel terrible." Having her apologize profusely for her dismissal of me only irked me even more.

"Are you finished?"

She looked momentarily regretful, then squared her shoulders and put a serene smile on her face. She didn't speak but nodded.

"Obviously, neither one of us had any idea who the other one was that night. Let's move past it and be the professionals I'm sure we both are."

"I'd like that," she said, looking relieved.

Did she really think it would be that easy? Probably. She wasn't the one that was going to have to stare at her tits every day knowing what the weight of them felt like in my hands.

"Great. I need to respond to my e-mails now, but after lunch I'd like you to bring me up to speed on what I missed while I was on vacation."

"Yes, sir. I'll make sure I have everything together."

"You do that." I walked into my office, closing the door and leaving the privacy film in place.

I didn't know what it was about this girl, but she got under my skin as easily as a scalpel would. What I did know was that I was overcompensating by being brusque with her, when everything in me was screaming to embrace her so I could feel her soft curves against my body again. Damn it. That train of thought led to me having to adjust myself.

I just didn't understand. It wasn't like I had problems getting women in my bed—I had my share of willing bed partners. And the odd time a woman wasn't interested? I just moved on and never gave her another thought. What was it about this one particular girl that had my shit in such a knot?

Whatever it was, she wasn't getting any leeway or perks from me at the office. I needed to see what Skye was made of—besides a rockin' body and kissable lips.

chapter three

Skye

I chose to eat lunch at my desk so I'd have everything ready for Mr. Steele when he got back.

When I'd looked up at the doorway earlier and recognized him, my stomach had dropped like it was a fifty-pound brick. Ditching a guy with blue balls was never a good way to start any relationship, but *especially* not if that guy was your boss.

Besides the whole stomach-dropping sensation, the minute I'd seen him my body went on high alert. And why wouldn't it? He was tall, lean, muscled, and had gorgeous, deep brown eyes. His three-piece suit fit him perfectly and did funny things to my insides. Everything about him screamed power and success. You didn't find that combination often in men my age. I wasn't sure, but I didn't think you found that often in men, period.

I needed to put all that aside though. I had no desire to be dating anyone, and I certainly would *not* be dating the boss. This was my first real job and I wasn't going to screw it up. In fact, I was going to excel at it.

As I finished up the last of my notes, he walked past my

desk and without stopping, said, "In my office. Two minutes."

I didn't bother replying since he was already in his own office by the time he had finished speaking. Since I'd started working here, all my co-workers had gushed about how great Mr. Steele was to work for. That he was fair, worked hard and played hard, but was generally easy to approach. In the few interactions we'd already had, I hadn't got that vibe from him—not even close.

Gathering my papers, I headed for his office and knocked on the open door. He didn't bother glancing up from his computer when he commanded me to "sit." Because he didn't say, I wasn't sure if I should close the door and hit the privacy switch. I opted not to and took a seat across from his wide desk, sinking into the black leather chair with chrome arm rests.

His deep brown eyes scrutinized me for a moment. I couldn't tell what he was thinking, since the expression on his face didn't change. After what felt like a million seconds strung together, he finally spoke, still with an unreadable look on his face.

"Before you bring me up to speed on what I missed, I want to make something perfectly clear." *This* didn't sound good at all. "I know you're new. Marci told me this is your first real job out of college, but there's a lot of responsibility that goes along with this position." I nodded confidently, but inside I feared that I was losing this job before it had really begun. "I need to be able to rely on you. I'm gearing up to establish a second office on the West Coast so I can start up an entertainment division of the firm. It'll mean some travel, long hours, and going above and beyond. I expect you to be my right hand, anticipating my needs before I do." He paused for what seemed like dramatic effect. "Is that something you think you can handle?"

I pushed out of mind whether or not his *needs* would ever extend into the bedroom. "You can count on me, Mr. Steele."

"We'll see about that. Now, what do I need to know?"

"Maureen Rigley will be in first thing Thursday morning."

He sighed and I looked up from my notes. His eyebrows were wrinkled as he continued to look at his computer. Obviously not a fan of Ms. Rigley. "What's the purpose of the meeting?"

"She didn't say. She called and asked to meet with you at your first available appointment so I scheduled her in."

His gaze left the screen and fixed on me. "If someone requests an appointment with me, it's your job to know why. How else am I supposed to be prepared for whatever concerns the client may have?"

My face heated in embarrassment. "I'm sorry. I won't make the mistake again."

"Clients generally don't ask to meet with me when they're happy," he said, his voice firm and unsympathetic. I nodded in response. "Now, what else? Hopefully you're not going to tell me I'm going in blind to *another* meeting this week."

We went through everything else he needed to know for the next twenty minutes, and although I was able to answer the rest of his questions, I wasn't feeling like I'd made a very good first impression. Well, second actually. When he finally dismissed me, I walked toward the door, eager to get out from under the microscope that was Landon Steele.

"Skye." The way he said my name stopped me in my tracks. It wasn't as dictatorial as it had been before. It was low, more guttural, and if I didn't know better, I would have thought it was full of lust. It sent a chill through my body, and I silently thanked the Lord that I'd worn a thick bra so he wouldn't notice my nipples pebbling at the sound of his voice. I turned to face him.

"Mr. Steele?" I said, a little too breathy for my liking.

Those intense eyes had me in their tractor beam and I couldn't look away. Jeez, I couldn't even blink. He broke eye contact first and looked back at his computer screen, the cold mask once again returning to his face. "Pull everything on Ms. Rigley's account. See if you notice anything out of the ordinary. I want to at least *try* to be prepared for our meeting on Thursday."

Ice entered my veins and just as fast as I'd gotten hot for him, I cooled back down. "Yes, sir."

"Close my door and flick the privacy switch on your way out."

I did as he asked and plopped into the chair at my own desk. All right, I'd made a small mistake by not asking why Ms. Rigley had wanted a meeting, but I was new and he didn't need to keep rubbing salt in the wound. I was a quick learner and it wouldn't happen again.

Hopefully, he was just overwhelmed after being out of the office for a couple of weeks. By the sound of it, we were going to be working closely together. I could only hope his attitude toward me would improve as time went on and he'd see I was capable of doing this job.

Landon

God, she had a great ass. The minute she'd gotten up from her chair to leave my office it was all I could focus on. That damn dress she was wearing showcased it perfectly...tight, high, and firm. The only question in my mind was whether she looked better from the front or the back, which wasn't a question I should be considering at all.

This girl was an itch I was dying to scratch. I was an expert at controlling my thoughts...it was how I'd built this business into what it was. The ability to bite my tongue when a client went spouting off had been an asset on more than a few occasions. But I needed to get my head on straight. I wasn't going to go there. Ever. She was my assistant and based on what I'd seen today, maybe not a very good one. Plus, the last thing I needed was a complication at work.

I had an upcoming presentation at a PR conference on the

West Coast, followed by a meeting with Calder Fox. The former child star-turned-movie star had run into some trouble lately. A year ago he'd been involved in a fatal car accident and a friend of his had died. Since then, there had been one salacious tabloid story after another, eventually landing him in rehab. If I could get the undoubtedly entitled punk kid as a client, it'd be my ticket into the entertainment industry. I'd finally be able to open up an office in California like I'd originally planned, had I not been so concerned about my mom that I wanted to stick around town.

Basically, I didn't need any distractions right now, and the fresh-faced new assistant whose look said high class while her body screamed 'fuck me, Mr. Steele' was definitely a distraction. What I did need was to get Skye out of my mind so I could concentrate on my damn job. I wasn't sure what it was going to take to do that.

The afternoon went by quickly as I caught up on everything I'd missed. Skye had drifted into my thoughts momentarily a few times, but I'd been successful at pushing her back out.

Before I knew it though, she was poking her gorgeous head in my office. "If that's everything for today, Mr. Steele, I'm going to be on my way."

I looked at the clock on my computer screen and saw that it was indeed quitting time—for some. I'd be here for hours yet, preparing for the rest of my week. "Have a good night."

"Same to you. See you tomorrow."

A few minutes later, Marci came in and plunked herself down in the chair on the opposite side of my desk.

"So, what did you think of Skye?" she asked.

Immediately, 'she's hot as fuck and all I could think of all day was bending her over my desk and shoving into her from behind' sprung to mind, but I didn't think Marci would want to hear that.

"I'm not sure yet," I responded instead, leaning back in my chair. Marci, who was quite a bit older than me, had been at the company from the start. Over the years we'd developed a friendship, and I often got the impression that she thought of me like a son. "I know it's her first job out of college, but what kind of other experience did she have? What's her background?"

"Well, to tell you the truth, her best experience didn't come from her schooling or any past employer but from her upbringing."

"How so?"

"She grew up in a political family. Her father's been involved in politics her entire life."

"Who's her father?" I asked.

"Mayor Summers."

I smacked my hand against the top of the desk. "I thought she looked familiar."

"I'm sure you've probably seen her in the paper with her dad. She knows better than anyone the importance of perception versus reality when it comes to the public."

"She probably also grew up with a silver spoon in her mouth and hasn't worked a day in her life."

Marci's lips puckered and she tipped her head, looking at me above the reading glasses she'd pushed down to the bridge of her nose. "Aren't you being a little hard on her? She hasn't been here that long and you've only just met her."

"She'd better be prepared to work, that's all I know. Things are only going to get busier and more demanding from here. Especially if I land Calder Fox."

"She was the best candidate for the job. I'm telling you, she has what it takes. You'll see." She smirked at me and rose from her chair. "Give her a chance."

I didn't say anything as she left. I'd give Skye a chance but it burned my ass. Her sophisticated appearance might impress the clients, but I had no interest in catering to a spoiled rich girl, day in and day out. She may have had experience under the glare of the media, but hard work was likely a foreign concept to her. I'm sure she grew up in the perfect family and had led the picture perfect life—

My phone buzzed in my pocket and I pulled it out. Figures. It was my not-so-perfect father calling. "Hey."

"Son." I hated it when he reminded me that we were related.

"Why are you calling?"

"Can't a father just call his son to catch up?" I remained silent but my silence spoke volumes.

He sighed heavily and asked, "Are we ever going to get past this?"

"Now is not really the time. I just got back in the office after some time off and I've got a lot to catch up on."

"Sure, I understand," he said, clearing his throat. "Maybe give me a call next week if you can."

"Sure thing." I hung up with a heavy feeling in my gut. A part of me hated this estrangement since we used to be close. I even looked up to him, once upon a time. But seeing my mom completely destroyed by his actions had changed everything. Whenever I thought of it, anger heated my face and my heart thrummed a fast beat in my chest. I just couldn't let go of the anger—not after what he did.

I leaned my head back against my chair and closed my eyes. I didn't have time to think about this shit.

chapter four

Skye

After the day I'd had, all I really wanted to do was go back to my newly rented apartment, open a bottle of wine, and relax while watching some trashy reality TV. Instead, I had plans with my dad to have dinner. My mom was at one of her many charity meetings, and rather than eat alone in their large house, my dad had opted to make plans with me. At the time it sounded like a good idea, but I was emotionally drained from the day.

I could call and cancel but I didn't want to disappoint my dad and, truth be told, I think he missed not having me around the house all the time. Although I loved them and we were really close, I hadn't hesitated to rent a place once I'd gained full-time employment a few weeks back. It was nice to finally feel like an adult, taking care of myself rather than having mommy and daddy doing it for me.

I walked into Monastery Restaurant to meet my father and saw him at a table in the back. We'd been coming here since I was a kid. It was tiny by the standards of most restaurants—it probably only had ten tables plus the seating at the bar in the main room—but it was homey and I'd always enjoyed coming here.

My father stood as I approached the table. "Hi, kiddo," he said as he bent down and placed a kiss on my cheek. Then he held me away from him by my shoulders and smiled down at me with approval. "It seems you're still surviving living on your own. Sure you don't want to move back home?"

I rolled my eyes playfully. We'd been over this a thousand times. "Good to see you too, Daddy. And you know I'm not coming home."

"But I miss seeing my baby girl every day."

"I'm not you're baby anymore," I said half-jokingly as I took a seat at the table.

My dad followed suit and then placed his hand over the top of my own and squeezed. "You certainly aren't. You've grown into a fine young woman. I'm so proud of you."

"Thanks." I blushed and looked down. My father's praise had always made me a little uncomfortable. I'd never felt entirely deserving of it, but had spent my life trying to live up to it. Maybe that was just the way it was with dads and daughters.

The waiter approached the table and took our drink orders. I didn't recognize him so he must have been a new addition. I could tell he recognized my dad—I'd learned the signs years ago. The frequent glances at my dad as he took *my* order, the extra smiles and pleasantries sent his way. Our waiter excused himself and my dad's attention turned back to me.

"So, how's the new job going?"

Of course my dad had picked the one subject I wanted to avoid. "I finally met my boss today."

"That's right. So, what did you think of him?"

"I don't know. He seemed okay. A little standoffish but it's not a big deal." I shrugged, trying my best to feign nonchalance.

"Sure you don't want to come work for your ol' dad?"

"You know I don't want any handouts. I'll make this work. I think he just had a lot on his plate, it being his first day back and all. I'm sure things will improve."

"If he's giving you a hard time, I want to know about it."

"Dad, I know you mean well but I don't want you interfering. I'm twenty-one. I don't need my daddy fighting my battles for me."

He reached across the table and gave my hand a squeeze again. "I know that, angel. I want to help if I can though."

"Really, dad. I'm fine."

"Okay, consider the subject closed." He put his hands up in a placating gesture.

After years and years in politics, I knew it came naturally to for him to swoop in to try and save the day, but I didn't want his interference.

The waiter returned with our drinks, took our food orders, and left us alone again. My dad looked across the table at me and I saw excitement brewing in his eyes.

"Dad, I know that look...what's going on?"

"Baby girl, I have some big news." Always the politician, he paused for dramatic effect. "I'm running for Senate."

I leapt out of my chair to give him a hug. "Daddy, I'm so happy for you! Finally. You deserve this. You've worked so hard and helped so many people throughout your career."

"Your mother and I have discussed it and feel the timing is right. You're out on your own and starting to live your own life. If I'm successful, your mother and I will have to move to Richmond."

"There's no *if* dad. You're more than deserving. I'm so excited! What can I do to help?" I'd been helping my dad with his political aspirations for as long as I can remember. Sometimes that meant knocking on doors and handing out flyers, and other times it meant picking up the phone and calling my way through the local phone directory. What it always meant was exemplifying the epitome of a well-raised child, complete with the proper manners, responses, and interest level whenever we were out in public or entertaining one of my dad's campaign contributors.

"Well, for a start you and Vic can join me at the announcement party. It's next Friday evening."

My smile faltered. I'd managed to avoid telling my parents that Vic and I had broken up, because I didn't want to deal with the barrage of questions I knew were sure to follow. Even though I had plenty of practice at maintaining my composure when I was uncomfortable, my dad knew me better than that.

"What's wrong?" he immediately asked.

"Vic and I aren't seeing each other anymore."

"Why? What happened?"

My dad was a fan of Vic and was pleased when we started seeing each other. I wanted to believe that it had nothing to do with the fact that Vic's father had been a large contributor to his campaign for mayor, but I knew that was probably wishful thinking on my part.

"It wasn't working," I said simply.

"How long has this been the case?"

I blew out a breath. "A while now."

"Your mother and I wondered why he hadn't been around the house much, but you always said he was working. Why didn't you just tell us?"

"I know how much you guys liked him. I just didn't want to get into it." That was the truth...I didn't want to discuss the details of our breakup with anyone.

"Do you think things will change? Could you guys work it out?"

"No, dad. It's over." My dad had no idea how much things had deteriorated between Vic and me—nor would he ever.

"I hope this isn't going to affect things when I ask his dad for a donation for my Senate run." He seemed to say it more to himself than to me but the comment still stung. I told myself that if he knew how Vic had treated me, the contribution to his campaign wouldn't have mattered.

"One shouldn't affect the other," I said.

"You're right. And you'll be there, correct?"

"I wouldn't miss it for anything." I pushed the vision of the last argument I'd had with Vic from my head.

"That's my girl. I suppose I don't need to tell you what an important night this is. Most of the guests will be people who've supported me in the past, but I've invited some other up-and-comers in the city to attend, hoping to build some relationships and additional donations to the campaign. I need you to be at your most charming."

I didn't take offense. It was a speech I was familiar with.

"This isn't my first fundraising party, dad. I've been doing this practically my whole life."

"I know, sweetie. I don't know why I even bothered to say that. You're an old pro like your dad by now." I *was* an old pro, which was the exact reason I hadn't wanted to tell my Dad about what Vic had done. Now it was even more important that he not find out.

Between thinking about Vic, my dad's expectations, and my new boss, I was starting to get a headache.

Landon

I pressed the intercom button on my phone to buzz Skye's desk. "Did you get through those reports that I gave you?"

"Yes, sir. I was just about to bring them in to you."

Huh. I hadn't expected that. I'd given her enough work to last her at least until the end of the day, if not into tomorrow morning.

Skye walked through my office door looking the opposite of the gray November day outside. Her dark skirt and pale yellow blouse emphasized the natural highlights in her hair as it swung in the ponytail she'd styled it in. I swear, every time she wore her hair like that all I could think of was taking her doggy style and using it for leverage.

She set the files on my desk, snapping me out of my perverted daydream. "Here you go."

It'd been like this all week. No matter what challenge I threw at her, she had met it. She hadn't turned out to be anything like I expected. She was intelligent and hardworking, and she certainly hadn't been looking for any special treatment because of who her dad was. Hell, she'd never even mentioned who he was. Maybe Marci had been right about her after all.

"Thanks for this."

"You're welcome. Do you have a minute, Mr. Steele?"

"What is it?" I asked, my attention suddenly caught by an e-mail that had just come in from my father. What could he possibly want?

"I took the liberty of moving some of your meetings around next week. You were due at Langley's on Tuesday at ten and then at Highgate at three, so I switched them around. That way you won't have to leave so early in the morning to beat rush hour and then when you head over to Highgate, you'll be heading in the opposite direction of traffic."

"That was good thinking."

"Also...the brochures for the cruise company came in. The ship captain's name was misspelled and Danny delivered them to the client before anyone looked at them. They were pretty upset when they called, but I assured them we'd handle it. I called the printer and managed to talk them into doing another run at no additional charge."

She was good. The guy that ran that company was the cheapest son of a bitch I'd ever come across. "How'd you manage that?"

She shrugged. "I may have mentioned that I could put in a good word for him with my mom. She's on the board of a lot of charities and they always have a need for printed material."

"Well then. Good job."

"Did you need anything else while I'm here?"

Yes. You sprawled out naked on top of my desk. "No, that will be all."

"Okay then."

"Close the door on your way out. Please." I had the urge to rub one off now. This imagination of mine was on overtime whenever she was around. God, I felt like such a fucking pervert, lusting after my assistant.

She did as I asked, but instead of unzipping my drawers, I turned my attention back to the e-mail. The old man wanted to get together for dinner. Sorry, pops. I was going to be too busy gearing up for the conference to squeeze you into the schedule. Whether or not that was true, it sounded good and allowed me to practice the art of avoidance, which I'd gotten pretty good at where he was concerned.

I knew eventually I would have to face him, but I didn't have time to deal with his bullshit right now. I had an empire to build and a sweet little secretary to get out of my head—the top one *and* the bottom one.

chapter five

Skye

I left work with a bounce in my step. I finally felt like I'd made some headway with my boss. He wasn't as gruff as he'd been at the beginning of the week, and over the past few days he'd even paid me a compliment or two on the work that I'd done.

I started across the parking lot to my car but stopped short when I saw Vic standing next to it. How did he have any idea where I worked? He looked different than when I'd last seen him. The same...yet different. He wasn't as clean-shaven as he used to be. His midnight black hair was longer and touched the tops of his ears. His lips curled up at the corners and he gave me a sheepish smile.

I started walking toward my car again, this time with purpose in my step. "What are you doing here? How did you find out where I work?" I stopped when there were a few feet left between us. He stepped forward and instinctively I moved back a step.

"I wanted to talk to you. I couldn't get a hold of you on the phone," he answered, ignoring my second question.

"That's because I blocked your number," I said, crossing my arms over my chest.

"Skye, I'm sorry I lost my temper." He sounded genuine.

There was a brief moment where I saw the guy standing in front of me as I had when I'd first met him. Fortunately, this was immediately followed by a moment where I flashed back to the night he'd pressed me up against his door, leaving bruises on my arm and a cut on my head. "I don't want to talk about it." I'd visited enough women's shelters with my dad over the years to know that if Vic didn't know how to deal with his anger, that would only be the beginning of his abusive behavior.

"Please. Can't you find some way to forgive me? Don't let it ruin us."

"There is no *us*. You made sure of that with your paranoia and constant jealousy. God, I couldn't go anywhere without you questioning where I'd been and who I'd been talking to. I have no idea why, but you never trusted me. Even though I never gave you any reason not to—"

"Look at you. You're gorgeous!" His voice rose as his emotions overtook him and I had a brief pang of fear. "Everywhere you go, guys are constantly checking you out. Are you really that blind? Who wouldn't want to be with you?"

"None of that matters. The fact is I was with you!" I stopped for a moment to gather myself. I knew from watching my father calmly deal with insane accusations from the press that letting myself get upset with Vic was not going to help the situation. After I knew I was completely under control, I lowered my voice and continued, "Until you put your hands on me in anger. I ignored all of the rest of the stuff until you did that."

He ran his hands through his hair. When he was finished, he looked even more disheveled than he had before. "Please. What can I do to make it better? I thought if I gave you some time on your own you'd come around." His eyes were pleading.

"There's nothing you can do, Vic. It's over."

Landon

I walked out the front of the building. It was a chilly evening but I took in a deep breath after having been stuck in an office tower all day.

I began making my way across the parking lot when I noticed Skye standing by her car. Her back was to me so I couldn't see her face, but the guy she was talking to was visibly upset. Or angry. I didn't know exactly. But his expression definitely told me that something was off with this picture. Normally I'd mind my own business, but I didn't like the way he stared at her while she was speaking. It was almost...predatory.

I stopped where I was, deciding to observe before I charged in there like I was her boyfriend or something. I had no right to interfere in her personal business, but the need to keep her safe kept my feet from walking in the other direction.

Skye went to walk around him and I figured she was done with the conversation. I was about to turn and head to my car when I saw him grab her arm. Even from the distance where I stood, I could see her flinch away from him. She tried to pry her arm from his grip but he held tight.

Before stopping to think I raced across the lot to get to her, anger burning in my chest. Seeing this guy manhandle her...I could break his fucking neck. As I came closer I saw the fear in Skye's eyes, and I swear it was all I could do not to beat the guy to a bloody pulp for causing her to feel that way.

"Is there a problem here?" I bellowed as I closed the final few feet between us. Skye looked over at me, startled. The guy removed his hand from her arm and glared at me.

"No problem," he said.

"Vic was just leaving," Skye said, her voice shaky and breaking in the middle.

"Why don't you get on your way before there *is* a problem?" I nodded in his direction.

"This isn't the end of this conversation, Skye." He backed away from her, his intense gaze still locked on her. Skye turned her head.

I stood watching him until he got into a black Beamer a couple of rows away and took off. Then I turned my attention back to the beauty I'd been concerned about when I'd come racing over here. She was still looking off into the distance.

"Skye," I said softly. She was deep in thought and I was afraid to startle her. My dad had taken me hunting a few times when I was young. I'd never really gotten into it, but I approached her the way I'd been taught to approach a deer—quietly, calmly, and with care so you didn't spook it. "Skye," I said again, a little louder this time.

She slowly turned in my direction and what I saw almost brought me to my knees. Gone was the young, confident woman who could handle anything at work I threw her way. Tears tracked down her red cheeks. Pain filled her beautiful blue eyes. She looked broken.

I wasn't sure whether it was because I was drawn to her or if it was because she reminded me so much of my mother after all the shit that had gone down with my dad, but I needed to comfort her. And despite the fact that I knew I needed to maintain the divide between employee and boss, I needed to comfort her right now.

I hugged her into my chest. I rubbed up and down her back in what I hoped was a soothing motion. Her tears turned into sobs. I wasn't sure if that was a good or bad thing. My suit jacket was open and I felt her tears soak through my shirt.

"Shh. It'll be okay. Whatever it is. It'll be fine." I continued trying to reassure her for a few minutes until she pulled away from my embrace. The emptiness I felt at no longer having her in my arms surprised me.

"I'm sorry for that. I'm so embarrassed," she said, looking up at me and wiping her wet cheeks. Mascara had pooled under her eyes. I reached out and ran my thumbs underneath her eyes to try to remove it. Our gazes locked and we stood motionless, just staring at one another. Our breathing was heavy and labored. The desire to lean in and kiss her was almost overwhelming, but besides it being inappropriate—she worked for me, for fuck's sake—I wasn't a complete douche. It was obvious that this girl had just been through the emotional wringer and I would never take advantage of that.

I removed my hands from her face and moved back half a step, breaking the spell. She blinked twice like she was coming out of a daze.

"Are you okay?" I asked.

"I'll be fine. I'm sorry I got so emotional. It won't happen again, Mr. Steele."

"Skye, cut the Mr. Steele shit. Who was that guy?"

She hesitated for a moment before speaking. "Vic—my ex." She paused for a moment and then quickly added, "We were broken up when you and I first met."

"Why was he here bothering you?"

She let out a huff of breath. "He wants to get back together. The feeling isn't mutual."

"Seems he can't take no for an answer." I gritted my teeth as the memory of him grabbing her arm flashed through my mind.

"He's pretty possessive. That's one of the reasons I broke up with him."

"What was the other?"

She blanched and the color drained from her face. "I don't want to talk about it. It's not your problem."

"Skye—"

"I can assure you that nothing like this will happen outside of work again. I'm sorry you had to step in."

I ignored her attempt at changing the subject. "Maybe you

should talk to the police about a restraining order if this guy won't quit bothering you."

"No!" she responded quickly. "That's not necessary, really. I'm sure after our conversation today he's realized there's no hope of us getting back together."

"Didn't sound that way to me. If he shows up here, or anywhere for that matter, I want to know about it."

"I appreciate that, but it's not your problem to worry about."

"I'm making it my problem. Got it?" Something about her brought out my inner caveman and screamed at me to protect her.

"You really—"

"Have you told anyone else about this creep bugging you? What about your parents?"

She was silent for a moment. "My dad has a lot going on right now. I don't want to bother him."

"That's what I thought. And that's your call to make, but now I'm the one who's going to help you deal with him." She opened her mouth to say something but I cut her off. "Don't make me pull rank on you." I smiled and she gifted me with a small smile back. Fuck me, but I liked being the one to put that smile on her face.

"Alright. If I have any more trouble with him, I'll let you know."

"Good. Now get out of here and go enjoy your night."

She smiled at me and without saying a word, climbed into her car. I stepped back and waited until she was out of the parking lot before making my way to my own ride.

It felt like I'd crossed some invisible line with Skye today, especially with my offer to take care of her ex for her. But what was I supposed to do? I was in PR and I knew who her father was. If that asshole kept harassing her, a restraining order would be the absolute last thing she'd resort to. The press would have a field day with that one, and it certainly wouldn't be good for daddy dearest's political aspirations. Somebody had to look out for her and that's all I was doing. *Yeah right, keep telling yourself that, Steele.*

Skye

I looked in my rear view mirror. Landon, I mean, *Mr. Steele*, was still standing there, watching as I drove away.

I was such a bundle of mixed and frayed emotions, I didn't know which to focus on. The anger that Vic had showed up at my work, the fear that had coursed through me when he grabbed my arm, and the embarrassment at knowing my boss witnessed the entire scene all seemed to be competing with the warm feeling in my chest when I thought of the look on Landon's face after he'd confronted Vic. It was a mixture of barely restrained fury at Vic and compassionate protectiveness directed at me.

As I drove through the busy streets of downtown Norfolk toward my apartment, I couldn't help but think that something had shifted between us in that parking lot. Or perhaps it had started earlier that day when he finally paid me a compliment on the hard work I'd been doing. What was I thinking? It was probably nothing. He was probably just a good guy who didn't like seeing a woman in that kind of situation.

At any rate, as embarrassing as my emotional breakdown in front of Landon had been, I was glad to have his support. My dad had so much going on with his run for Senate, he didn't need any additional stress. And if Vic continued to be a problem, I wasn't sure what I would do. A restraining order wasn't an option. It would bring too much attention to my dad's campaign and he'd worked too hard for me to blow it because I'd chosen to date an asshole. I refused to be a burden to my father.

What I needed was some girl time. Ellie was due back in

town late tonight and the timing couldn't be better. She'd only be here for a few days and I'd planned to invite both her and Katie to come over to my place. Drinks with my girls was a necessity.

Ellie had been travelling with Mason while he was on tour and her home base was now in Los Angeles. I missed having her around all the time. We'd been roommates all through college and then lived near each other for almost a year after we graduated. It was strange not being able to see her whenever I wanted. But as her friend, I couldn't have been happier for her. She was deeply in love and Mason was a great guy. The press around their romance had calmed down some, and she felt confident now that she could handle whatever came their way. It would be good to see my bff in person again.

After I pulled in to my parking spot, I quickly fired off a text to Ellie and Katie, inviting them over the following night. Ellie was likely flying and wouldn't get the text until tomorrow, but Katie got back to me quickly to say she was in. I let out a deep sigh. A night with the girls was exactly what I needed.

chapter six

Skye

I was excited to show the girls my new place. It wasn't anything super fabulous, but the one-bedroom condo suited me fine. It was all mine and I now made the money to pay for it. I'd been a daddy's girl all my life, but I was finally standing on my own two feet. Never mind the fact that the past couple of weeks I felt like I was standing on five-inch stilettos with broken ankles.

I made sure to leave work on time so that I'd be able to stop and pick up the ingredients for chocolate martinis on the way home. I placed everything on the kitchen counter and looked around the apartment. It was small but the open floor plan ensured that it didn't feel claustrophobic. It also helped that the living room wall was floor-to-ceiling windows with a view of the Elizabeth River in the distance. A set of doors led to an outdoor balcony. It was small and could really only fit two chairs, but it was nice to be able to get some fresh air when I wanted. My place was still sparsely decorated, with only a light gray sofa, an arm chair, and a dark wood coffee table. Although my parents had offered to chip in and help me pay to fully decorate the apartment, I really wanted to do it myself, and I knew my friends wouldn't care one way or the other.

I walked to the bedroom and changed out of my work wear before slipping on a pair of yoga pants, a fitted white tank top and throwing my hair up into a messy bun.

Twenty minutes later I was relaxing on the couch watching my own brand of guilty pleasure—The Real Housewives of Orange County—when there was a knock at the door. I bounded up from the couch, excited to see my girls. We spoke all the time but I felt like it'd been forever since we'd all been in the same room together.

I swung the door open wide and we all immediately squealed—the high-pitched girly kind that probably could only be heard by dogs. Our squeals were followed by a long group hug, until they finally made their way into my apartment.

"It's so good to see you guys!" I said. Ellie looked as gorgeous as ever with perhaps a little more bronze glow to her olive skin. Life in California obviously agreed with her. It was Katie's transformation that had me in awe though. She looked like she'd lost even more weight since I'd seen her a few weeks ago. "Katie, you look amazing!"

"Doesn't she?" Ellie agreed.

"Thanks, girls! This is what starving yourself and working out twice a day will get you."

"How much weight have you lost now?" I asked.

"I'm down about fifteen pounds so far. Fifty more to go!"

Shortly after Mason and Ellie had gotten back together, he'd invited Katie and me out to a video shoot. He thought we'd get a kick out of it which we totally did, except for one embarrassing incident when Katie was mistaken for a plus-size model from a nearby shoot. Since that day, she'd vowed to make a change in her life and it seemed she was making good on it.

I was glad to see her adopting a healthier lifestyle, but I hated that she'd had to go through *that* to propel her into it.

I'd told her at the time that she should be flattered someone had thought she could be any kind of model, but she hadn't seen it that way. I didn't think she needed to change, but she did seem happier than the last time I'd seen her, so it must be a good thing.

"Come on in, guys. There's not much to see really, but it's mine."

Ellie was the first to speak. "Skye, this is great! You'd never believe that you just moved in a few weeks ago. Where's all the boxes?"

"Old habits die hard. It's all about appearances."

"Oh, the life of a mayor's daughter," Ellie said with a laugh.

"I've been in my place for a year and this already looks more put together than mine ever will," Katie said.

"That's because you're a slob," I said to her.

"This is true," she agreed.

"I was thinking we could order in. There's a great Chinese food place around the corner. And I've got everything to make us some chocolate martinis." One of the best things about being out on my own was being able to choose my own menu.

Ellie turned to Katie. "Can you have that?"

"Damn straight. It's gonna cost me an extra few hours at the gym this weekend, but it's worth it to partake with you bitches."

"Such a poet," Ellie said, shaking her head and giggling.

I went to grab my cell phone from my purse to order dinner while Ellie and Katie took care of our drinks. We settled in, waiting for the food to arrive while sipping our martinis, and a sense of contentment came over me. It was the first time in weeks that I hadn't felt either agitated or antsy. This was what I wanted. To be surrounded by friends, sipping on drinks in my own apartment. Free to do as I pleased. Away from my controlling ex-boyfriend and as out of the spotlight of politics as I could manage with my father being who he was.

"I miss you girls," I said. Tears burned behind my eyes.

Not missing a beat, Ellie said, "Skye, what's wrong?"

"Nothing, nothing. I'm just so happy you guys are here. So how's life with Mr. Rich and Famous?" I deflected.

The smile that overcame Ellie's face made me envious. Not in a jealous I-wish-she-didn't-have-that-way. In a wistful way, where I hoped that someday there'd be someone to put the same smile on my face.

"Life with Mason is incredible. All the traveling takes some getting used to, but I'm glad that we're back in L.A. for a few months while he works on his new album. It'll be good to stay in one place for a while."

"Except when you come to visit us," Katie said.

"Which you're going to do often, right?" I added.

"No doubt about it." Ellie winked.

Ellie filled us in about life on the road and some of the cities her and Mason had visited on tour. When the food arrived, instead of sitting at the breakfast bar, we all opted to eat off our laps in my living room.

"So Katie, any more dating disasters?" Ellie asked.

"Oh my God, you guys. If I have to go out with another live-at-home loser, I'm gonna shoot myself."

"Hey!" Ellie and I both said in unison.

"I just moved out of my parents' house, thank you," I said.

"That's different. I like dating older guys. I'm sorry, but if you're in your late twenties and still living with mom and dad, something's up." We both nodded in agreement. "Even worse if you have to borrow mom's car to pick me up for our date."

"You can't be serious," I giggled. Katie sent me a death glare.

"Where do you find these guys?" Ellie asked with an amused tone.

"Online mostly. It's like searching through a second-hand shop for an almost new pair of Manolo Bhlaniks. I'm looking for a diamond in the rough."

"You are not leaving me with much hope for re-entering the dating world," I said.

"I haven't even told you about the guy who sent me a picture of his penis in a strappy high-heel sandal."

"What?" Ellie screeched.

"It was impressive, actually. I'd say he'd fill a size ten for sure, but seriously—who does that?"

"Do you have the picture on your phone?" I asked.

"Of course," Katie replied.

"Well, let's see it!" Ellie said.

Katie grabbed her phone from her purse, scrolled through it for a moment, and finally turned her phone to face us.

"Oh. My. God," I said in disbelief and then started to laugh.

"It actually almost looks like a foot in there. How is that possible?" Ellie asked, laughing.

"It took me a minute, too," Katie said.

"So do you consider that a foot fetish, a shoe fetish, or something else entirely?" I was laughing so hard that it was all I could do to get the words out.

"Where does a guy even get the idea for that? Like, is he sitting around the house one day thinking, 'I wonder what my dick would look like in a pair of Jimmy Choo's?" Ellie said.

"Do you think he wears the shoes, too?" I questioned.

"Skye, take a look...he *is* wearing the shoe," Katie pointed out.

"I think she means on his actual feet," Ellie said, giggling.

"All I know is I don't want my lady bits anywhere near a guy that's had his penis in a fungus factory like a shoe."

"Oh God. Can you imagine?" I said, disgusted by the thought.

"I wonder what it would look like in a peep toe..." Ellie said and trailed off, looking like she was actually trying to picture it in her mind.

"Hmm...kind of like a peep-penis shoe," Katie said.

"I wonder if instead of heel supports he uses ball supports?" We all laughed together until we literally couldn't laugh any more. Finally, Katie said, "Anyway, like the mayor's daughter has any trouble getting a date with a decent, *employed* guy."

Before I could tell her that no one, employed or otherwise, had asked me on a date recently, Ellie cut in. "Have you heard from Vic at all since you split?" She may have kept tight-lipped about her dislike of Vic while I was still dating him, but I expected now that he wasn't in my life anymore, I was going to get the unedited version.

I'd given both my friends a surface-level rundown of the events leading up to the demise of Skye and Vic. Looked like it was time to pony up.

I filled them in on Vic's increasing jealousy and how he'd begun keeping tabs on me, and how it had led to the blowout of epic proportions when I finally decided I'd had enough. I purposely left out the part about him getting violent because, knowing Katie, she'd track down his address and castrate him. So really I was just keeping my friend from an impending assault charge.

"Well, I'm glad he's out of your life. I never liked him," Ellie chimed in when I was done.

"I'm aware," I deadpanned.

"We need to find you a rebound guy," Katie said.

I laughed. "I'm going to take a break from the male species for a while."

"Won't that be a little frustrating?" Ellie asked.

I scrunched up my face. "What do you mean?"

"She means, you'll be sexually frustrated because you're not getting laid."

I picked up our dishes off the coffee table and walked them over to the kitchen. "Believe me, that's the last thing on my mind these days. I have enough on my plate with my new job and my demanding boss."

"How is the new job, by the way?" Ellie asked.

My cell phone rang from its spot on the coffee table and I involuntarily stiffened, my first thought being that it could be Vic. I walked back to the living room and picked it up, When I saw a number I didn't recognize, I couldn't help but wonder if Vic had gotten a new phone. A chill crept up my spine at the thought that he might go to such lengths to get me to answer his call. It continued to ring in my hand while I contemplated who else it could possibly be.

"Aren't you going to get it?" Ellie asked. The look on her face told me that she knew something was wrong.

I tried to recover by putting a smile on my face. "Of course." I pushed the button that would answer the call and put it to my ear. "Hello?" I said a little hesitantly.

"Hi, Skye?"

"Mr. Steele?" He was the last person I expected to find at the other end of the line. I felt relief at hearing his voice but also the stirrings of desire. I tried to push down the former.

"Listen, I'm sorry to bother you when you're off the clock but something important has come up."

"It's not a problem. What can I help you with?" I supposed this was the type of thing he'd meant when he said I'd be working hard and at all hours.

"I'm working from home and some important contracts just came in for the Withers account. I've signed everything and normally I'd just bring them into the office with me in the morning, but as you know, I have that meeting in Richmond first thing. The client needs an original set messengered to them before eleven. I wondered if it would be okay if I dropped them by your place? I'd be more comfortable if they were in your hands so I know they'll be taken care of."

"Of course. That's no problem. I'll make sure they go out first thing tomorrow."

"Thanks, I knew I could count on you. I'll be by in five minutes. I have plans tonight and I'm just headed out. I'm not too far from your place."

"You know where I live?" I asked.

"Relax, Skye. I had to look your number up in the personnel files and jotted down your address in anticipation that you'd say 'yes.'"

I imagined Landon didn't hear many 'no's' from women. "Of course. Sorry. Well then, I'll see you when you get here." I ended the call and placed my phone back on the table.

Shit! Landon was going to be here any minute and I was dressed in yoga pants and a tank top. As much as I told myself I didn't care if he found me attractive or not, I knew deep down it was a lie.

Katie interrupted my thoughts. "Who was that on the phone?"

"My boss. He has to come by to drop some contracts off."

"Does he always make house calls?" Ellie winked at me.

"Ew, El. Gross. He's probably some middle-aged, balding guy with a paunch. Right, Skye?"

I looked at Katie. "Um...not exactly."

"Oooh, this sounds interesting. Dish," she said.

"There's nothing to dish."

"I'm calling bullshit. Your neck is red. It only gets red when you're embarrassed. What's this boss of yours like?" Ellie asked.

"I don't know. A regular boss, I guess." I shrugged, trying for nonchalance.

They were both looking at me like they didn't believe a word I said. Couldn't blame them. *I* didn't believe a word I said. But what was I supposed to do? Tell them how every time he said my name it sent a chill up my spine—in the best way possible? Tell them how much I'd tried to remember the feeling of having his arms wrapped around me and my cheek pressed into his firm chest? No chance. There was no way anything was going to happen between us, and I'd never hear the end of it if my friends knew.

There was a knock at the door and a shot of nervous energy flew right to the pit of my stomach. I took a deep breath, as deep as I could without Ellie and Katie noticing, and went and opened the door.

Landon stood there, wearing a pair of dark jeans and a gray button-up shirt. It was only the second time I'd seen him in anything other than a perfectly pressed designer suit. He looked even better now than he did dressed to the nines. More approachable. Less the stern businessman. He raked his eyes up and down my body slowly, taking everything in with those assessing dark eyes of his. The air left my lungs as his gaze traveled over my chest and stayed there for just a second longer than it should have. God, what I wouldn't give for his gaze to be his hands and to feel them on my bare skin. *Mind, meet gutter. Nice to meet you, gutter. I have a feeling we'll see each other often.* My thoughts seemed to take a one-way detour straight there any time he was within a few feet of me. His deep voice drew me from those thoughts.

"Did you even look through the peephole before you opened the door?" he asked brusquely before stepping into the apartment.

"I was expecting you. You told me you were on your way, remember?" I turned to see that he'd noticed I had company. The girls were staring up at him with wide eyes and apparent admiration. Katie's lips turned up at the corners. "These are my friends, Ellie and Katie," I said, motioning to them.

"Nice to meet you," Ellie said.

"Skye was just telling us all about you," Katie said. I glared at her, letting her know that her meddling was not welcome.

"All good, I hope." His smile widened and I could see that his charm was working its magic on my friends.

"Nothing but," Katie said and winked. I was so going to kill her after he left.

Landon turned to face me so that his back was now to the living room. "Sorry, I didn't know you had company."

"It's no problem. Do you have those contracts?"

"Right here." He passed me a thick folder marked with the logo for Steele & Associates.

When I looked up from the folder, I saw Katie in my peripheral vision with her hands in front of her making a pumping motion and sticking her tongue in and out of the side of her cheek. Oh my God, if he turned around right now, I would never get my chance to murder her because I'd die of embarrassment first.

"Thanks. I'll make sure they go out first thing in the morning."

Landon lowered his voice and leaned in so that only I could hear him, which I appreciated after I heard what he had to say. "You really need to check who's at your door before you just open it. What if it was your ex? As it was, I didn't even have to buzz in."

I looked up to his eyes and felt the instant draw I always did whenever he was near. We were compelled toward each other but both trying to resist the pull. "You're right. The locks don't work properly on the front doors. I'll be more careful," I just about whispered.

"Make sure you are." He turned to look back at the girls. "It was nice to meet you. Sorry to interrupt your night."

"You can't stay for a drink?" Ellie asked. Gah! Not her, too.

"Thanks but I have plans." He glanced down at his watch. "And actually, I'd better get going. She won't be happy if I keep her waiting."

I ignored the pang in my chest that he was out with another woman tonight. I had no right, and if I let myself go there, it'd be running through the back of my mind all night.

I walked to the door and opened it, pressing myself against the wall so he could get past. "Right, well. I guess I'll see you in the office tomorrow."

He walked in my direction but stopped when he was in front of me. "Thanks for taking care of this for me. Oh, and you look cute out of your usual duds." He smiled, gave me the once over again, and walked out the door without looking back.

chapter seven

Landon

How was it possible that she looked just as fuckable in a pair of yoga pants and a tank as she did dressed like the class act I saw at work? Damn. I shifted in my seat to adjust myself as I pulled up in front of the restaurant. I was late and she wouldn't be happy. Punctuality was important to her and this wouldn't be the first time that work had held me up.

I walked into the brightly lit restaurant and saw her sitting at the table by herself, checking her phone. Probably looking to see if I'd texted. As if she felt my eyes on her, she looked up and smiled as I made my way over to her. It was so good to see that smile back on her face.

"Mom, hi. Sorry I'm late." She stood and I gave her a big hug. When she pulled away, she patted my head like she'd been doing since I was young. Secretly I hated it but I'd never had the heart to say anything. Yep, I was a certified mama's boy.

"You work too hard, Landon. I assume it was work that kept you?"

I held her chair out for her to sit and then made my way to my own seat. "I had to drop some contracts off before I came here."

"How is work going?"

"Plugging along. I've got a big meeting coming up in L.A. and if things go well, I'll be opening an entertainment division out there."

"That's fantastic! I'm so proud of you, sweetie. You've worked hard and I'm glad to see it pay off for you."

"Thanks, Mom. So where is Vance tonight?"

"He's got an early day tomorrow so I left him at home." She laughed and I couldn't help but recall a time not that long ago when I thought I'd never hear that sound again. She met Vance almost a year ago. Since then, I'd slowly gotten glimpses of the woman my mom used to be before her husband betrayed her and she was left with nothing. These days she was pretty much back to her old self.

The waitress came over and blatantly eye-fucked me in front of my mother while she took our drink and meal orders. She chewed on the end of her pen with her hip cocked out to the side and smiled. I was polite but did nothing to encourage any further attention from her. After she left, Mom and I caught up with each other until our meal arrived. Once we started digging in, I decided it was time to bring up the subject I'd been putting off since I arrived.

"So...dad has been calling me a lot more lately."

The hand holding her fork paused mid-air on the way to her mouth. "Really? How is he these days?"

I saw a brief shadow pass over her face. "Alright, I suppose. I didn't inquire, to be honest." She nodded in understanding. "He keeps asking me to get together with him."

"Why don't you?"

"You know why...after everything he did—"

"Landon." Her face was drawn and serious. She set her fork back down on her plate. "I understand better than anyone the issues you have with your father. But maybe it's time to let some of that go."

"I can't believe that you of all people are saying that."

"I know you'll likely never have the relationship with your dad that you once did. But he is your father and you only get one. Better some kind of a relationship than none at all. I think you'll regret it later on in life if you don't at least try."

I ran a hand through my hair in frustration. "Why? Why should I give him a chance after what he did to you?"

She pursed her lips and I saw tears form in her eyes. "What he did to *us*, honey. His betrayal didn't just affect me. I'm so sorry that you had to step in and be my rock after everything happened. It wasn't fair to you."

"Mom, don't apologize."

She reached out and covered my hand with her own, squeezing it gently. "I love you so much for doing it, but you don't need to worry about me anymore. I'm okay. You're not betraying me if you want to have a relationship with your dad."

She always knew what my greatest fears were, even before I realized them myself. Until this moment, it didn't occur to me that one of the things holding me back was the fear that any relationship between my dad and me would be a slap in the face to my mom after how much he'd hurt her.

We sat in terse silence for a minute before she picked her fork back up off her plate. "Give it some thought. That's all I'm saying."

I nodded. I would do as she asked—there wasn't anything I wouldn't do for the woman sitting across the table from me—but I couldn't imagine what would have to happen to bridge the Grand Canyon-sized divide that had been forged between my dad and me.

chapter eight

Skye

I let go of the door and watched as it closed on its own. Stunned, I just stood there, unsure how to take his parting comment. It was the first personal thing he'd said to me outside of the Vic situation. But "cute"? Is that really how he saw me? That sounded like something you'd say to child.

"You must have to wear your period panties to work every day with that guy," Ellie said, breaking into my thoughts.

I made my way back to the living room and plopped down on the couch. "It's not like that..."

Katie laughed. "I'd let that guy bend me over a desk any day of the week."

I blushed, visions of me bent over Landon's desk, skirt hiked up to my waist, panties around my ankles now swimming through my thoughts.

"Seriously, Skye. Why didn't you tell us he was so hot?" Ellie asked.

I remained quiet.

"Because she likes him is my guess."

I glared over at Katie. "Okay, maybe I've had an inappropriate thought or two about him. So what?"

"Ah-ha! I knew it!" Damn—if I were a book, Katie could skim through and still pick out every spoiler.

"You're not thinking of pursuing anything with him are you?" Ellie asked.

"Of course not. He's my boss." I'd be keeping what happened between us at the bar to myself.

"Just save it for the spank bank then," Katie said.

"Oh my God, Katie!" Was her filter completely nonexistent?

"So what did he say when he whispered in your ear? Sweet nothings?" Ellie asked, smirking.

My face must have belied the seriousness of what he'd said because both of my friends' faces suddenly looked significantly less amused. I knew I needed to tell them about what happened in the parking lot. Even though I still didn't want anyone to know about the shoving incident, I didn't feel right keeping all of it from my best friends.

"He was telling me to make sure I use my peephole before I open the door."

"Why would he be concerned about that?" Katie asked, sounding genuinely confused.

I let out a sigh. "Vic showed up at my work. I don't know how he knew where I'm working, but he met me out at my car as I was leaving to try and persuade me to give him another chance."

"I don't understand...why would your boss be concerned about that, and why would he be telling you to check the peephole because of it? What exactly happened?" Ellie asked. Her face was serious and she looked as if she was ready to let all hell break loose if I gave her even the smallest reason.

"We argued and it got heated. Mr. Steele intervened."

"That asshole! I knew I didn't like that guy when you started dating," Ellie about yelled.

"I'm aware of how you felt about him."

"I'm sorry, Skye," she said, gentling her voice. "I'm not trying to make you feel worse."

"I know you mean well."

"Has he bothered you since?" Katie asked, her eyebrows scrunched together.

"No, I haven't seen or heard from him. It doesn't hurt that I blocked his number. That's why I was hesitant to answer my phone earlier. I didn't recognize the number."

"You weren't going to tell us, were you?" Katie accused.

I shook my head in response, avoiding eye contact with either of them.

"That's ridiculous. If you can't talk to us about it, who can you talk to?" Ellie asked, sounding a little hurt.

"I didn't want to bother you guys with it. You both have such great things going on right now. Besides, it's been dealt with," I assured them.

"Hot boss to the rescue," Katie said and we all laughed. Even though she often said the wrong thing at the wrong time, sometimes Katie knew exactly what to say to lighten the mood.

A couple of hours and several martinis later, we all sat huddled around my laptop, ogling pictures of Ellie's boyfriend, Mason. He was a celebrity, well known for his hip-hop music so pictures of him weren't hard to come by. Months ago, this sort of thing would have bothered Ellie to no end, but she'd grown more accustomed to dating someone in the limelight. Although I received nowhere near the level of attention Ellie and Mason had to deal with, I knew it could be hard to take at times.

Ellie was laughing along with us when Katie shouted out, "Let's Google your new boss, Skye! See if we can dig up any dirt."

I rolled my eyes at her. What did she think she was going to find? "Go for it. You're probably only going to find a bunch of boring PR press releases and maybe some local coverage of the company."

And that's exactly what she found...at first. There was plenty of stuff about his meteoric rise in the local business scene. There was also stuff about his plans to expand his business outside of the area. But what caught *my* attention was in the social section of the local newspaper, which stated that my boss was known to have been out on the town with one woman one week and another the next. It was also made clear that Landon was the most eligible playboy around.

When had I begun to think of him as Landon instead of Mr. Steele? I shook my head to clear the fog from the alcohol.

"Well, no real surprise that he's getting laid on a regular basis," Katie said.

"Of course he's getting laid. Look at him," Ellie said, pointing to the screen and giggling.

I knew he was my boss and I shouldn't be having the thoughts about him that I was, but I didn't want to think about him with other women either. It made my stomach lurch.

"Why do you have that look on your face?" Ellie asked.

"What look?"

"The one that says you wish *you* were the one getting boinked by him," Katie said, throwing a piece of popcorn at me. Since I'm obviously an open book to her, I'd better have it translated into Italian so Katie couldn't read it quite so easily.

"I do not."

"Oh, please," she said.

The martinis must have loosened my tongue. That's the only explanation I have for the confession that came next. "Okay, fine. Maybe I've thought about him like *that*, but it's not a big deal. Who wouldn't?"

"No judgement here," Ellie said. "I don't know how you could work next to that man all day and *not* have those thoughts."

"You guys should have an interoffice romance," Katie said as if it were both simple and obvious. "You could sneak into the elevator and hit the stop button—"

"Ah! Enough," I said and covered my ears. Great, now I had images of Landon bending me over his desk *and* taking me in the elevator. The ride up to the twenty-fifth floor would never be the same. Damn you, Katie.

"Maybe you guys could make something work. I work for Mason," Ellie said and shrugged.

"True. But you started working for him *after* you guys got together. Big difference. No one would ever take me seriously. They'd all assume any acclaim that came my way was because I was servicing him in the bedroom. Not to mention what the press would do with that information if they found out."

"What does the press have to do with it?" Katie asked.

"My dad. Any mistakes I make directly affect him and his political career. I haven't told you guys yet but he's going to run for Senate. If Landon and I ever got together, they could twist it into something it wasn't. Questions would arise about how I was raised if it people thought I was trying to sleep my way to the top. And inevitably they'd start asking my dad if he agrees with my decisions. I could never put him in that position. He's worked too hard for me to screw it up for him. You just never know how the press will try to spin things...they're too unpredictable."

"Your dad is running for Senate? Wow..." Katie said, trailing off.

"So you just bang him for a bit," Ellie said and laughed.

"Not going there. Besides, I have no interest in a guy that's out with a different woman every week. My picker is off. Otherwise, how do you explain all that time I spent with Vic?"

"Good point," Ellie said.

"No, next time I'm not letting my hormones do the picking. Next time I'm going to use my head instead of my heart."

"It's hard not letting your picker pick the pecker your hormones are lusting after. Good luck with that," Katie said and we all laughed hysterically, partly because of the alcohol and partly because Katie was...well...Katie.

chapter nine

Skye

"Everything looks wonderful," I told my dad as he encased me in a big hug. The ballroom at the Marriott Waterside had been decorated in blue and white. Balloons were everywhere and several long buffet tables held an assortment of cuisine. It all looked delicious but I already had to squeeze myself into this navy evening dress, so there was no way I'd be touching any of it tonight. An orchestra was onstage playing, while a man with a fantastic deep voice sang.

"Sweetheart, you look fabulous," my mom said. She looked as put together as ever with her blond hair back in a French twist. She wore a black evening dress that reached all the way down to her feet, and her blue eyes sparkled with excitement. She hugged me in close and whispered in my ear, "Your father mentioned that you and Vic aren't seeing each other anymore. I'm sorry that things didn't work out."

When she pulled away, she looked at me with concern. "It's okay, Mom. It really is for the best."

"Okay then. I'm sure you'll meet a nice, suitable fellow soon enough."

"I'm sure I will." I wanted to move past this topic of conversation as quickly as possible, so I turned toward my dad and asked, "So, who needs a dose of my sparkling personality this evening?"

"You leave it to me to separate the people here tonight from their wallets, honey. You do what you always do and we'll be fine."

"Okay, Daddy."

I turned to take in the rest of the people in the room. Some I knew and had seen over the years at events similar to this one. Others were complete strangers to me, and I'd have to make sure to work the room in an effort to introduce myself. The majority of the people here were much older than me. Politics wasn't exactly a pastime of many people my age, nor did many of them have the money it took to be a guest at one of these fundraisers.

Taking as deep a breath as my restrictive gown would allow, I gave my parents a small wave and walked into the crowd, ready to charm as many people as I could into supporting my dad and his bid for the Senate. It wasn't work to me anymore. I knew what was expected and had been doing it for so many years that it was second nature.

A couple of hours later, I stood in line at the bar, hoping to get a cold glass of water. I didn't drink at these events, even though legally I could now. I never wanted to make an error in judgement because I'd overindulged.

The line was a long one, as it usually was when an open bar was involved. I stood, shifting my weight from foot to foot, trying to give some relief to my poor feet. Four-inch heels might look killer on, but they were just that—killer.

When my turn finally came, I made my way to the bar and was about to order when a man came and stood beside me.

"Excuse me, I..." My voice trailed off as I realized that the guy who was standing there, looking hot as hell in a black tuxedo and bow tie, was none other than my boss. His hair was more slicked back than usual and his grin was way wider than I'd ever seen it, but it was definitely him.

"Fancy meeting you here," he said.

My sex clenched and I attempted to control my heart rate, which had flown off the charts at the sight of him. "I could say the same to you, Mr. Steele," I said, grinning back at him. I was beyond happy that I didn't accidentally call him 'Landon', which would have been as inappropriate as the thoughts I've been having about him.

He leaned down and whispered into my ear, "You look absolutely stunning this evening." He was close enough for me to feel his warm breath on my exposed neck. A shiver raced through my body. I'm sure he noticed and I felt my face heat under the intensity of his stare.

"Thank you." The bartender saved me from having to say anything more when he approached to take our order. After he'd handed me an ice water and Landon his whiskey sour, we made our way to the edge of the dance floor.

"Looks like you've gotten a good turnout tonight," he said.

"I think my Dad is pretty pleased."

"Not to mention the guest list. There are some really influential folks in this room."

I nodded, unsure what to say. I wasn't used to this conversational version of Landon. I'd only had dealings with him as the blunt and straightforward boss, followed by the protective gentleman who appeared when I'd had the run-in with Vic. He was at an event hosted by my family, so were we considered boss and employee here? Colleagues? Or simply two people the same age, talking at an event where the average age was close to sixty?

"You never did say why you're here?" I asked, turning to face him. He did the same and the look on his face had me catching my breath for a moment.

He looked almost...in awe. His deep brown eyes were wide as he took in all my features. His chest heaved and it sounded as if his breathing became heavier. "I'm here because I agree with your father's politics and also because it's a great place for me to network with other business people in the community." He'd adopted the persona he usually saved for dealing with me in the office.

He paused for a moment and looked like he was struggling internally with something before he spoke again. "I watched you from across the ballroom, Skye. You're a natural at working a room. Everyone you speak with is completely enamoured in your presence. Can't say I blame them."

"You watched me? Why would you watch me?" I asked quietly, as if we were sharing a secret between only ourselves.

He broke eye contact and shook his head slightly like he was clearing his thoughts. Damn, what I wouldn't give to be able to see into his mind at that moment.

chapter ten

Landon

For fuck's sake. This girl had me wound tighter than all shit and all she did was look up at me with her blue eyes and innocent expression. The fitted V-neck navy dress she wore exposed just enough cleavage to get the juices flowing and my imagination going. From across the room I'd seen the way her gown dipped just past the middle of her back, and I couldn't decide which view was sexier. *Moving on.*

"Watched may have been the wrong word. Noticed is more like it." I was full of shit. Watching her was exactly what I'd been doing but no chance in hell I was going to answer her as to why. That was a minefield I didn't want to walk across. Life would be much simpler if I wasn't attracted to her. Someone needed to tell my dick that because it was semi-erect pretty much any time she was within view.

"I see," she said. "Why didn't you mention that you'd be here tonight?"

I shrugged. "Would it have made any difference to you?"

"I...I guess not."

The truth was I hadn't mentioned it because I wasn't sure

I was going to end up coming. I knew it'd be difficult to see her outside of the office and I'd considered just avoiding the party—and the inevitable attraction I'd feel when I saw her all dolled up—but this evening was too good an opportunity to rub elbows with the business owners in this town. I hadn't built my company into the success it was by avoiding uncomfortable situations.

The band finished up the fast-paced song they were playing and began with a slow song whose melody I recognized as Frank Sinatra's 'The Way You Look Tonight.' I placed my hand on Skye's shoulder. I shouldn't have but I couldn't help myself. Her proximity and the light floral scent of her perfume filled my senses and drew me in. I'd use whatever excuse I could to touch her.

I removed my hand from her shoulder and held it out to her. "May I have this dance?"

Her eyes flicked up to mine and widened. I took her drink, setting both of ours on a nearby table. She said nothing for a moment and then hesitantly put her hand in mine. "Of course."

The feel of her small hand in mine reminded me of how petite and fragile she really was. I walked her out to the middle of the dance floor and pulled her into my arms. My hand grazed the smooth skin on Skye's warm back and I felt her suck in a breath. We locked eyes and began moving in time to the music.

We exchanged no words but I was acutely aware of every point of contact between our two bodies. I held her closer to me than was probably appropriate, but at that moment I didn't give a shit. I'd take what little I could get, when I could get it. I wouldn't have another excuse to press my body to hers any time soon—if ever.

She didn't seem to mind. I wasn't sure if I was just telling myself that because it's what I wanted to believe, but her crystal blue eyes still hadn't broken contact with my steady gaze. My eyes finally dipped down to her lips which were slightly parted. *Fuck.* What I wouldn't do to be able to taste those lips right now.

I was lost in my thoughts, focused only on what kissing Skye's lips would lead to next, so I didn't even consider the fact that my dick was growing harder underneath my tuxedo pants. When I felt Skye pause for just a split second, it brought my focus back to her. I looked up to see her gazing up at me with wide eyes.

Shit. Motherfucking shit. I cleared my throat. "I'm so sorry, Skye."

Her cheeks grew pink which was cute as hell and didn't help the situation in my pants—not at all. "It-It's fine. Really."

I hadn't felt like such an idiot since the time I'd inadvertently gotten a hard-on while talking to my sixth-grade teacher...while wearing jogging pants. I felt like *that* kid again.

"I didn't mean any disrespect," I said.

"I know," she said softly.

"It's just...like the song says, the way you look tonight..." In an attempt to lighten the mood, I began singing the lyrics to the chorus into her ear. I didn't sound anywhere near as good as the guy on stage, but based on the full-body shiver she had in my arms, she didn't seem to mind.

She pulled back and looked up into my eyes. "Thank you for the compliment."

"I only speak the truth."

Movement from the edge of the dance floor caught my eye and I glanced up. Vic was standing nearby, watching us with his arms crossed over his chest. His mouth was drawn into a firm line and his face was about the same shade of red as the last time I saw him. Something told me that wasn't his skin's natural color either. I instinctively pulled Skye in closer to me and tightened my arms around her.

"Landon, what is it?" she asked.

"Nothing."

"Then why are you holding me in a vice grip?"

"Sorry." I loosened my hold on her a bit as we continued

our slow turning to the music. I knew exactly when she spotted him because her body became rigid beneath my touch and there was a flash of fear in her eyes. "What's he doing here?" I asked with more venom in my voice than there should have had been.

"He's probably here because his dad owns a large investment firm and has been a big supporter of my father's campaigns. I should've realized he'd still be expected to come even though we broke up."

"I made it pretty clear to that asshole last time I saw him that he needed to leave you the hell alone. Unless you want him here?" Damn. Even I could hear the jealousy in my tone.

"Of course not. Let's just ignore him and he'll probably go away."

"Not likely. He's headed this way," I said. Skye turned to look and when he was few feet from us, we stopped dancing.

You could practically see the effort required behind the guy's clearly fake smile. "Fancy seeing you two here—together."

"We're not here together, Vic, we're just dancing. You know as well as anyone that I have a job to do at this party," Skye snapped.

I took a step toward Vic and rose up as tall as my six-foot-two-inch frame would allow, hoping to make the few inch difference between us feel like a bigger divide than it was. "I thought I made it clear that you shouldn't be bothering Skye the last time we spoke," I said in a menacing tone.

Skye put a hand on my arm. "Not here. This is my dad's event and I can't afford to cause a scene," she said quietly.

"Which is exactly why this asshole is here trying to talk to you now."

Vic put his hands up in a placating gesture. "Relax. I was only stopping by to say 'hello' to Skye. I've already spoken to your father this evening. Seems he was quite disappointed to hear about our breakup."

"Actually, I told him about it myself. He did like and

respect you but we're done, and I don't need to explain to *you* why," she said. "So please just leave me alone, Vic."

"We may not be dating anymore, but I don't see any reason why we can't still be friends. Unless your new boyfriend here has a problem with that." He gestured to me with his hand—a hand that I wanted very much to break.

I looked to Skye and saw that her cheeks had turned red. "He's not my boyfriend, he's my boss. Now stop embarrassing me."

"Sorry, it was hard to tell the difference with the way you two had your bodies plastered together."

"This conversation is finished, Vic." Skye turned and left the dance floor.

Because it was obviously important to her to have this event for her dad go off without a hitch, I said nothing to the douchebag and turned to follow Skye, who was making her way toward the exit. It didn't escape me that even though she wanted to get the hell out of here, she didn't walk at such a fast pace that she drew attention to herself. She was a girl accustomed to having people watch her in public.

When I finally reached the hallway, I looked left and saw her skirting through a doorway. I approached and saw that the sign outside said it was a bridal waiting room.

I knocked on the door and was met with silence so I knocked again, this time louder. Still nothing. "Skye, I know you're in there."

"I just want to be by myself."

"Skye, let me in. I just want to make sure you're okay."

"I'm fine. Please...just go back to the party."

"I'm not going anywhere until you let me in." I heard the lock click and she quickly swung the door open, motioning me in. She had tears on her cheeks and looked so goddamn vulnerable that I wanted to pull her into me and rock her gently to soothe her frayed nerves.

"I'm fine, really. You don't have to worry about me."

"Clearly, you are not fine." I gestured to the tears still on her cheeks.

She threw her hands up in the air, spun around, and stomped to the other side of the room. "Okay, I'm not fine. Is that what you wanted to hear? But *you* don't have to worry about me. It's not your problem." She sounded angry now. I'd rather see her anger directed at me than have to witness the woman I'd come to know as such a capable person looking so desperate and alone.

"It is my problem. You work for me."

"Exactly! You're my boss and this is the second time I've broken down in front of you. It's completely embarrassing, not to mention unprofessional."

I narrowed the distance between us with a few long strides until I stood before her. She wouldn't look at me but I took my hand and nudged her chin up until she did. "You, my dear, are the consummate professional and you've been nothing but at work. And whether you think it's my business or not, here's the thing—I'm making it my business. So you can either tell me what's really going on right now, or the two of us will be spending the rest of the party in here until I convince you otherwise."

Her eyes bore into mine. Their crystal blue color looked like ice, but I could see the fissures in them. She said nothing. I returned her look without breaking eye contact or saying a word. She wasn't going to win this one. Eventually the ice in her eyes melted away until she looked lost and alone again.

"Tell me what's going on. You're too upset for it to just be about running into an ex," I said softly.

She said nothing for a beat and then finally, "He almost caused a scene that would have been the talk of the town. It would have ruined the party and I couldn't stand to be the one that put a blemish on my dad's run for Senate."

She was a shitty liar. I'm sure all that was true but she was holding back. "That's crap. I saw fear in your eyes out on that dance floor when you first saw him. Why?" I put my hands to her cheeks and wiped away her tears with my thumbs. She closed her eyes momentarily, like she was enjoying the sensation of my hands on her. At least that's what I'd let myself believe anyway.

"When we broke up, it was messy. Things didn't go well."

"What does that mean?" I asked, hoping it didn't mean what I thought it did.

She took a deep breath in, as if gathering the courage to go on. "The night I broke up with him, he got a little physical." That motherfucker was as good as dead. I dropped my hands from her face and let them hang at my sides, my fists automatically flexing. "He didn't hit me or anything. He just grabbed my arms and pushed me against the door. I hit the back of my head and it left a small cut."

My guts twisted as I listened to her try to make it sound like it wasn't a big deal. My mind really went spinning when she said, "I'm so embarrassed." She dropped her face into her hands.

"What the fuck do you have to be embarrassed about? Some asshole puts his hands on you and *you're* the one feeling like you did something wrong?" I pulled her hands away from her face as gently as I could in my riled-up state. Rage burned so hot through me that it was all I could do to stand in one spot. I wanted to punch something—preferably *someone*. I wanted to hurt Vic like he'd hurt her, only about ten fucking times worse. But I had to keep that impulse in check. The last thing I wanted was for Skye to be afraid of me.

"I don't know why I'm embarrassed. I just am."

I took her into my arms and squeezed tightly. Unlike our last hug, instead of keeping her hands pressed up against her, she wrapped her arms around me and squeezed me back.

God, she felt so fucking perfect in my arms. It was as if a small piece of me that I didn't even know went missing was now back where it belonged. I didn't want to let her go, but I needed to look into her eyes when I said this to her. I pushed her away from me and gazed down into those pools of blue that were so easy to get lost in.

"Listen to me. You did nothing wrong. It is *never* okay for a man to lay his hands on a woman in anger. Never. You have nothing to be embarrassed about. Do you understand?" She nodded. "Does anyone else know what happened?"

"No. You're the first one I've told." Figures. If there was one thing I'd learned about Skye, it was that she thought of others before herself.

"You can't keep shit like that to yourself. I'm sure if you'd told your dad, he never would have even let the guy into the party."

"You're right, he wouldn't have. But I can't tell him. Vic's father is one of his largest contributors. I'm not going to burden him with this."

"Your dad would want to know."

"You can't say anything. Please. You have to promise me, Landon."

A warm feeling filled my chest at hearing her call me by my name. I don't even think she realized she did it. I hesitated for a moment as her eyes pleaded with me. "Fine. As long as you promise me you'll tell me if he tries to make contact with you again."

"Deal," she said.

"I have to tell you, Skye, it's all I can do not to go out there and rip his throat out."

"But you won't because you know how important this night is to my father and how important my father is to me." She said it as a statement of fact.

"That's the only reason that asshole's not visiting the hospital tonight, believe me."

"I really have to get back out there before people start to wonder where I am."

"Okay, but I'm sticking around the rest of the night to make sure he doesn't bother you again."

"You really don't have to do that; I was just caught off guard. I'm fine now that I know he's here."

"I realize I don't have to, but I am. I won't bother you. I know you have to make the rounds, but know that I'll have my eyes on you the rest of the night."

I noticed the way goosebumps traveled up her arms after I said that, but I pretended not to.

"Fine then. Thank you. I have to freshen up before I go back out there."

"I'll leave you to it." I walked toward the door without looking back, because if I did I wasn't sure I'd be able to resist the urge to wrap my arms around her again.

The rest of the night passed without incident. I didn't speak to Skye again, but she was in my line of sight at all times. Vic must have left after our little encounter because I didn't see him again. I had a feeling he wasn't going to let go of Skye that easily though.

When I got home, I went right for the liquor cabinet and poured myself a Scotch. Actually I poured several, hoping to drown out the images I had festering in my head of Vic laying his hands on Skye.

I was a barely controlled atom bomb waiting to take out anything and everything in my path. I had to remind myself several times how that would only make things worse for Skye—how it would only cause her more pain.

The lines between us were blurring. Hell, they'd probably been blurred since the beginning. If it wasn't clear before tonight, then it was crystal clear now. When I'd first met her, I'd made the asshole assumption that her life had been picture perfect and even mildly resented her for it. The more I'd gotten to know her, the more I realized she had her own burdens to bear, most of which I'd never known about or ever considered.

I wasn't sure what it was about her that brought out a

caveman instinct to protect her. Yeah, she was hot as fuck and it was all I could do to control my impulse to touch her whenever she was near, but it was more than that. She was intelligent, quick on her feet, and knew immediately how to put anyone at ease who had the pleasure of being in her company. Being a politician's daughter, I'm sure she'd had enough practice, but it was more than that—it was just her. That's why seeing the fear in her eyes when she'd spotted Vic and the thought of him harming her...FUCK!

I threw my glass across the living room, where it struck the wall, leaving a dent and shattering to the floor. It was well past midnight and I was half in the bag, but I needed to do something. Since my first choice—beating the shit out of Skye's douchebag ex—wasn't really an option, I decided I'd go for a run to try and clear my head.

As I exited the glass doors of my condo building, I sucked in the cold air and began to run at a steady pace. Halfway through my run, I knew it was no use...no amount of pounding the pavement was going to remove Skye from my thoughts.

chapter eleven

Skye

The rest of my weekend was uneventful. Thankfully, Vic made no further appearances other than in my dreams, where the night of our breakup played out over and over. Only this time, Landon showed up before Vic could hurt me.

As I walked toward the back of the office on Monday morning my nerves were working overtime. I didn't know what to expect when I saw Landon. Things felt different between us. I was still his employee, and although I wouldn't exactly call us *friends*, there was definitely more than just a work relationship going on between us.

As I got ready this morning, I vacillated between wanting to dress to discourage any attention from Landon and dressing in a way that I thought he'd like. In the end, I decided on a tailored skirt and blouse, not unlike what I usually wore.

I was responding to a few e-mails when I heard murmurs of "good morning" to Landon throughout the office. Swallowing my nervous energy, I stood when he entered the reception area that led to his office. I wasn't sure what to expect from him and didn't know if he'd bring up what had happened at the party. I needn't have worried because it was business as usual.

"Good morning, Mr. Steele."

"Good morning, Skye. I need these papers couriered over to the client this morning and you and I need to figure out what we still have outstanding before the conference and the L.A. meeting. Plan on a working lunch in my office."

"Yes, sir." With that, he dropped the papers he'd referred to on my desk, walked into his office, and closed the door behind him. It was obvious he didn't want to be disturbed when he activated the privacy screen.

I told myself that it was a good thing he'd gone back to being just my boss, but the disappointment was difficult to ignore. It *was* a good thing though. Any more displays of the "sensitive and caring" Landon and it was only going to be more difficult to convince myself I wasn't interested in him.

Having to be at work every day pining over your boss would be complete hell. Who was I kidding? I already had a front-row, center aisle view of what that was like.

This was a good thing. Maybe if I thought it enough I would begin to believe it.

Landon

Skye ordered me a soup and sandwich for lunch, and a grilled chicken salad for herself. She surprised me when she sat down on the couch in the sitting area of my office. "Thank you for the other night," she said, looking down at the coffee table, where she was organizing the food.

I said nothing for a beat and then, "Thank you for opening up to me."

"You make it easy. You're really good at the comforting thing."

I didn't tell her that I had lots of practice trying to put the pieces of a broken woman back together. "Well, I'm glad you felt like you could talk to me since you hadn't told anyone else." I forcibly pushed down the anger that threatened to bubble to the surface again.

She looked up from the table at me with a depth of sincerity that you see from few people in life. "I do feel like I can talk to you. As crazy as that sounds."

I got up from my desk and walked over to join her. Instead of sitting in the chair across from her, I sat down beside her on the couch. She looked up at me, the surprise evident on her beautiful face. My thigh grazed hers as I shifted to get comfortable in my seat. "Why does that sound crazy?"

"I shouldn't have said anything. Forget it." She turned her attention back to the coffee table and our lunch.

I brought my hand to her chin and gently forced her to look back at me. "Why is it crazy that you feel like you can talk to me?"

I sat and waited for her answer, staring into those crystal blue eyes. It may have been minutes or only seconds that went by—I couldn't tell you. For a woman used to portraying the image she wanted the public to see, she did a lousy job of hiding her emotions from me. She looked unsure and vulnerable.

"We didn't exactly start off on the right foot...sometimes it feels as if you're always testing me. Like maybe you don't trust my judgement or my capabilities, let alone want me to confide in you about something in my personal life."

The last thing I wanted to do was give her the impression that I didn't have any confidence in her. I only wanted to be sure she could handle the job and wasn't some rich princess used to having everything her way. I felt like an asshole, because in trying to keep her at arm's length from my raging hormones, I'd managed to make her feel like she wasn't good enough. When the truth was the complete opposite...I held more reverence and was more drawn to her than any other woman before. And there was the *real* problem.

I scrubbed a hand along my jaw, thinking of what exactly I could say without giving myself away. So far she'd been a saving grace to me in the office and I didn't want to make her uncomfortable. I did want her to know that I was here for her if she needed me though. Especially when it came to Vic. She looked at me expectantly, her eyes wide.

"I'm sorry if I've given you that impression. Look, you're doing well here. I'm happy with how fast you've caught on to everything and I feel like I can rely on you to take care of things for me. I've just got a lot going on trying to make inroads into the entertainment industry and I'm sorry if I made you feel that way. I do like you, Skye. A lot." I couldn't help myself. She was seated so close to me that I could smell the fresh floral scent of her perfume. I reached up and cupped her face, stroking my thumb along her cheek. "I'm here for you if you need to talk...about Vic. Or whatever."

I swear she held her breath as I stroked my thumb along her soft skin. I could tell I'd made her uncomfortable. I dropped my hand quickly and leaned forward to grab my lunch off the table. She didn't say anything so I tried to lighten the mood by moving the conversation along to safer topics.

"So, have you booked our flights out to L.A. yet?" I asked.

"I did. We leave on the Sunday at 8 a.m. and fly back a week later."

"Perfect. I'll have a car pick you up at your place at 5:30. We can go to the airport together."

"Okay."

"You should bring clothes that are suitable to go out during the evenings. It's possible we may have to schmooze a potential client, and meetings in L.A. usually happen over dinner or at a bar, not in an office building."

She nodded her head but I could tell she wanted to say something by the way she was biting her bottom lip. Damn, that was sexy. "Mr. Steele, do you think we'll have plans on Saturday night? The conference will be wrapped up, and I was hoping to make plans with some friends I know in Los Angeles. But if it's a problem, I can cancel."

"I don't suspect it'll be a problem. As long as we're able to wrap up all our business with Calder's people before that." Relief flooded her face at my words.

"Thank you. My best friend moved out there a few months ago and we've always celebrated our birthdays together, so her boyfriend's planning on taking us for a night out." She hesitated a moment before she continued, looking uncertain. "Would you want to join us?"

I raised an eyebrow. That was unexpected. I tried to squash my excitement at her invitation. Jesus, when had I become such a pussy?

"You don't need to invite me. I'm sure I can find something to occupy my time."

"I know I don't need to...I just thought it might be good for business. I'm sure wherever we're going will be crawling with people from the entertainment industry. Maybe you can make some contacts."

"Your friend works in the entertainment industry?"

"She's dating Mason Nash. Works for him, too."

"Really?" I knew exactly who that was. His music was played a lot at the clubs I went to with my buddies. These days work was so demanding though that I rarely had time to see any of my friends.

She nodded. "It's a newer relationship but they seem pretty serious. Anyway, you're welcome to come. Maybe you'd even have fun." She nudged me in the side with her shoulder.

"I have the ability to have fun, Skye. There's more to me than the person you see here in the office."

She lifted her brows. "Oh, I know," she said and it looked like she was stifling a laugh.

"What does that mean?" I couldn't help but smile back at her.

"Well, you were certainly all kinds of fun the night we first met. Plus, I hear you're quite the ladies' man," she said in a teasing tone.

That was not what I was expecting, and it didn't please me—at all—that she saw me that way. "I see," I said in a clipped tone.

She seemed to catch on to the change in my mood and tried to change the subject. "Anyway, I'm going to put the final touches on your presentation for the conference this week. I'll send it to you as soon as I'm done."

"You do that."

We ate in tense silence for a few minutes before we got back to business and discussed what needed to be done before we headed west. Skye expertly avoided the topic of our first encounter and whatever she'd heard about me to make her think I was a man whore. Question was, did it bother me that she thought of me that way because I was her boss, or was it more than that?

chapter twelve

Skye

I left Landon's office and released the breath I'd been holding as I slumped down into my chair.

Stupid. Stupid. Stupid.

Why had I commented on him being a ladies' man? What the hell had I been thinking? We'd been having an amiable lunch together and I went and ruined it by opening my big mouth. It was like my brain synapses misfired when I was around him, and I forgot the years of practice I had at shifting conversations *away* from uncomfortable topics.

It had definitely pissed him off, too. Maybe he didn't want anyone at work to know what he did in his personal time? I couldn't imagine that was it. It wasn't exactly difficult information for the girls and I to find.

But really, what did he expect me to think after our first encounter? Whatever the reason, I'd be steering clear of all talk of his personal life from now on.

The week after Thanksgiving, I was taking the elevator up

to Steele and Associates when I heard Landon's voice call out to hold the elevator just as the doors were closing. I quickly hit the button to keep them open and he jogged into the enclosed area. His entry made it seem like all the oxygen had been sucked from the room, and I was acutely aware of how close our proximity was to one another. I stepped back until I bumped into the wall behind me.

"Morning, Skye," he said, his voice raspy. It sounded as if he'd just woken and hadn't fully brushed off the effects of sleep yet. There was nothing sleepy about the smile he gave me though, which instantly turned my insides to mush.

As I glanced at our reflection off the steel elevator wall, Katie's words from weeks earlier popped into my head. Heat rose to my face and I had never been more thankful that mind-reading wasn't an actual skill people possessed. Images of Landon and I discarding our clothing, of him pressing me up against the back of the elevator and lifting me so that my legs circled his waist, of his mouth on my—

"Are you feeling okay? You look a little flushed." Landon's voice cut through the sexy scenario I'd created in my head and embarrassment flooded every pore in my body.

"Yes, I'm fine. It's a little warm in here." I unbelted my coat and unfastened the top few buttons as Landon hit the button for our floor. The elevator started its ascent.

He cleared his throat. "Seems the cold weather has finally found us. Do you like it, or did you prefer it warm and wet?" He nodded toward my jacket before his gaze shifted slowly down the length of my body.

Before I could say anything, the elevator made a funny noise and shook before coming to a complete stop.

Oh shit. No, no, no, no, no. I wasn't claustrophobic or anything, but being confined to a small space—especially one where I was alone with Landon for an undetermined amount of time—would require more restraint than my body could muster in this sexually-charged environment.

"What the hell?" Landon began pressing buttons and

when nothing happened, he pulled out his phone. "Damn. No signal."

I searched through my bag until I found my own phone. "I don't have a signal either."

Landon let out an aggravated sigh and pressed the emergency call button. A moment later, a grainy voice shattered the heavy silence. "Hello? How can I help you?"

"It seems our elevator has stopped. Can you send someone to get it going again?"

"I'd be happy to, Sir. Can you please tell me what car number you're riding in?"

We both looked around the confined space until I found a small metal plate with a long number stamped on it. I pointed it out to Landon and he walked over and began reading the numbers out to the attendant.

"Very good, Sir. We'll have someone there to get you out as soon as possible. When I have an update, I'll let you know."

Landon turned to face me. "Are you okay?"

I laughed a little. "I'm not claustrophobic, if that's what you mean."

He gave me his panty-dropping grin and it was all I could do not to let out an audible sigh and gaze at him with stars in my eyes—as ridiculous as it might have sounded. And trust me, I knew it sounded ridiculous.

"I suppose we should make ourselves comfortable. Doesn't sound like we're going to be getting out of here any time soon."

This was a dream come true and my worst nightmare, all rolled into one. Being forced to be this close to him, just the two of us for God knows how long...I couldn't think of anything I'd wanted more. At the same time, not being able to act on any of the things I was feeling was pure torture and the not-so-dull ache between my legs was proof of this.

It was like bringing a child to the window at the pet store and showing them the new puppy. Isn't it cute? Isn't it sweet?

Wouldn't you like to have it? And then telling them they were going home empty-handed.

Landon drew me out of my thoughts—again—when he started to take his coat off and placed it on the floor. "I don't know about you, but I'm going to have a seat while we wait."

I really needed to stop drifting into lala-land around him, or he was going to start thinking there was something wrong with me. "Good idea," I said, removing my own coat and placing it on the ground. I preferred a trip to the dry cleaners with my coat over standing in these heels any day.

I'd chosen to wear a dark gray, cowl-neck sweater dress to work today. It was chic and classic, and I liked the way it accentuated what little curves I had. I sat down carefully so as not to showcase the goods to him. We sat facing each other on opposite sides of the car, both our legs stretched out so that our feet were positioned near the other's hips.

"How you girls wear these damn things is beyond me," Landon said, nodding his head at my choice of footwear. I had on a pair of three-inch black pumps with a cute little bow at the back near my ankle.

I laughed. "We do it for you guys...you do know that, right?"

"Is that right?" He chuckled and ran a hand up and down his jaw. God, that was so sexy. What I wouldn't do to feel that dark stubble underneath my own fingers.

"Of course. How do you think my legs would look in this dress if I wore flats with it?"

He smirked at me and looked me square in the eye. "I have a feeling you'd look just as gorgeous either way, doll."

I wasn't sure how to take that. I was sure he didn't mean it the way I wanted to pretend he did, but that didn't stop the blush from creeping into my cheeks. "Thanks," I said, a near whisper.

His heated gaze met my own and once again all oxygen seemed to have fled the room. At this rate, we'd die of oxygen deprivation if they didn't bust us out of here pretty soon. I was distracted from that alarming thought when Landon picked up one of my feet and placed it in his lap. "Look at these things...what is this heel...four inches?"

I giggled and it sounded nervous even to my own ears. I hoped Landon hadn't noticed. "You are such a man. No, that's actually only three inches."

He laughed in return, his chocolate eyes shimmering with mirth. "Still, three inches can't be easy to take."

"I've taken more before."

"I'm sure you have."

Wait. Were we still talking about high heels here?

His hand moved from propping up my shoe for inspection to my ankle, where he lightly pinched my tights and said, "And these things can't be comfortable to wear."

I shrugged, trying to seem nonchalant, although I was acutely aware of the way his thumb had begun to rub back and forth across my ankle. "They're not so bad." Damn. That sounded way too breathy, even to me.

His hand slowly began to explore further up my leg and then back down again. Each time he'd move it up, I found myself wishing he'd let it climb a little higher. Finally, he leaned forward and his hand crested my knee. I sucked in a breath and held it. His eyes flicked up to mine as if asking for permission and when I didn't deny him, his hand caressed my inner thigh just above my knee.

He scooted closer to me and leaned forward. The heat from his body radiated into mine and the smell of his cologne was intoxicating. I closed my eyes as he approached—

Suddenly, the elevator car jerked to life and began its ascent again. A voice came over the speaker, "Everything should be fine now. We've got you on your way. Sorry for the inconvenience."

Startled by the voice, as well as what had almost occurred, I panicked and jolted to my feet, accidentally hitting Landon underneath the chin with my knee when I stood.

"Oh my gosh, I'm so sorry!" I bent over to see if he was okay.

He remained seated on the floor and rubbed his jaw. "No permanent damage done." I couldn't help but wonder if he was talking about his jaw or what had happened between us in the last few minutes. He slowly moved to stand, grabbed both of our coats, and passed me mine.

"Thanks." I couldn't even look him in the eyes when I said it.

Finally, after what felt like for-friggin'-ever, the elevator doors opened to the Steele and Associates reception area. I immediately left the confines of the car and headed to my desk without waiting for Landon.

I was putting my purse in my desk when Landon stopped in front of me. Oh God, he wasn't going to talk about what went on in *there* right *here*, was he? I looked up to find him standing there with an amused grin on his face. Good to know I was so damn amusing.

"We're going to need to put some extra work in for the conference presentation over the weekend. Let's do it at my place. I'm sick of staring at the four walls of my office. I expect you there Saturday morning. I'll get you the address."

I swallowed the fist-sized lump that had formed in my throat. "I'll check my schedule."

He looked down at me with a knowing grin. "You do that."

He and I both knew I'd be there, but he didn't need to know how much I looked forward to it.

chapter thirteen

Skye

Nervous as hell, I stood motionless outside the door of Landon's condo on Rader Street. Ignoring my body's response to him in the office was one thing. I wasn't sure how I was going to do it when it was just the two of us at his place—and very much alone.

I'd pondered what to wear all morning. Should I go casual? He was still my boss. Would he expect me to look professional even though it was the weekend? If I dressed up, would he think I was trying too hard and wonder why I wasn't more relaxed? I had settled on a pair of dark skinny jeans with knee-high black boots, paired with a fitted, cream-colored, V-neck sweater. It was nice looking but not exactly casual.

Hiking my bag that carried my laptop and all of my accompanying work high onto my shoulder, I knocked on the door. Moments later, Landon answered. Yep, I must have done something wrong in a past life because I was definitely being tested. He wore an aged pair of jeans, faded in all the right spots and hanging low on his hips. The lean muscles of his upper body were on full display in a charcoal long-sleeved shirt. Basically, he looked mouth-watering, panty-drenching good. Crap.

He smiled wide. "Skye. Come on in." He moved back so I could enter and grabbed the strap of the bag off my shoulder as I passed him. "Allow me."

"Okay, thanks."

I looked up to take in the space that Landon chose to call home, surprised to see it didn't have the same chrome-heavy contemporary look as our office. He was certainly doing better than me because his living room, kitchen, and dining room were at least three times as big as my own. Hell, he even had an actual dining room with seating for eight. What really surprised me though was the warmth of the space. Dark hardwood floors worked well with the light brown walls and dark leather furnishings. Vintage advertising posters were enlarged and decorated the walls. The place looked lived-in but neat, and it was apparent that he took pride in his home.

"Can I get you a drink before we get down to it?" he asked, taking my jacket from me as I shrugged it off.

"Maybe just a water."

"One water coming up. Be right back."

I walked into the living room and took a seat on the couch, watching Landon as he headed to the kitchen.

"Your place is really nice. Not what I expected."

He made his way back to me with a glass of water in his hand and raised an eyebrow at me. "What did you expect?" he asked. He sat down on the other end of the couch and placed the water on the table in front of us.

I shrugged. "I don't know. I guess more like the office décor."

He shook his head. "I want my personal space to be comfortable. Some place to unwind and forget about everything else going on in my life."

"It's definitely comfortable and decorated better than my place." He laughed. "Really. I can put an outfit together like no one's business, but interior decorating was a gene I didn't inherit."

"Well, thanks for the compliment."

There was something different about Landon today. He was more relaxed. More himself, I guessed, though I didn't know for sure. The stoic businessman who usually made an appearance at the office was gone. In his place was an at-ease, approachable guy. I liked this version of him.

"Should we get to work?" I asked.

"Sure thing."

I pulled out my laptop and some of the notes I'd made regarding the presentation he was giving at the conference. His topic was how to grow your PR business and he'd previously indicated that he was focusing on his sales technique and how he identified and signed new clients.

We went over the conference schedule for a while and finally turned our attention to the presentation. "I've included everything you've given me in the PowerPoint, but I thought it might be a good idea to expand on some of the ideas." I was nervous that he wouldn't welcome my suggestion and my mouth went completely dry. I grabbed my water off the table and drank a good amount.

Landon cocked an eyebrow. "How so?"

"Well, the attendees might benefit from seeing a bit of what you did with the clients after you landed them. It's one thing to get a client, another to keep them."

He leaned forward with his elbows on his knees. "What did you have in mind?"

"What if we use a couple of case studies with some of the more innovative things you've put in place? Take, for instance, the event you did for the Elizabeth River Tour Company and Riley's Seafood Restaurant. How many people would've thought to have people go fishing from the tour boats and then bring their catch into Riley's to be prepared for dinner that night? Bringing two clients together to benefit them both was ingenious."

"How did you even know about that?" He furrowed his brow.

"I went through the old files when I got the idea and pulled out the ones I thought would work well."

"Good work, Skye. Even if the only thing the attendees get out of it is to start thinking outside the box, it would be worth including in the presentation."

"My thoughts exactly."

"We'd have to get permission from the clients."

"Leave that to me." Landon gave me one of his lopsided grins that sent a small pang of need to my core. I gave him my most dazzling smile, hoping to return the favor, regardless of the fact that I should be wishing for no such thing. "I've been charming people my entire life, Landon. I can handle it."

His eyes heated and he held my gaze. "I don't doubt it for a minute."

The mood suddenly turned serious. I cleared my throat. "Do you mind if I help myself to some more water?"

"Not at all."

As I made my way over to the kitchen area, I felt Landon's eyes follow me. I may or may not have encouraged it by shaking my ass a little more than necessary as I walked.

After refilling my glass, I paused to take a look at the pictures housed in a large entertainment unit. There were a few of him that looked like they were taken in high school. He was cute even back then and was probably already a ladies' man when the pictures were taken. "You used to run track?" I asked, pointing to one where he was wearing a track outfit and holding a trophy.

I heard the leather creak on the couch and felt his presence as he came to stand behind me. Our bodies weren't touching, but I swear I could feel a current pass in the small space between his body and mine.

"Yeah. I still run actually." I felt his warm breath on my neck when he spoke, and I could smell his expensive cologne.

The scent wasn't familiar to me but it was divine. I could stand there all day inhaling it.

"I run, too. There's nothing better to clear your head."

"Exactly."

I stepped to the side a bit to check out some more of his photos. I wanted to know more about him—wanted to see beyond the mask he usually wore at work. There were a few photos of him and someone who I guessed was his mom. He was younger in a couple of them, but the last one looked to be more recent. His father was noticeably absent. I decided it was better not to bring it up, since I had no idea if his father was even alive or not. If he was alive and well, the fact that he wasn't represented among the photos in Landon's home sent up a red flag regarding the status of their relationship.

Perched on a shelf on the other side of a flat-screen TV was a picture of Landon leaning against a candy-apple red 1970 Chevelle 454 SS, complete with white racing stripes.

No. Friggin. Way.

The 1970 Chevelle had long been my dream car. While most girls sat in their bedrooms in high school daydreaming about the quarterback, I'd been picturing myself behind the wheel of this exact car, driving on the open road, windows down, music pumped without a care in the world.

"Is this your car?" I asked, trying hard to contain my excitement.

"Yeah. That's my pride and joy. It was my first big purchase when the company started to do well."

"I have to tell you how insanely jealous I am. I could beat you over the head right now."

"Sweetheart, any time you want to beat my head, you just say the word."

My cheeks flamed at his obvious innuendo. Somehow we'd fallen back into the pattern of sexually suggestive banter, which seemed to be our go-to these days. I looked over to

Landon and noticed he seemed to be amused by my embarrassment. He was forgetting that two could play at this game.

I turned to face him and jutted my hip out to the side, then ever-so-slightly stuck my chest out toward him. "Maybe you can take me for a ride some time," I said as breathy as possible without sounding like a complete idiot.

"Unfortunately, she's put away for the winter. That said, I'd still love to take you for a ride."

My breath caught. I looked up into his chocolate brown eyes and saw that they were heated and darker than they usually were underneath his half-drawn lids. That only stoked the fire within me.

"I bet you know how to give a girl a good ride," I said, holding his gaze. Goodness knows I'd been daydreaming about it myself for weeks now.

"I've been told I give a damn good ride. It's all how you work the stick, and I've always had requests for more when I'm finished."

I licked my lips at the picture he was painting with his words. Landon's eyes caught the movement. His hand shot out and cupped the back of head.

Fear and equal parts anticipation coursed through my veins. I wanted so badly for him to lean in and kiss me—to push his tongue through the seam of my mouth and take me in a fierce and knee-buckling kiss. He stood there unmoving, except for the rise and fall of his muscular chest from his deep breaths. His eyes roamed my face, but I'm not sure what he was looking for. If it was permission—he had it. However, as quickly as he'd placed his hand on me, he withdrew it.

"Why don't we head over to Doumar's for a break and then get back to this?"

The change of subject and his mood transformed so quickly that my lust-fogged mind had trouble keeping up. His professional mask was effectively back in place and it saddened me a little to see the easygoing man I'd spent the afternoon with disappear once again. In our short time together today I'd learned that there was a depth of complexity to Landon that wasn't apparent at first.

"Um...sure. Just let me grab my coat."

chapter fourteen

Skye

We drove to Doumar's in Landon's Audi RS5. It was sleek and screamed success, reminding me of the "office Landon." I realized then that his vehicles mimicked his personality. One, smooth and sleek, while the other was laid-back and up for a good time.

Doumar's had been a staple in Virginia for more than a hundred years. It was a family-owned diner that specialized in homemade ice cream and burgers. Throw in a little old school curbside service and it was one of the most popular spots in Norfolk, due to its yesteryear charm and made-to-order food and drinks.

Since it was chilly out, we decided to eat inside. It was unusually quiet for a Saturday, so we were able to slip into an empty booth right away. One of the waitresses, Betty, approached our table with a set of menus and plopped them down on the table. She'd been working here as long as I'd been coming.

"I don't suppose y'all need these, but I brought 'em anyway. Skye, Landon...it's good to see you both. Though I can't say I've ever seen you in here together." She put a hand to her ample hip and looked between the two of us. Betty always remembered her customers. I just didn't realize that Landon was one of her regulars, too.

I looked across the table and Landon seemed as surprised to see that Betty knew me as I was about him.

"You come here a lot?" he asked with a smirk on his face.

"Since I was a little girl."

"That's right. I've known you both since you were wee high," Betty said, holding her hand up to her waist. "What can I get you for...the usual?"

"Yes, please," we both said at the same time.

Landon looked over to me and laughed. "Thanks, Betty." He turned his attention back to me after she took off to put in our orders. "My parents used to take me here on the weekends when I was little to watch the waffle cones being made. I loved watching old man Doumar press and roll them. He even let me try my hand at it a time or two."

"Me, too! But I did such a horrible job, after a few tries he never let me again."

Landon gave a small chuckle and then looked out the window, staring off into space. He looked contemplative...like he was reliving and enjoying some long ago memory. He'd mentioned that his *parents* had taken him. The pictures of him and his mom in his apartment came to mind, and I decided to take my chances and bring up his family. "So...do you have any siblings?"

He turned his head to look at me once again. I couldn't help but notice the sad tilt to his mouth. "No, there's just me. Apparently after I came along, my parents didn't think they'd be able to handle any more. I guess I was quite the handful."

I smiled, picturing the younger Landon I'd seen in some of the pictures, giving his parents a run for their money. "I couldn't help but notice the pictures of you and your mom in your condo, but you just mentioned your parents..." I trailed off as I saw a shadow pass over Landon's face. He recovered quickly, the mask firmly back in place.

"I don't talk to my dad much anymore."

"Oh, I'm sorry."

He shrugged, trying to feign nonchalance, but I saw how tense his muscles were from across the table. "It's no biggie. He did some things a while ago...it hasn't been the same since."

I didn't get the feeling he was open to discussing exactly what those "things" had been so I changed the subject. "Well, I know you have excellent taste in cars, you were an accomplished athlete in high school, and you love Doumar's as much as I do. What else do I need to know about you? I'm enjoying discovering the man behind the mask."

Landon raised his eyebrows. "The man behind the mask?"

I gave him the best 'duh' look I could. "You have a much cooler veneer about you in the office. Very professional, mind you, but you wear your emotions behind a mask. It's hard sometimes to tell if you're pleased or irritated with me."

"Really?"

"Come on."

"Honestly, I think it's probably because I'm so focused at work. I've worked hard to get my company where it is and losing focus could mean I lose business. It's important to me that if a client or two bails, it wouldn't put the entire company in peril. I have to think about the people working for me who rely on their jobs to pay the bills."

Everything he said sounded genuine and of course, as an employee, it was good to hear. But there was something more behind that last statement, though I couldn't say what exactly. "I'd say you don't need to worry about that. You already represent a wide range of businesses, and if things go as planned in L.A., you *really* won't have anything to worry about."

"Exactly. That's why it's so important we nail that meeting with Calder."

Before I could respond, Betty set our plates down in front of us. I looked at her and smiled my thanks, but when I heard Landon laughing on the other side of the table, I looked across the booth. He was focused on our plates and when I looked down, I saw why. Apparently, we each had the same "regular"—minced pork barbecue sandwich and a glass of limeade.

"What are the chances?" I asked.

"It *is* the best thing on the menu so probably pretty good," he said. "Thanks, Betty."

"No problem, sweets. You two enjoy."

After she'd walked away from the table, I raised an eyebrow to Landon. "Sweets, huh? I'd say someone has an admirer."

I figured he'd respond with some equally playful banter...um, wrong. He fixed his gaze to me, and when he said his next words, they were weighted with meaning. "Who do you think my admirer is?" He was stone-faced, serious, and seemed to really be looking for an answer. I couldn't very well raise my hand like I was in third grade and shout "me, me, me!" I didn't know how to respond, so I did the only thing I could think of—I took a giant bite of my sandwich to occupy my mouth.

Landon smirked and seemed happy to let me avoid the question. "I've only ever seen you eat salads and other healthy shit at work. I'm surprised you're walking on the wild side with that sandwich." His hands were occupied with his own giant sandwich, so he nodded his head down toward my plate.

"I confess to being a bit of a granola girl, but I can't help myself when I'm here. And I've been known to take a walk on the wild side a time or two, you know."

You know? Of course he knew. I'd been groping his crotch in a public hallway before I even knew his name. He clearly had the same thing running through his mind because a knowing grin spread across his face.

"Oh I know, Skye. Believe me...I think about your last walk on the wild side quite frequently."

The floor could open up into a giant sinkhole and swallow me whole anytime now. I felt the blush spread up my chest and onto my face, making my ears burn. Landon just laughed at my expense, apparently happy that he'd rendered me speechless.

The rest of our lunch passed mostly in silence, partly because we were both thoroughly enjoying our meals and partly—at least for me—because I didn't want to venture back into the territory of the conversation we'd abandoned. I felt, quite simply, like an idiot. My comment had been in jest. I really didn't have much of a wild side. Certainly not one I was comfortable with anyway. My experience with Landon at Fahrenheit had been about the craziest thing I'd ever done.

We finished up and said our goodbyes to Betty, who made us promise that we'd be back to see her soon. I got the sense that she thought there was more between us than a working relationship, but I was too embarrassed to address it in front of him. The next time I came in by myself, I'd make sure she knew the score.

When we returned to Landon's place, we took our respective spots back on the couch and got back to work. Hours later, I had a stiff neck and aching back from being hunched over my laptop, so I stood to stretch.

I raised my arms over my head and bent to the side slightly, feeling a rush of cooler air across the strip of my belly where my shirt had risen. I thought nothing of it until I looked down at the couch where Landon was still seated.

His eyes were fixated on my exposed stomach before they darted up to meet my own. I slowly lowered my arms back down and kept my gaze trained on his. He stood from the couch, looking like a predator about to devour his prey. And oh, did I want to be devoured. In that moment, I would have thrown caution to the wind and let him. But instead of leaning in to kiss me as I hoped he would, he placed both of his hands on my upper arms and turned me slowly so that my back faced him.

chapter fifteen

Landon

The need to pull Skye into my embrace and ravage her mouth was burning like a hot coal inside my stomach. But I couldn't do that. I shouldn't. And yet I still needed my hands on her—needed some kind of connection to her physically, if I was going to be able to take my next breath.

"Um...Landon. What are you doing?" she asked softly, almost a whisper.

What *was* I doing, for fuck's sake? Blurring the line again, that's what. It was a thin, almost non-existent one to begin with. Hell, it was like I'd been trying to etch a line in concrete with a stick since the moment I saw her in my office.

"You're tense. Let me massage you for a minute," I found myself saying, despite the argument going on in my head.

"You really don't have to," she said, but the tone of her voice made it obvious she didn't mean it.

"I feel guilty for keeping you here all afternoon and on a Saturday evening." That was complete bullshit. I didn't feel an ounce of guilt. Instead, I felt privileged that I was able to spend the entire day in her company. The day had been amazing and I could easily picture us doing this on the weekends...spending time together, hanging out, learning more about each other, sharing shit with one another. I couldn't remember the last time I wanted something more than a temporary fling or a one-nighter with a chick, though if I had to guess, it was probably in high school before my parents' divorce.

I moved my hands up to her shoulders and began squeezing and kneading gently. Her muscles were tense and a lot of ideas about how I could help her relax came to mind.

None of them appropriate.

When I moved my hands closer to her neck, I touched bare skin. I continued massaging, and at one point she leaned her head back slightly, a small moan escaping her perfect lips. Thank God I wasn't pressed up against her or she would have felt my reaction to the sound she just made. After a few minutes, her muscles became loose and I knew I was pushing my luck to continue on like this. A man only had so much self-control.

I removed my hands from her body, hating that I had to do it. But I was her boss, and as much as I wanted her, I didn't want either of us in a position where working together would become a problem. Because, let's face it—I was the owner of the company, and no matter what happened between us or how uncomfortable things got if they didn't work out, I wasn't going anywhere. She'd be the one who'd have to leave. And since she was the best assistant I'd had so far, I didn't want to lose her. Plus, I could already see what an integral role she was going to play in helping me handle a second office on the West Coast.

I couldn't—and wouldn't—screw all that up just because my dick wanted a taste of what it wasn't entitled to.

I cleared my throat and adopted my professional demeanor. When she turned to face me, I said, "I suppose you should be going now."

From the look on her face, I'd say she was a little taken

aback. "Oh...okay. Sorry, I didn't realize you had plans. I guess I should have figured since it's Saturday night. I'll just get my stuff together and get out of your way."

She was doing that cute rambling thing she did when she was nervous. It only made her more endearing to me—unfortunately.

She bent over to grab her laptop and papers off the table, putting her perfect ass on display. My dick actually twitched just thinking of what it would look like if I peeled those tight jeans down her legs, followed soon after by whatever undergarment she had on under them. I'd step between her legs and—

"Landon?" Skye's voice brought me back to the present.

I shook my head to clear the inappropriate thoughts. "Sorry, what?"

"I said the next time we're working late and you have a date or something, just let me know and I'll be sure to get out of your hair."

I couldn't help the small smirk, knowing full well she was fishing for information. I also couldn't help that it pleased me, even though alarm bells should be going off in my head.

It would be easier to go with her assumption, but I didn't want to lie to her and for whatever reason, I didn't want her to think there was anyone else. There wasn't. I'd never looked for a relationship. In fact, I avoided them at all costs. Why hand all that trust over to someone and give them the power to destroy you? The only risks I took were in my professional life, not my personal one. So far, that approach had been worked well for me and paid major dividends. Yes, women warmed my bed on a frequent basis, but I was always upfront that it was going nowhere beforehand. I didn't need the drama that a woman scorned would inevitably cause.

That being said, I decided to go on a fishing expedition myself.

"I don't have a date, but I assumed that you probably had plans of your own on a Saturday night."

"Actually, I don't," she said. "Since Vic, I haven't wanted to start dating again and all my friends had plans of their own tonight."

I tried to ignore the feeling of relief that washed through my veins at her declaration of not wanting to date. Tried, but failed.

"Well, that might be a good idea for the time being, given the last douchebag you went out with." I was a self-serving asshole for saying it and trying to cement the idea in her head, especially when I didn't plan on pursuing her.

I could live with it.

"How do you really feel?" she said and chuckled a bit.

"Sorry, but that guy is bad news." Her eyes lost the sparkle that was normally there and she looked to the ground. I tipped her chin up with my finger. What was it about this girl that made it impossible for me to keep my hands to myself? "Hey, what is it? What did I say?"

"Nothing. What do you mean?" she said, obviously trying to play it off.

"Nice try, Skye. But you lost some of your sparkle for a second there. What were you thinking of?"

She stared into my eyes for a moment before responding. "It's nothing. Just remembering some of the drama before we broke up, that's all."

"You sure?"

She nodded and looked thoughtful for a moment. "What did you mean I lost some of my sparkle?"

I mentally berated myself for saying too much. There was no easy way out of this one. Fuck it—I'd just have to say exactly what I'd meant. "You have this thing about you, this sparkle in your eyes that draws people in. It's just your natural charisma...a vibrancy that you lose when you talk about him. It's like there's no life in your eyes. Like you're no longer...you."

I cupped her jaw with my hands and ran my thumb lightly over the smooth skin of her cheek. Damn it. I had to kiss her— I had to.

I leaned in slowly, letting her know my intentions so she could pull away if she wanted. She didn't. Instead, she leaned in and our lips met in the middle. The kiss was chaste at first until I ran my tongue along the seam of her mouth, seeking entry. She acquiesced and when our tongues touched, the match was struck and passion roared to life like a flame. I moved my hands down to cup her ass and press her into me. When she felt my hard shaft press into her, she moaned and wrapped her arms around me. One hand found my hair and she tugged it in her grip, while the other dug into the muscles in my back. We continued on for several minutes until we finally pulled away and stood apart from each other, both sucking in lungfuls of air.

"I'm sorry. I shouldn't have done that. I just love that the classy, polished façade falls to pieces when my hands are on you."

"I don't know why that is. I seem to lose all sense of right and wrong when I'm around you," she said, still slightly breathless.

"I'm sorry if I've made you uncomfortable. It's just...I've been thinking about kissing you again since that first time, when I didn't even know who you were. Am I the only one?"

She said nothing, and just when I thought she was going to up and leave without answering, she shook her head slightly. "What does it mean?" she asked, sounding less confident than I'd ever heard her.

"I suppose it means we're attracted to each other. Beyond that...I don't know."

"Nothing can ever happen. I work for you."

"Believe me. I've told myself the same thing more than once. That fact seems to have trouble permeating into my brain."

"Well, it can't ever happen again." She sounded like she was trying to convince herself more than me, but I simply nodded my agreement. "Okay then. It was just a momentary slip and that's all. No need to discuss it again. We're both adults. I'm sure it won't be an issue for us in the office."

"Of course not. Again, I'm sorry if I made you uncomfortable." I ran a hand through my hair.

"Consider it forgotten." She smiled her practiced smile at me, one she'd probably worked on since she was a young girl. I really despised when that smile was directed at me.

She gathered the last of her things and rushed toward the door. I followed her, hating how awkward things had become between us.

"I suppose I'll see you at the office on Monday morning then," I said.

"Enjoy the rest of your weekend." She turned to open the door and stopped with her back still to me when I spoke.

"We'll probably have to work a couple nights next week. I hope that's not a problem."

"Of course not. Why would it be?"

"Probably best if we worked from the office instead of here." She nodded, still not turning to look at me. "Alright then, I'll see you later."

She opened the door and left without giving me a backward glance.

This was exactly why I needed to get her out of my head for good. As I mixed myself a whiskey sour, I debated calling up one of my buddies for a night out on the town, but for some reason the idea held little interest for me. What the hell was wrong with me? There was a time when I'd drink away the stress of the week or find some random hot piece of ass to relieve the tension—or a combination of the two. I guess I'd have to go with the drinking for now, since the only one I wanted to work out my stress with had just walked out the door.

Regardless, there was no doubt that the sexual tension between us was escalating. Something was going to give—and soon.

chapter sixteen

Skye

I stood in the elevator to head down to my car, still shell-shocked. As much as I'd been hoping for it, I hadn't expected him to kiss me—not really.

My head was spinning. It was hard to keep all of Mr. Mercurial's personalities straight. Intense, to-the-point business man in the office, relaxed, approachable guy at home, and demanding then standoffish after he had his hands on me. The crux of the whole thing was that I liked all those sides to him and appreciated all the complexities that went into making Landon Steele exactly the man he was.

The elevator dinged and the doors opened. I made my way to my car deep in thought, barely noticing my surroundings.

The more I tried to resist my attraction to Landon, the harder it became. I hadn't wanted to involve myself with him for fear it would affect our working relationship, but it seems that not acting on my feelings was achieving the same result. Maybe I'd just follow his lead from now on. If he wanted to keep things all business, I'd deal. But if he made a pass at me again, I'd know for certain that he was as attracted to me as I was to him.

I'd been taught my entire life to consider the consequences of my actions, but perhaps it was time for me to act like the carefree, twenty-one-year-old I should be. My dad had his career and I'd never do anything to purposely jeopardize it, but I had my own life now and had to live with my own decisions. Maybe a fling with Landon was just what I needed to remember how fun it could be without all the drama that was my relationship with Vic.

After all, we were both adults—how complicated could things get?

The first part of the week was business as usual between Landon and me...that is, until Wednesday evening. We had to work late to finish the final prep for our trip to L.A., and because there had been a problem with the heat in the office all day, it was completely sweltering.

"Are you sure you wouldn't rather do this at your place or mine? It's so hot in here," I said when I entered his office.

"Here is fine. We'll manage." He'd taken his suit jacket off, removed his tie, rolled his shirt sleeves up and undone several buttons, revealing a small portion of his muscled chest.

I'd taken off the opaque tights I'd worn under my dress earlier that morning, as well as the tailored jacket I wore over my mod-style tank dress. I was still overheated so I'd tossed my hair up into a messy bun on top of my head. If anyone came into the office, we certainly didn't look like a professional pair.

"Where do you want to start?" I asked. I put a mock copy of the handouts I'd put together for his speech in front of him on his desk.

He picked one up and looked it over. "These are good. Have them sent over to the printers and shipped to the hotel in L.A. so they arrive before the conference."

"Will do."

"What else do we need to go over?" he asked.

I came around to stand beside his desk and placed some notes in front of him that I'd put together for our meeting with Calder Fox. "I thought you could look these over and see if there are any other points you think are worth mentioning. I talked to some of the Account Reps and listed some examples of the crisis management work our office has done in the past."

Calder was a child star turned up-and-coming movie star who'd recently fallen from grace. Everyone was slating him as the next Tom Cruise, but his reputation had taken a nosedive with the recent revelations of how he was spending his free time. A recent rehab stint hadn't helped.

Landon looked over the papers and seemed happy with what he saw. I loved seeing him like this...professional businessman, in control, and completely focused on what he was doing. The cologne he wore slowly permeated my senses the longer I stood beside him. I loved that smell. It was so sexy and so...Landon.

He picked up a pen off his desk and went to mark up my notes. He began writing but the pen had run out of ink. He swirled it around in a circle on the page as if some ink would magically appear. "Damn. This one's out. Can you pass me that one?" he asked distractedly, pointing to the other side of the desk.

I reached over to grab the pen. As I was about to hand it to him, it slipped from my fingers and fell to the floor. I started to bend over to get it when Landon said, "I'll grab it."

I went back to looking at the notes on the desk, trying to figure out what he thought needed correcting when I felt his hand's feather light touch against my ankle. I stilled immediately. It must have been a mistake. He had to have accidentally brushed against me when he was reaching for the pen.

What happened next was no accident.

He ran his hand from the inside of my calf up to my knee

and back down again. I sent up a small 'thank you' prayer that I had decided to shave that morning.

I glanced down to my side. He was looking up at me with half-drawn lids. I didn't say a word and couldn't move as he continued his slow assault on my senses.

My breath quickened and my dress suddenly felt altogether too restrictive. This time when he brought his hand back up my leg, he passed over my knee until his hand was up under my skirt, mid-thigh.

"Your skin is so smooth. It's like silk or cashmere or something. I've never felt anything like it."

My pussy throbbed in anticipation, wanting him to touch me there. How could it not? His large hands climbed a little higher but still weren't touching me where I needed him to most. I swear, if he didn't do something to ease the ache soon, I was going to go bat-shit crazy.

I let out a rough exhale of air and leaned forward, placing my hands on the desk in front of me so that I was slightly bent over. That must have been all the invitation he needed. When his hand finally crept back up my leg, he brought it all the way up to the juncture of my thighs.

I glanced back at him again. He was seated in his chair, still with one hand all the way up under my skirt. His large erection was pushing against the seam of his pants. It was such a turn-on to think that I did that to him—that I put him in that state.

His fingers made contact with the silk of my thong and rubbed lightly from front to back. The slight friction gave me little satisfaction. It was all I could do not to grab his hand myself and push him roughly against me.

Without warning, he removed his hand and stood up. "Don't move," he said with an authoritative tone. He adjusted himself before he began to walk toward the door. God, watching him touch himself, even just that little bit, was so freaking hot. He closed the office door, flipped the privacy switch for the glass, locked the door, and turned back to look at me.

I hadn't given a second thought to the fact that his office door was open. It was late and everyone had gone home, but who knew whether security or the cleaning staff were around? I was normally a girl who examined every angle and every possible outcome before I did anything. I just completely lost my head around this guy.

Landon said nothing as he made his way back over to me, but the look on his face was one of possession. He wasn't asking for permission for what he was about to do. He was taking what he wanted.

About. Fucking. Time.

chapter seventeen

Skye

He surprised me by sitting back down in his chair and sliding it so he was directly behind me. Without a word, he grabbed the hem of my dress and lifted it so my skirt sat around my waist. My ass was pretty much on display since the pair of thong underwear I'd worn provided little modesty.

"I knew you'd have a great ass. Do you have any idea how long I've fantasized about seeing it? It's as perfect as I imagined. You flit around here with your fitted dresses and your tight skirts on, and some days it's all I can do not to sport wood when I look at you."

I felt my underwear grow wetter with each word that escaped his lips. "Landon, please."

"Please what?"

I was growing desperate for his touch—for him to relieve the ache that was threatening to consume me whole and drive me mad. I pushed my ass back a bit in an effort to make it clear what I wanted. A throaty laugh escaped him.

"I'll give you what you need, sweetheart. But first I want to take a good look at this pussy."

My knees almost buckled right there. I'd never had anyone be so blatant and crude with me. What surprised me was how much it turned me on. He pushed my legs farther apart and pulled my thong halfway down my legs so it was stretched between my knees. I felt his hand at my back exerting pressure, causing me to bend over some more.

I was glad I didn't have to look him in the eyes as I was having a moment of slight embarrassment at being so completely on display to him.

"Oh sweetheart, you are so fucking wet. Your pussy is aching for me. Do you have any idea what that does to me?"

Embarrassment. Gone.

Something about this guy made me throw all reason away and urged me to do naughty things. My inner sex kitten had come out to play.

I moaned. I couldn't help it. I swear I was in danger of his words alone bringing me to climax.

After what seemed like minutes of him looking at me, he finally brought his fingers from one end of my sex to the other. After a few strokes I was moaning into the desk, my need for him at an all-time high. I was about to lose my mind when he slowly, gloriously, sunk his fingers into me. His thumb brushed up against my clit and he began to move his fingers in and out of me.

"My fingers are dripping with you. It's so. Fucking. Hot." He punctuated each word as his fingers pushed into me. His thumb was tracing an invisible pattern over my clit. I couldn't hold still any longer and began to move my ass back into him, wanting him deeper, harder, faster.

His breathing grew more labored behind me. "That's it, baby. Fuck my fingers like you want to be riding my cock right now."

I threw my head back and moaned, not caring if someone was outside the door emptying garbage or not.

What. The. Fuck. Ever.

Landon stood behind me and I heard him playing with the

belt on his suit pants, followed by his zipper. I didn't know if he was going to push himself into me, and honestly, in that moment, I didn't care. All I cared about was getting the release that I so badly needed—the release that had been building and building while working alongside Landon all these weeks.

He must have been stroking himself because he moaned, and I felt the head of his rigid shaft hit my ass cheek each time I pushed back onto his fingers.

I was so close. The tension in my body was almost ready to snap...if I could just—the taut coil inside me shattered and I moaned as my orgasm overtook me. I squeezed my eyes shut as Landon's thumb continued his ministrations and he wrung the last of that blissful feeling out of me.

When my mind came back to the present, I heard Landon panting heavily and with a groan, he found his own release. I felt warm liquid coat my ass and he briefly pushed the head of his shaft into one of my cheeks.

It was silent except for the sound of the two of us trying to catch our breath. I wasn't sure what to do. How had that just happened? What I should say? What did it mean, if anything? A thousand questions swam through my mind.

"Wait here for second. Let me get something to clean you up." I heard him pull up his zipper and refasten his pants. When he walked around me to leave the office—shutting the door behind him as he left—I didn't have the guts to look up at him. I couldn't bear it if I saw him looking at me with regret.

A minute later, I heard the door open and close again. He used what I guessed was a wet paper towel from the bathroom to wipe the evidence of his release off me, and then dried me off with another. When he was finished, I quickly pulled my underwear back up, smoothed my dress down, and turned to face him.

The look of regret I feared wasn't there. Instead, he gazed down at me with awe, or reverence maybe. Whatever it was, in that moment it scared me. Because maybe we were going to do this. Maybe he wanted to try to make something work between us.

My last decision on who to date had turned out to be a disaster. And now here I was fooling around with my boss. Bad decision after bad decision. I was in a job I liked, in an industry where I wanted to make my mark, and here I was risking it all because I wanted to bone my boss.

Stupid. Girl.

No matter my intentions, whenever I was around this man, my hormones took over and reason went out the window.

Landon cupped my cheek. "Skye, I—"

"We should get back to work. We still have a lot to get through."

He looked like he was going to argue with me for a second and go back to whatever he had wanted to say, but I couldn't deal with it right now. If he said it was a mistake, I'd be heartbroken. And if he wanted to push for something more, I wouldn't know what to say because I didn't *know* what I wanted to happen.

"If that's what you want," he said, his tone clipped.

I nodded my head, turned back to the desk to grab the papers we'd been working on, and headed over to the seating area at the other side of the office. No way could I stand at that desk again tonight and have any chance of concentrating on work. Not with my thong still wet, courtesy of Landon.

chapter eighteen

Landon

Sitting across from me, Skye looked as poised and put together as she always did. I had no idea how she managed it, when only an hour ago she'd been writhing against me and moaning her pleasure. I had a semi every time my mind wandered back to what I'd done to her at that desk. I'd probably get jack shit done the rest of the week, since my desk now served up a constant reminder of the carnal woman who momentarily abandoned her controlled demeanor.

As she reviewed the notes I gave her, I had the opportunity to study her without looking like the creep that I probably was. The temperature in the office was still hotter than hell, and since our little escapade, Skye's normally porcelain skin had a noticeable flush to it. She had her legs tucked up under her in the chair and was absently chewing on the end of her pen as she read. Her heart-shaped pink lips looked as kissable as ever. Her hair was tousled up on top of her head in one of those makeshift bun things that girls wore. It was messy but cute. The fine hairs at her neckline had curled up a bit.

"Those are nice earrings," I blurted out.

It took her a second, but she looked over to me when she realized I'd said something. "Sorry?"

I motioned toward her. "Those earrings. They're nice. Not something you see a lot of girls wear." Jesus. I sounded like a sap. What guy noticed what earrings girls wore? Truth was— we didn't. I only noticed these things about her.

"Oh, thanks." One of her small hands reached up to touch one of the earrings in question. "They're vintage. I kind of have a thing for vintage stuff."

"They suit you."

She looked at me for a moment. "Thanks." Then she turned her attention back to her papers and I did the same, deciding to spare her my interrogation for the time being. It was clear that she didn't want to address what had happened between us, so I'd let her off the hook—for now. But we *would* have to deal with the situation between us, sooner rather than later. The sexual tension and my affinity for her were growing stronger each day. I figured it would've lessened by now but the opposite was true.

Every day I got a better idea of what a treasure the woman sitting across from me was. I just had to figure out what I was going to do about it. What kind of idiot discovered hidden treasure and then threw it back into the sea?

That Sunday we arrived at the JW Marriott in downtown Los Angeles before lunch. I'd arranged to stay in the Chairman suite and booked the adjoining room for Skye. We were here for a week, and I hated being stuck in some small hotel room with only a bed and small desk, day after day. I wanted something comfortable to retire to before we had to head out for the hobnobbing required while we were in town.

When I walked through the suite doors, I was happy to see that the room was as spacious and comfortable-looking in person as it was when I'd looked it up online. There was a living area with a flat-screen TV on the wall, which opened up to a dining room with a large, wooden table. This would be a good place for Skye and me to work while we were out here. Beyond that was the master suite, which would be perfect for unwinding after a long day—or collapsing from exhaustion, as the case might be.

A knock came from the door of the adjoining room. I set my bags down and went to open it. Skye walked in, not at all looking like we'd been traveling for hours and were dealing with a time change. Her hair was back in a ponytail and she wore a pair of black leggings and a white shirt. I think chicks called them tunics or something. Whatever it was called, she looked casual, comfortable, and sexy as all hell.

"Wow. Looks like I need to speak to the boss about getting an upgrade in my accommodations," she said, laughing.

"There's a reason you have an adjoining room. You're welcome in here any time. I'll leave this door unlocked; come and go as you please. I figured you'd want your own...room."

She smirked and turned from perusing the room to look at me. "That's probably best." She took a walk around the suite to check it out. "So, we have a free day. What do you want to do?"

"Actually, I took the liberty of booking us one of the cabanas by the pool. It'll probably be the only day we'll have to do something like that. What do you think?"

"It's only seventy degrees out. Won't we be a little chilly?"

"Did you bring a swimsuit?"

"Well, yeah."

"Then we'll be fine. The pool is heated and the cabanas have heaters too. I think the whole pool deck does."

She shrugged. "Okay then. Let me change and I'll meet you down there in a few."

It was an unseasonably warm day for December in L.A. so the pool deck was busy. I was relaxing on the chaise inside the cabana after giving my drink order to the waiter when I saw Skye making her way across the pool deck. She had on a pair of sunglasses and a floral cover-up with long, billowing sleeves. When she reached the cabana, she smiled wide and dropped her beach bag onto the coffee table in the center.

"The waiter just left. I didn't order for you because I wasn't sure what you'd want," I said.

"I think I'm going to take a dip in the pool. Do you mind ordering me an iced tea when the waiter comes back?"

"Sure thing."

She slid off her sandals and then proceeded to pull her cover-up off over her head.

I was in trouble.

I was in so much fucking trouble if I thought there was *any* way I might get through this trip sleeping only a few rooms away from her when she looked like *that*.

Her swimsuit was a gold one-piece that had a slit all the way down to her belly button and a belt around the waist. I'd been imagining what she'd look like completely naked since I'd first seen her. This swimsuit was giving me a pretty good idea, but apparently my imagination hadn't been doing her justice.

She smiled at me before heading over to the pool and diving in. It was clear she had no idea the effect seeing her in that tiny bit of fabric had on me. That or she hid it well. Now I'd be trying to hide the wood I'd no doubt be sporting all afternoon.

The waiter returned and I ordered Skye's drink. A few minutes later, he dropped it off just as Skye was returning to the cabana. He did a double-take as she came up behind him. I couldn't blame him but it still fueled my competitive nature, seeing another man appreciate her rocking body. Even if she wasn't mine.

I tipped him a couple of dollars and said, "We're good for a while. Thanks." Skye smiled her megawatt, draw-every-man-to-her-within-twenty-feet smile as he passed by her to leave.

Fuck me, but I loved that smile. "How was the water?" I asked.

She grabbed a towel off one of the tables and began to dry herself off. "Warmer than I thought it'd be. We got lucky it's such a nice day out today."

"The warmers help, too," I said, motioning to the heater in the roof of the cabana.

"There is that." She laughed, her entire face lighting up.

She really was breathtaking...and pure...full of light. When I was with her, I forgot about the pressures of growing my business and my strained relationship with my father—everything else just faded into the background and I was just here with her...in the present. And none of the other shit mattered.

When she was done rubbing that damn towel over every inch of her porcelain skin, she came to sit beside me on the couch and grabbed her drink off the table. I watched as she took the straw between her lips. This had to be some form of foreplay torture. First the swimsuit, then rubbing herself down, and now this? As she sucked the liquid down, I began to get hard just thinking about what those lips would look like wrapped around the end of my cock.

I couldn't watch her a second longer. I pulled the drink away from her mouth and she gave me a quizzical look. "We need to talk."

"Okay..."

We'd both avoided any conversation about what had happened that night at the office. I planned to bring it up during our long flight over here, but the timing didn't feel right. Now we were in a cabana in the middle of a packed pool, and although this didn't seem the place to delve into what was becoming an increasingly complicated situation, I guess it was as good as any.

Skye set her drink on the table in front of us and turned her body to face me. Stretching out one leg in front of her, she draped it over the top of my lap. She shifted and I knew the moment she felt my semi because she looked up at me with what could only be described as a minx-like look. This girl knew exactly the effect she was having on me.

"What did you want to talk about..." She moved her leg down onto my lap further, brushing up against my shaft before continuing, "...Mr. Steele?"

"Jesus, Skye. I think it's pretty obvious what I'm thinking about at the moment."

"You do have a point," she said and gestured down to my lap.

I ran my hand along the back of my neck, when what I really wanted to do was run it from one end of my shaft to the other. It seemed Skye was in a flirtatious mood and wanted to test the boundaries of our relationship. I wonder what she'd do when push came to shove?

I ran a hand slowly up and down the length of her leg. Her breathing hitched when I reached mid-thigh so I knew I was getting to her. "You have a quite a way with words today. You'd better watch yourself or I might think of a few other things that mouth of yours would be good for."

"Don't beat around the bush...get straight to the point. What else do you think I could use this mouth for?" She moved her calf back and forth over the rapidly growing bulge in my pants. The friction against my cock had me straining against my shorts.

"For starters, this." I pulled her in by the back of her neck and brought her mouth to mine. Our lips touched, but instead of feasting and ravaging her—as was my impulse—I took my time, slowly nibbling her bottom lip before running my tongue along the seam of her mouth. She immediately opened to me and our tongues met. The kiss was slow and sensual, but we each vied for control. She may have started this cat and mouse game, but I wasn't about to let her call the shots.

Her hands came around my neck and tangled in my hair. The sensation of her pulling my hair made me want to get her on her back and push into her but I restrained myself. Just barely.

I broke our kiss. She was looking at me, breathing deeply, her chest heaving. "Go close the curtains," I said. She didn't argue and I watched as she took her perfect little ass to the other side of the cabana and pulled the privacy curtains across, sealing us into our own little paradise.

She walked toward me and before I could say anything she kneeled in front of me. Fuck me. What happened to the sweet little princess I knew in the office? Why was I even asking? I didn't care right now. I loved that I brought out this wild side in her—a side I suspected she didn't even know she had.

"What are you doing?" I asked, my voice cracking at the end.

She licked her lips and looked up at me. "Getting to the point, of course, Mr. Steele." She grinned and started to pull my swim trunks down. I lifted a bit to get them out from under me. She moved them down until my cock sprang free, mere inches from her face.

"My, my. They don't call you 'the man of steel' for nothing, do they?"

I swallowed. Hard.

And then she swallowed my cock. Okay, not literally, but she didn't take her time exploring me. No, she went right for it until the end was pushing against the back of her throat. It was the exact opposite of everything I would have expected from her.

I groaned and fisted a hand in her damp hair. She dragged her tongue along the bottom of my cock. As she pulled up, she swirled her tongue over the tip as it left her mouth. It was exquisite torture.

"Fuck, Skye. Why are you doing this?"

She fisted the base of my shaft and ran her hand up and down its length. I groaned and let my head fall back.

"Are you complaining?"

I lifted my head back up and looked at her. She had a smirk on her face and licked the tip of me when we made eye contact.

"Not a chance. I just don't understand. Since we fooled around the other night, you haven't wanted to discuss it. It was like you just wanted it to go away." It was all I could do to form a coherent sentence and not focus every ounce of my energy on what her hand was doing to me.

"You really want to talk about this *now*?" She stopped moving her hand and I was near desperate for her to continue her brand of torment on me.

"Right. Later. But we *will* discuss it." My hand was still in her hair and I applied a light pressure to let her know that I was more than willing for her to get back to what she'd been doing.

She wrapped her lips around me and once again sucked me into her warm, wet mouth. Then she dragged her lips up and down my cock, my nerve endings begging for release. Instinctively, I gripped her hair tighter but let off a bit for fear of hurting her. I was close. Fuck, I was so close. A part of me couldn't wait to explode inside her, and the other part wanted to drag this out as long as humanly possible.

I brought my other hand into her hair and she increased the pace. When she pushed my swim trunks to the side a bit and moved a hand in to cup my balls, I was done for.

"Shit. I'm gonna come." Skye made no effort to take her mouth from me. She pushed me all the way to the back of her throat and then moaned. The vibration coupled with her playing with my balls sent my release rocketing up my shaft.

I moaned as I poured more and more of myself into her. She took it all without complaint. After I'd rode out my orgasm, I removed my hands from her hair and pulled her up onto my lap so she was straddling me.

I nuzzled my face into her neck. "That was...damn. I don't even have words."

She brought her hands around my neck and weaved them into my hair. I pulled back to look at her.

"You don't have to say anything," she said and gave me a

chaste kiss on the lips. "We should probably open the curtains before people start to wonder though."

"As if they aren't already with all the moaning and groaning going on in here."

"I don't think we were that bad," she said as she rose to go put the curtains back in place. I lifted my swim trunks back up. She pulled the curtains open and sunlight streamed back into the cabana, diminishing the intimate atmosphere that had been present only moments earlier.

"So do you want to stay here for the rest of the afternoon or is there something else you feel like doing? This is our only day to relax, so we might as well enjoy it," I said.

She came and sat beside me, grabbing her drink from the table. "I saw something about the Melrose Trading Post in one of the brochures in my room. It's a flea market. You're probably not interested, but I wouldn't mind checking it out." She shrugged.

"I'll check it out with you."

"Really?" She smiled, looking surprised.

"Sure, why not? What are you in the market for?" I asked.

"Well, you already know I like vintage stuff. Some of my best finds are at places like that. I wouldn't mind picking up something for my apartment. I haven't had much of a chance to decorate it since I moved in."

"I'm sure it looks fine."

"Says the guy with a home that looks like it could be featured in *Architectural Digest*."

"It didn't happen overnight. I've been there for a couple of years," I assured her.

"Even so. I hate coming home to such a sterile environment every night."

"Alright. Why don't we head up to the rooms and I can order us something for lunch while you're getting ready?"

She put a hand on her hip. "Are you saying I have a lot of work to do before I'll be presentable in public?"

"What? No...I—"

She laughed, cutting off my attempt at backtracking. "I'm kidding. I want to jump in the shower anyway so that sounds good."

"Alright. You head up and I'll be right behind you after I let the waiter know we're leaving."

"Perfect."

No, she was perfect, I thought, as she got up to grab her cover-up and put it back on. Or pretty close to it. She put her sandals on, grabbed her bag, and turned back to me.

"I'll come over to your room when I'm ready. Would you mind ordering me something light? Say a grilled chicken salad or something?"

"Will do."

"Thanks." She turned and made her way around the pool and back into the hotel.

My gaze followed her until she was out of sight. Skye was poised and polished when she needed to be, but when it was just the two of us, there was another side to her that intrigued me more and more every day. That was what worried me.

chapter nineteen

Skye

I should have probably taken a cold shower after the cabana.

Instead, I stood under the hot spray thinking back on my split-second decision, clearly not well thought out considering the fact that we'd pretty much been in public. But I'd wanted to please him—mission accomplished.

I couldn't even say how many times I'd thought back over my experience with him in his office over the past few days—I'd lost count. Because it *had* been an experience. I'd never had a man give me so much pleasure in my life and the orgasm had nearly been my undoing, leaving me feeling vulnerable and spent.

Maybe my courage had come from the fact that we were in a city where no one knew me or my father. I don't know. But it *had* taken courage to get down on my knees in front of him. When I'd looked up and saw his expression, I knew it was the right decision. The mask that was normally in place had disintegrated. Sitting above me had been a man on the precipice of losing control. His hooded coffee-colored eyes looked almost feral, as if his entire existence relied on what I would do next.

I had never been that bold with another man. Ever.

In fact, I'd never enjoyed pleasing a man through oral sex so much. I felt like I was in control and had some power over him. And I knew very few people had any type of power over a man like Landon.

I was in the moment when I was with him. I liked that. I was accustomed to being in my head most of the time—considering outcomes, weighing options, determining consequences. It wasn't like that with Landon and I found myself wanting to enjoy that feeling a little while longer.

I hurried to finish my shower and finished getting ready, throwing on an Aztec print tank top and a pair of fitted jeans with gold strappy sandals. It was unseasonably warm, but I thought it might cool off later so I threw a light sweater into my tote before heading to the adjoining room to meet Landon.

His eyes roamed my body when he saw me enter and my breath caught. I'm pretty sure we were both thinking of ditching the flea market outright and just falling into bed with each other. I wasn't completely opposed to the idea but I had no idea what *this* was between us. I was afraid if we spoke about it, we'd ruin it. At present, I was happy to close my eyes, put my hands over my ears like a two-year-old, and say "la-la-la-la-la, I can't hear you."

"You look wonderful," he said.

He was one to talk. Landon wore a pair of dark jeans that fit him perfectly and a black button-up shirt with the sleeves rolled up. It wouldn't surprise me if people took him for an actor or model, being that we were in L.A. If the public had any idea of the orgasm he could give a girl, they'd think he was a porn star.

"Thanks. You, too."

He motioned to his jeans. "These old things?" Hmm...seems Landon knew exactly how good he looked in those jeans. "Lunch is over on the dining room table."

"Great. Have you already eaten?"

He looked a little sheepish. "Sorry. I waited for a bit but I was famished."

I laughed. "It's not a big deal. I took longer than I thought I would. Sorry." I didn't mention that I'd been so slow because I'd been reliving our time spent in the cabana.

"It's not a problem. I'm going to check my e-mails while you eat, and then we can head down to the lobby to catch a cab."

"Sounds good."

Forty-five minutes later we pulled up in front of Fairfax High School, where the flea market was held every Sunday. Rows upon rows of tables lined the parking lot. I felt like a crackhead in a meth lab. There was nothing I loved more than finding hidden treasures amongst a load of crap. We exited the cab and though I offered to pay, Landon refused.

We stood at the end of a long row of tables. He turned to me, looking a little overwhelmed, and asked, "So, where do we start?"

"Have you ever been to one of these before?"

Landon shook his head. "I think my mom may have taken me to a few when I was younger, but I really don't remember. I did most of the shopping for my place online."

"Well, you just start at one end and work your way up, then back down the other side. Price is always negotiable. If you see something you like, don't act too interested and never ask the price on that item first. Ask about something else so it doesn't seem like you can't live without the thing you're really interested in."

He laughed. "So you've done this a time or two."

I nodded. "I'm in my element here. Come on." I didn't know what possessed me, but I took his hand and led him to the first table. He didn't pull away and I found that I liked the feeling of having my hand in his—maybe too much.

After finishing one row of tables and finding nothing of interest, we started in on the opposite side. I immediately noticed an old photo frame that was etched copper with a beautiful green patina over it. I'd considered adding accent pillows in that color to my gray couch at home, so the frame would be another necessary pop of color in the room. After asking about a couple of other items on the table, I inquired about the frame to the older gentleman manning the table.

"That there's seventy-five dollars."

I looked at him skeptically. "For a picture frame? You've got to be kidding."

"You have any idea how much copper costs these days?"

"That may be so, but it's still not worth anywhere near seventy-five dollars."

"Well, what are you willing to pay for it?"

"What are you willing to part with it for?"

"How's sixty dollars sound?"

"Expensive." It'd been my experience that vendors were usually happy getting close to half of what they started out asking, so I started my price below that.

"I'll give you twenty."

He scoffed at me. "Keep dreaming, doll."

"Alright, twenty-five."

"Fifty."

"Twenty-eight."

"Forty-five."

"No way. Thirty and that's as much as you're going to get from me."

"Make it thirty-five and you have a deal," he said.

I pretended to think about it for a moment and then nodded my head. It was more than I would have liked to pay for it, but it was unique and I hadn't ever seen a frame quite like it. I wasn't leaving here without it. The man began wrapping up my frame in newspaper. I looked around to see where Landon had run off to and spotted him a few booths down, eyeing something on one of the tables. He must have felt my eyes on him, because he looked up and gave me a smile. It was warm, genuine, and full of adoration. I felt like a giddy schoolgirl that something as innocent as a smile could get me so excited. I smiled back and he walked over to me.

"You find something?" he asked when he reached me.

"A copper picture frame."

"Your girlfriend here drives a hard bargain," the man working the table said.

I was about to correct him on his assumption when Landon spoke up. "She knows how to get her way, that's for sure. You should have seen her earlier this afternoon."

I blushed and the man on the other side of the table laughed, not having any idea what the reference was. He passed me the bag with my purchase in it.

I started to walk in the direction of the table where Landon had been looking, but he put his hand on the small of my back and turned me the other way. "Weren't you looking at something down there?" I asked.

"No, but I thought I saw something in this next row that I liked. Come on."

We made our way past a few more tables when I heard my phone ring in my bag. I fished it out and brought it to my ear.

"Hello."

"Aaaah! Are you in L.A. already?" It was Ellie. It felt so good to hear her voice and know that we were in the same city together and not on opposite sides of the country from one another.

"I am. We got in this afternoon. I'm just at a flea market."

"Yet another reason I love you. You come to the city with places like Rodeo Drive and you end up at a flea market."

"I hadn't thought about that," I said and laughed.

"Listen, I'm calling to see if you're free to catch a bite to eat tonight?"

"I thought you were tied up?"

"I was supposed to be, but our meeting got canceled and

now Mason is off to meet with the guy he's thinking of hiring as his new manager."

"So it would just be the two of us?"

"Damn straight!"

"Say no more. When and where?"

"I can come get you."

"No, no. I can make my own way wherever we're going."

"Alright then...oh! Let's meet at Pink's. I haven't had a chance to go there since I've been in L.A. It's world famous."

Ellie always made me laugh. For the size of her, you'd never know how much food that girl could put away. "Is there going to be anything there for me to eat?"

"Probably not. But don't worry, you won't have a coronary from one bad meal."

I laughed again. Good thing I'd opted for the salad at lunch. I'd definitely have to make an effort to get a run in tomorrow. "Alright. Can you text me the address?"

"Sure thing. Want to meet there in...say, a half hour?" she asked.

"Perfect. See you then."

"I'm so excited!"

"Me, too." And I was, but it wasn't until I hit 'end' that I realized that meant I'd be ditching Landon at the flea market. "That was Ellie," I said to him.

He looked amused, the corner of his lip twitching up slightly. "Sounds like you were making plans."

I cringed. "I'm sorry. I didn't even think. You're welcome to join us."

He put his hands on both of my shoulders, and I suppressed the shudder that almost ran through my body at the feel of his hands on my bare skin. I knew exactly what those hands were capable of. "Go enjoy a night with your friend. I know you miss her."

"I hate to ditch you here when it was my idea."

"Don't worry about it. You won't have another chance to

see her until your birthday celebration Saturday. I'm going to stick around and keep looking for a bit."

"Are you sure?"

"Positive. Go. Have fun."

"Okay. I won't be late."

"Skye, I may be your boss but I'm not your babysitter. As long as you're ready to attend the first seminar at nine tomorrow morning and in shape to be there, I'm not going to complain."

"Thanks for being so understanding."

"Don't mention it. Now go." He looked down the row to the front of the school. "There's a couple of cabs waiting out front. Go grab one."

I nodded and headed to the front of the school, smiling to myself.

chapter twenty

Skye

The cab pulled up in front of Pink's and I saw Ellie already standing out front waiting for me. She had on a pair of fitted khakis with pockets down the legs and a t-shirt with a light sweater on over it. She looked happy—radiated happiness, actually. And it was nice to see, given what the first half of her year had been like.

I paid the cab driver, grabbed my tote from the seat beside me, and exited the vehicle. Ellie immediately squealed when she saw me and ran over, giving me a big hug.

"It's good to see you, too," I said as she rocked me back and forth in her arms.

"I'm so excited you're here. I can't wait to celebrate our birthdays together next weekend."

"Me either." I hooked my arm in hers as we made our way to the line. One quick look up at the menu and I knew I'd definitely have to make time for a run in the morning. Once we'd both ordered and gotten our food, we decided to sit outside on the patio since it was still fairly nice out. I had an entire winter in Virginia to endure and was all about spending as much time outside as possible. Native Californians may not have thought it was that warm out, but I thought it was perfect.

Ellie picked out a table and put her chili dog and fries down. I opted for the turkey burger and a bowl of chili. It looked good but it was no sandwich from Doumar's back home, and I didn't know if it would be worth all the extra calories. Watching Ellie mow into her dog, I was envious. I didn't pack any extra weight, but that was only because I worked at it by watching what I ate and exercising regularly. I swear Ellie could consume whatever she wanted and still keep the pounds at bay.

"How was the flea market? I don't see anything with you so you must have come up empty."

I shook my head while I swallowed a bite of the turkey burger. Damn. I could understand why this place had been around for more that seventy years. If the turkey burger was this good, I could only imagine what the real burgers tasted like. "I got a picture frame. It's in my tote."

"Cool."

"So how are things with Mason?"

She smirked. "Things are good."

I laughed. "How are things *outside* of the bedroom?" I asked and she joined in my laughter.

"Things are good all around. We're getting settled and Los Angeles is starting to feel less foreign to me now that we've been in one place for a while."

"Do you like where you guys are living?"

She shook her head as she chewed. "It was a process finding a place we both agreed on. But now that we're in there, I'm happy."

"Any word on what Mason has planned for Little Mac?" Ellie didn't like discussing what had happened last summer, but I'd been wondering if and when Little Mac would be getting what was coming to him. As far as I was concerned, the fact that he'd drugged Ellie's drink and made it look like the two of them had been intimate, just to piss of Mason...well, he deserved whatever Mason had planned for him.

A shadow passed over her face. "No. I've brought it up a few times, but he says he's taking care of it and he doesn't want me involved. I trust him so I've stopped asking about it. It puts him in a bad mood the rest of the day whenever I mention it."

"I see."

"Anyways, you'll have to come by before we go out on Saturday and see the place. We can get ready together. It'll be like our college days."

"That'd be great. I can't wait to see it."

"Is your boss still joining us?" I couldn't help the blush that crept onto my face when she mentioned Landon. And like any best friend would, she immediately called me out on it. "So...what's the story?"

"No story." I tried to feign innocence but Ellie wasn't buying it.

"Bullshit. Spill."

I let out a sigh. It would be good to talk to someone about what was or wasn't going on between Landon and me. Plus, I could use her opinion on the situation. "Did Katie ever tell you about the night she dragged me out to the bar after Vic and I broke up, and she got me wasted to try and get me back into the dating game?"

"The night you got puked on? How could I forget?"

"Well, that's not all that happened that night."

"Okay..." Ellie's forehead creased.

"That was actually the first time I met Landon. He tried to pick me up at the bar, we made out, and then I freaked and took off. I didn't see him again until I found out he was my boss."

Ellie dropped her burger onto her tray. "And I'm just hearing about this now, why?"

"I was embarrassed. It's not like me to act that way and I

didn't think I'd ever see him again. There was no reason to mention it."

"What happened when you found out he was your boss?"

"I was mortified, of course. But what was I supposed to do? It's a good job at a growing company and a great start to my career."

Ellie's eyes were as wide as saucers and she leaned in to listen more intently. "What did Landon say? Did he recognize you?"

"Right away. It was clear from the look of shock on his face when he walked in the room."

"Oh my God, I would have paid good money to see this go down."

I playfully smacked her arm from across the table. "It's not funny!"

"Oh, yes it is." She laughed and I waited for her to compose herself. "How are things between you guys now?"

I relayed everything to her and when I was done, she sat at the other side of the table with her mouth hanging open. "This guy must really be something. I would never have expected you to be fooling around with your boss. Katie, maybe. But not you."

"Exactly. When I'm with him, I don't think of any of that stuff. It's like I don't even know who I am anymore—like I'm a stranger in my own skin. At the same time, I'm enjoying myself and it feels so right to just live in the moment for once in my life."

"Why didn't you call me while all of this was going on if you were feeling so conflicted?"

"You're so busy with Mason's schedule and everything, and I didn't want to be a pain in the ass."

Ellie picked my hand up off the table and squeezed it. "I may not be able to sit on the end of the bed while we swap stories anymore, but that doesn't mean I'm not here for you. I'm *never* too busy for you."

I needed to hear that. Ellie had been a constant in my

everyday life for so many years now that I couldn't help feeling lonely without her around. We were each growing into our adult lives...I suppose it was bound to happen. We wouldn't be each other's number one priority anymore, but hearing her say that nothing had changed between us made me feel better.

"I'm just so confused. I don't know what to do. I have no idea what *he* wants to do. He's tried to talk to me about it a couple of times, but I always change the subject."

"Don't you want to know what he's thinking?"

"I do. I'm just scared. What if it's not what I want to hear? It's become more than just fooling around for me. I'm having real feelings for him."

"Then that's something you need to know before you keep doing what you're doing with him—before you get hurt." I nodded. I knew she was right. "Do you want to pursue something more serious with him?" she asked.

"If I'm honest with myself deep down, I've been longing to belong to him for a while now. He's such an amazing guy. He's so intelligent and savvy with his business, but when it's just the two of us, there's this side of him that's so sweet and caring. And when we're fooling around, well..."

"Don't leave me hanging. Well...?"

"He's kinda...dominant a little. And vocal," I said, looking down at my hands in my lap.

"Nice! Well, if that's the way you feel, why don't you tell him?"

"Because if he feels the same way, that's when things are going to get *really* complicated."

"Sounds like that's already happening, Skye," she said softly. "What exactly are you afraid of?"

"Of what the people at my work will say, about what will happen to my job if it doesn't work out between us, about what my dad will think and whether it will affect his run for Senate, of Landon not feeling the same way...that I'm just another girl to fool around with to him. Should I go on?"

Ellie got up and moved to my side of the table. I turned to

face her and she put a hand on my shoulder. "I know you're scared and believe me, I get it. I do. I had all those same reservations last summer, but my only regret was that I didn't tell Mason sooner how I felt. If you really like this guy, I think you have to tell him. Otherwise, someone is going to get hurt."

"I know. I'll say something this week. I don't know how, but I'll find the courage to bring it up."

Ellie gathered me into a hug and we sat like that for a few minutes before I let her go. It felt so good to have my best friend with me again. Reluctantly, I eased out of the hug, and after catching up some more, she took me back to the hotel. I resisted the urge to see what Landon was up to and went straight to my own room and got ready for bed, acutely aware of his presence on the other side of the wall..

chapter twenty-one

Skye

I had set my alarm for early the next morning so I could head down to the gym to get a run in on the treadmill. I preferred running outdoors, but I hadn't researched the area and didn't know what route to run. I couldn't take the chance that I wouldn't be back in time for the first seminar of the day. This was my first work conference and I wanted to prove to Landon that I could handle it and showing up late to the first event was not the way to do it.

I grabbed a bottle of water from the room, cringing inwardly because the thing probably cost six dollars. The gym was pretty empty with only a few middle-aged men working out on some of the weight machines. I chose a treadmill on the far left, as far away from the other workout equipment as I could get. A lot of guys thought gyms were like bars—ripe for picking up women. I was only here to get a good run in before I started my day.

I was a mile into my workout and getting a good sweat going when I saw someone take the machine next to me out of the corner of my eye. Music pounded through my ear buds so I pretended not to notice and kept running, looking straight ahead at the screen broadcasting the early morning news.

A moment later, I felt a tap on my shoulder. I pulled one of my ear buds out and with an irritated look on my face, turned to see who was disturbing my workout.

Landon stood on the machine next to me, smiling. He put his hands up in a placating gesture. "From that look, I'm guessing you're not a morning person."

"Landon. Sorry, I thought you were just some guy coming over to hit on me."

"That happen often?" he asked. He sounded slightly irritated when he said it. Interesting.

"Sometimes. It's part of the reason I usually prefer to run outdoors."

"I see." He put his water in the drink rest on the machine, hit some buttons, and started jogging. "How was your visit with your friend?"

It took me a minute to think of a suitable response, since I suddenly found myself preoccupied by his lean, muscular arms. He swung them as he jogged, the muscles tensing and bunching. It was all very distracting.

"Um...it was good. Nice to catch up with her. She invited us over to her and Mason's house for drinks before we go out Saturday night."

"That sounds fun."

I was panting a bit now as we talked since I was further along in my run. "You cannot pitch him on our services when we're there, Landon. I'm serious. I don't want him to think that's the only reason we're there." My voice came out sterner than I'd meant it to.

"Do you really think I'd do that? I may be ambitious, Skye, but I'm not a complete ass. I wouldn't put you in that position."

"Sorry, I didn't mean it like that. It's just a touchy subject. I don't want him to think I'm trying to use his relationship with my friend for my own gain."

"I'll be on my best behavior."

I laughed. Well, as much as I could while I was trying not to suck air. "Good."

"So when is your actual birthday anyway? All I know is that you and Ellie have been celebrating it together since you were college roommates."

"My birthday is this Friday and Ellie's is the end of next week."

"I'll have to keep that in mind." He had a sheen of sweat covering his body and damned if I couldn't get my mind out of the gutter, because all I kept wondering was how salty his skin would taste if I ran my tongue along it. Maybe Katie was right and I did need to get laid. My inner monologue sounded like a teenage boy's these days.

We ran in silence until I finally worked up the nerve to ask something I'd been wondering about for a while. "If you've always wanted an entertainment division to your PR firm, why didn't you start it up out here in California rather than Virginia?"

I looked to my side to see that he'd pursed his lips and creased his eyebrows. "It's a long story."

"And one you don't want to share, I'm guessing?"

"Not this early in the morning."

Alright then. I knew to let the subject go so I did, and we remained silent for the rest of our run.

The day had gone well. It was my first real conference, although I had an idea what to expect since I'd accompanied my dad to a bunch of political stuff over the years. Still, I couldn't help feeling a little like a fish out of water a few times throughout the day. Steele and Associates certainly wasn't the largest or most successful PR firm represented at the conference, but it seemed many of them knew who Landon was.

We'd just finished up dinner with the members of a PR

firm from Denver and had decided to grab a quick drink in the hotel bar, The Mixing Room. It was late evening and still pretty busy, but we managed to find two seats together along the bar.

The bartender approached us almost immediately. "For the lady?"

"I'll just have a glass of wine, please. Do you have a good cabernet?"

"Absolutely. For you, Sir?"

"I'll just take a beer. Stella, please."

"Coming right up."

Landon leaned his elbows on the bar in front of him and turned to look at me. "So, what did you think of your first full conference day? Was it what you expected?"

"For the most part. I thought the seminars this morning were more interesting than the ones this afternoon, but overall they were all well done."

"I agree. But then again, 'Accounting for HR Professionals in the Information Age' never really sounded that exciting to me to begin with."

I laughed. "That's true. We're probably just lucky we were able to stay awake."

"Here you are." The bartender placed our drinks in front of us. I grabbed my purse off my lap.

"Keep your money. I've got it," Landon said and placed some bills on the bar.

The bartender picked up the bills, thanked Landon, and walked away.

"Are you sure?"

"Positive."

"Okay, thanks." I brought the glass to my lips and took a small sip. The wine warmed my insides as it made its way down into my belly. This was exactly what I needed to unwind after a long day, and one that I'd be repeating for the next four days in a row. "So what's the PR crowd like at these things?" I asked.

"What do you mean?" He bunched his eyebrows.

"You always hear how wild and crazy the crowd at some of these conventions can get. So far this bunch seems pretty tame."

"There's a few stories I could share with you, believe me. The only good part about people making stupid decisions at a conference like this is that everyone in PR knows to keep their mouths shut."

Flashes of the two of us in the cabana the day before raced through my mind. Did he consider what happened between us a stupid decision?

"What about you? Ever made some dumb choices at one of these things?" I asked.

Landon took a pull of his beer and set it down on the bar before answering me. "I've been known to make a bad choice or two before," he responded with a shrug.

I told myself that he wasn't talking about the situation between us. I'm not sure I believed myself, but I put on a brave face and didn't let my unease show. I changed the subject before how I really felt slipped through the cracks.

"Are you ready to tell me why you didn't start out by opening up shop in L.A.?"

"It's a long story. One you'd probably rather not hear."

If he thought that would get me off topic, he was mistaken. The only thing he'd done was pique my interest more.

"I do want to know or I wouldn't have asked."

He let out a deep sigh. "You asked about my relationship with my dad a while back." I nodded, encouraging him to go on. "When I was in my junior year of high school, my dad lost his job. He'd been the Vice President of Sales at a chemical manufacturing plant the whole time I was growing up. He made a good living...good enough that my mom didn't have to work. Anyway, when the economy went to shit, they let go of a lot of the top heavy management salaries, including my dad."

"That must have been tough for him."

"I'm sure it was, only instead of being a man and telling

his family what had happened, he hid it from both me and my mom. He pretended to go to work every day but really went to the bar to drown his sorrows and seek comfort for his fragile ego by banging a bunch of other women."

"Oh my God." I placed my hand over the top of his and squeezed. He'd been looking straight ahead at nothing but turned to look into my eyes. He held my gaze for a moment and I saw the hurt there. Raw pain was still present years later from his father's betrayal.

"Yeah, well that's not all. My mom eventually found out because one of the girls he was banging showed up at the house looking for him. She was pregnant and apparently my dad had been dodging her calls. She'd had enough and tracked him down. When my dad came home from 'work' that night, my mom confronted him and he admitted to everything."

"I can't imagine. That's so awful, Landon. So...you have a half brother or sister?"

He shook his head. "She ended up losing the baby."

"I'm sorry."

"He also dropped it on us that we were losing the house. He'd gotten behind on the bills while he was pretending to go to work every day, and we only had another thirty days before the bank was foreclosing. My mom was a homemaker. She'd never handled any of the finances. I guess she never thought she had anything to worry about, and if she did, she figured my dad would tell her."

"How did your mom handle everything?"

He blew out a large breath. "Not well. She was devastated. Sunk into a depression. Some days she didn't even leave her bed. After all of that went down, I knew I'd have to take care of my mom from there on out. She wanted to stay in Virginia because her sisters, her parents, and all her friends were there. I couldn't leave her behind. Not until she was on her feet and more like her old self again."

"How is she doing now?"

"Better. Much better. She's been dating the same guy for a

while. She's found a job she likes...which is why I can go after these entertainment accounts now."

"I'm glad to hear she's getting past it. She must be proud of the success you've become after everything you had going on."

"Everything with my dad....it's made me a little fanatical about building my own business. My dad worked for his employer for twenty years and it didn't matter. They cut the cord like it was business as usual and didn't give a second thought to what would happen to him after that. I wanted my fate to be in my own hands. I didn't want to give the power to take everything away to some Poindexter with a calculator in accounting."

The puzzle pieces were moving into place...why there were no pictures of his dad in his apartment, his unrelenting drive to build his business, his lack of any mention of a serious relationship in his past. I wasn't sure what I'd do with the information, but I was glad he'd confided in me.

"Do you have any relationship with your Dad at all?"

"Barely. It's strained." He ran a hand through his hair, leaving the brown strands unruly.

"It must be difficult to forgive him."

Landon nodded, just barely, and didn't say anything for a while. He picked at the label on his beer and then finally broke the uncomfortable silence. "It's hard to forgive someone who caused you and someone you love that much pain. I grew up thinking I had the perfect little nuclear family, and then because of some shithead decisions on my dad's part, it was all ripped away from me."

I took my hand and rubbed Landon's back. I wanted to offer him comfort and couldn't bear to see him like this. It was a total one-eighty from the strong and capable man I'd come to know.

"Maybe in time it will get easier," I said. Because really, what did I know? I came from the type of family Landon had just described. I couldn't imagine what that type of betrayal from a parent could do to someone—talk about baggage.

He turned to look at me and gave me a small smile that didn't hold any promise. "Maybe."

"Well, thank you for telling me. I don't get the feeling you confide in many people like that."

This time he turned his entire body to face me and looked at me like he was searching for something. "No, I don't. I haven't talked to anyone about that in years. Thanks for listening." He brought his hand up to my cheek and brushed it lightly with his thumb. The sensation of his hand deepened the intimacy of our conversation and I was no longer cognizant of everyone around. As cheesy as it sounds, it really was like they all faded away into the background.

Landon held my gaze and after a minute, dropped his hand and swung himself back around to face the bar. "Have you been able to confirm our meeting with Calder's people on Thursday evening?"

Whoa. Whiplash. I swear, sometimes I felt as if his quick change of subject was a test to see if I could keep up.

"I spoke to his manager during the lunch break today. We're all set to meet at Casa Vega at seven."

"Terrific. If we can land him as a client, it'd be a big inroad into the L.A. scene."

"We'll land him," I said with total confidence. We'd done our research, developed a plan of attack, and were prepared for the meeting.

"I like your confidence. Every appointment I take, I go in with the attitude that I'm getting the business. Otherwise, what's the point?"

I laughed. "You really need to work on your self-confidence, Landon. It's very lacking."

Before he could respond, a shriek of "Landon" came from the other side of the bar. I turned to see a woman with a lot of curves—the top half she didn't appear to have been born with—approaching from the other side of the bar. She was exotic-looking with creamy brown skin and long, straight black hair parted in the middle. She smiled as she made her way over and it turned up the corners of her dark brown eyes and highlighted her plump lips.

"Who is that?" I asked. It was clear from the way she was sashaying over to us that she wanted Landon in her bed.

"Jia Mendez. She works at a PR firm in New York. She'd be one of those bad decisions I referred to earlier."

Oh, correction. *Back* in her bed. Instantly, my guard went up and if I'm honest, I wanted to claw her eyes out.

Irrational, I know.

But if this woman was coming over to try and repeat the past, she and I had a problem—regardless of whether I had any right to feel that way or not.

"Landon. My God, you look better than ever," she said when she reached us and leaned in to give him a hug. It didn't escape my notice that she pressed her tits into his chest on purpose, or that the hug lasted longer than it should have.

"Jia, good to see you again. I'd like to introduce you to Skye Summers. Skye works as my assistant." It rubbed me the wrong way, being referred to like that. It was completely true but it made me question if that's how he *really* saw me.

I stuck my hand out to shake hers, not letting the smile I'd plastered on my face falter at all. Not one bit. "Nice to meet you."

She took my hand in a lackluster way and gave me the once-over. She must have figured I was no real competition for her, because she quickly turned her focus back to Landon as if I didn't exist. Leaning into him and almost forcing herself between his legs, she ran a finger down his chest seductively. "We have a lot to catch up on," she said, licking her lips. She actually licked her fucking lips.

Landon smiled at her but it didn't reach his eyes. One point for Landon.

He took her hand off his chest. "We do. I haven't seen you since last year. How have you been enjoying the conference?"

"It's been good. I'm hoping that events this year will top last year's, if you know what I mean."

That was my cue to exit. I had no interest in torturing myself, watching this beautiful creature try and use her siren call on Landon.

"I'm going to head on back to my room. It was nice to meet you, Jia." I turned and slugged the last bit of wine in my glass, grabbed my purse off the bar top, and hopped off my seat. "I'll see you tomorrow," I said, looking at Landon.

"Are you sure? Why don't you stay?"

I shook my head. "I'm tired and I want to get up for a run early tomorrow so it's best if I go."

"Alright. I'll see you in the morning then." The stupid smirk on Jia's face showed how pleased she was that I was leaving the two of them alone. I walked away without another word.

When I reached my room, I shut the door that connected our two rooms and locked it. In my heart, I didn't believe that Landon would be taking Jia back to his room tonight, but on the off chance that I was wrong, I'd be crushed if I heard her crying out his name in the middle of the night. Better safe than sorry.

chapter twenty-two

Landon

The next morning I dragged my ass out of bed for a run before the conference started. After I managed to make it clear to Jia that I wasn't interested in banging her again, I'd sat at the bar later than I should have, tossing back the beers and thinking of both Skye and my father. I had a bit of a hangover going, but I wasn't about to let that throw me off my game for the day. At least my presentation wasn't until the following day.

When I walked into the exercise room, Skye was at the same machine she'd been at the day before. It was busier than it had been yesterday, and this time someone was on the only machine next to her. I opted for the machine two down and she glanced to her side when I climbed up on the machine. I smiled and she gave me a short smile back and then turned to look straight ahead again. Was she pissed at me? Something was definitely off.

As I racked up the miles, I pondered what could be bothering her. Granted, I was of the male species and we weren't always the most clued into a woman's way of thinking, but I started to wonder if she was pissed about Jia. I'd been uncomfortable the way she'd been so blatant in front of Skye, but that was just Jia. Surely Skye didn't think that something had actually happened last night? Even if I wasn't sure where things stood between the two of us, did she really think I'd do that? Yeah, I could be an asshat at times, but I wasn't a complete douche.

The guy running in between us decreased the pace on his machine to a slow jog. Great, he was cooling down. Once he left, I'd take his spot and feel her out.

A few minutes later when the machine beside her was free, I hit the stop button on my own and took the one directly beside her. She turned and did a double-take when she saw me there.

"What are you doing?" she asked.

"I wanted to talk to you. Something wrong?"

She shook her head. "Why would something be wrong?"

"You just seem different this morning."

"We've barely said two words to each other. How could I seem different?" There was definitely something up. The tone of her voice was off—she sounded stiffer and more removed than I'd ever heard her sound.

I pondered what I was about to say and then just decided to go with it. "Nothing happened, you know."

"Sorry?" she said.

"Last night, between Jia and I. Nothing. Happened."

"It's not any of my business."

I'd had enough of this. Any time I tried to talk to her and figure out what the hell was going on with the two of us, she avoided the subject. I hit the stop button on her machine. She turned to face me, eyes wide with a shocked expression on her face.

"What are you doing?"

"This has to stop."

"You did just stop it. Want to tell me why?" She put a hand on her hip now that the treadmill had stopped moving.

"Not this," I said, gesturing to the treadmill. "You. Don't think I haven't noticed that you've avoided talking about what is or isn't going on between us. Did you really think I'd take her back to my room after everything that has happened between us over the past couple of weeks?"

"I agree that we need to have a discussion about the situation," she said and it wasn't lost on me that she didn't answer my question. "But do you really think *this* is the best place for it?" She waved a hand, indicating the number of people working out within earshot.

She had a point. This wasn't exactly the most private of places.

"Fine. But the first opportunity where we have more than twenty minutes alone together, we're discussing it."

"Fine." She hit the button to restart her machine. When she'd gotten back up to speed, she spoke. "For the record...no, I didn't think you'd bring her into your bed last night, but I wasn't sure."

I couldn't tell if that was a vote of confidence or not, but I realized then that I wanted to prove to her I was someone she could put her trust in.

The next couple of days were packed with seminars, lunches, and dinner meetings. My presentation went exceedingly well, thanks in large part to all of Skye's prep work. She'd had some good ideas about what to include and seemed to know what I needed before I even knew myself.

It was late Thursday afternoon when we found ourselves back at my suite with a couple of hours to kill before our meeting with Calder. We were prepared so there wasn't much more we could do.

As much as I wanted to bring up the subject of what was happening between us, I decided to wait until after we got back to the room tonight. This was an important meeting and I needed to be in the zone. I wasn't sure how my conversation with Skye would play out and I didn't want to be distracted in the meeting in case it went poorly.

So instead of telling her I wanted to see where this thing between us was going, I suggested we order room service since the meeting tonight would likely be over drinks, not a meal. We sat on the couch in the living area. I watched some sports highlights while Skye checked her e-mail on her laptop. The door was open between the two suites and I swore I heard something coming from her suite. I muted the TV and listened. Yep, it was her phone. I turned to see that she was too engrossed in typing something to notice the ringing.

"Is that your phone?" I asked.

She didn't look up from the computer. "Hmm?"

"Skye." I waited until those gorgeous pools of blue met mine so I knew she was paying attention. "Your cell is ringing in the other room."

"Oh. Thanks." She set her laptop down beside her on the couch and jogged over to the doorway. She walked back in, scrolling through her phone. "Missed it." She came to sit beside me and brought the phone to her ear.

"Hi, Daddy. Did you just call?"

After a pause, she continued, "It's okay. I know how busy you are trying to get the campaign off the ground."

I tried to act like I wasn't listening, but it was hard with her sitting a few feet from me. I didn't want to unmute the TV because that would've been rude, so I pretended like I was reading the ticker scrolling across the bottom of the screen.

"Daddy...you know I'm in Los Angeles for work. I don't get back until really late Sunday night."

Another pause. "Honestly, it's not a big deal. I know you're burning the candle at both ends. We can do something next week."

A longer pause and then she sighed. "Sure. Text me his name and number and I'll see if we can set up a time."

I frowned slightly, wondering who she was referring to.

"Okay then. I'll call you when I'm back in town."

"Love you, too. Bye." She ended the call and set her phone on the coffee table. "That was my dad."

"I heard. Everything okay?" I asked.

"Yeah. He was calling to see what I was doing for my birthday. He wants me to go to my parents' house for dinner. Then he was apologizing profusely that he hadn't called sooner."

"He must be busy trying to get everything set for his Senate run."

"He is. I don't want him to feel bad. It's really not a big deal." She shrugged.

"You two obviously have a good relationship." She looked uncomfortable now. "It's not a big deal. I realize not everyone has the shitty relationship that I do with their father."

"I know. I just feel like maybe it was a little insensitive of me to call him back in front of you, since I know how it is with you and your dad."

I reached across the couch and put my hand on top of hers. "It wasn't. Trust me, it doesn't bother me anymore."

She gave me a look that told me she didn't believe a word I said. "The man who opened up to me about his dad wasn't someone who didn't care about his father. It's clear you still care about him."

I let out a sigh. How could she see through me so easily? And why didn't it scare me anymore that she did? "I do wish things were different between my dad and me, but I don't see how I could forgive him. He acts like nothing is wrong, like when we talk there isn't this gigantic fucking thing between us. It's like he wants me to pretend it never happened."

"Maybe he just doesn't know what to say..."

"Maybe. Anyway, what else did your dad want?"

"Oh, nothing really. Some reporter from the paper wants to do an interview with me. Something about what it's like to be raised in a political family."

"Do you have to do a lot of those types of things?"

She shrugged. "Not too many. Usually they just want a quote or a quick sound bite. Nothing major."

"Well, if you need any help from a PR guy before your interview, you know who to come to."

She laughed. "I think I'll be okay. There aren't many skeletons hiding in my closet."

chapter twenty-three

Skye

We walked into Casa Vega, a well-known restaurant in L.A., and I immediately loved it. The place was dimly lit with brick walls and circular booths built into the outer walls. The seats were leather with a masculine feel. Red tablecloths with white napkins completed the look. The smell of authentic Mexican food permeated the place and although I'd already eaten, my stomach grumbled.

Landon approached the hostess to ask about our reservation and waved me over a second later. She led us toward one of the booths in the back corner. Calder and his manager, Chelsea Thompson, were already there. Wowza. He was as attractive in person as he was on the big screen. More so even, maybe. His blond hair was pulled back into a short ponytail but I knew it reached close to his neckline. I had to try hard not to stare. His manager was an attractive woman who looked to be in her late thirties with long brown hair, a fake chest, and startling emerald-green eyes.

We all made our introductions, placed drink orders—Calder noticeably ordered a club soda—and sat down in the booth.

"How are you enjoying Los Angeles?" Calder asked. He directed his question at me with a lopsided grin that promised trouble. The fun kind. This guy just oozed charm and confidence, and I had no doubt that the media reports of his philandering were more than likely true.

Though it was me he'd asked, Landon was the one who answered. "It beats Virginia this time of year," Landon said. We continued with small talk until the waitress brought out our drink orders.

It was clear Chelsea wanted to get down to business. "So, what do you think you can do for Calder that countless other PR teams haven't already tried?"

Landon didn't miss a beat. If I was impressed by how well he handled being on the hot seat when he did his presentation yesterday, I was even more in awe now. He was a man with his eye on the prize. He'd narrowed in on his target and he was going to kill or be killed.

"Easy. We're going to tell the truth."

"Excuse me?" Chelsea said. She looked a little incredulous and I had to bite my lip to hold back a laugh.

It struck me as odd that Calder had chosen to take a backseat during this part of the conversation. Chelsea was definitely the one running the show here.

"Instead of the lie-and-deny approach, we're going to get it all out. Tell all the tales that need telling so that there's no fear of anyone else stepping forward with a legit story that could undo any progress we make with Calder's public image."

"People *will* still step forward with stories though," she said.

"True. But after they hear what Calder has to say, they'll have no credibility. People won't believe it could possibly be true after everything else he'd already admitted to. What would be the point of him admitting to the worst and then leaving something out?"

Finally, Calder piped up. "Why do I have to tell anyone

anything? Let them think what they want. I don't give a shit. I just want to act."

"That's all well and good, but you know as well as I do that we live in a celebrity and consumer culture. And you, my friend, are the product. Like it or not," Landon said.

I saw my chance to further drive the point home so I spoke up. "If you want to continue to work in this town, we need to spin some of the press in your favor. Unfortunately, it matters to producers and studio heads what the public thinks of you—regardless of how talented you are."

Calder seemed more interested now. "So you'd want to do what? Have a press release?"

Landon shook his head and then surprised me by looking to me to take the reins. I used my softest, most sympathetic voice. "No. We need to book you a spot for a one-on-one interview, where people can see the sincerity and remorse in your eyes so they know you're telling the truth and that you're repentant. The public loves to see a superstar fall from grace, but even more than that, they love seeing that star rise from the ashes. And *that's* exactly what you're going to do."

Calder and Chelsea shared a glance. There was something behind it but I couldn't decipher what. "Do I really have to tell everything?" he asked, not sounding like the oozing-with-confidence guy I'd just met.

"Everything," Landon confirmed. "And you need to continue to stay sober and stay out of trouble. After that, Chelsea here needs to get you booked on something...a movie or a TV show...something for your big comeback."

"What if people think he's an even bigger asshole after he admits to everything?" Chelsea asked.

Landon shrugged. "I'm not going to lie...it could happen. Hell, it will happen for some people. But the majority will like that you came clean and are trying to help yourself. If there were parties with porn stars—you say it. If you were snorting lines off a hooker's tits—you say it. If you were showing up late to set because you were strung out the night before—you say it. You say *everything* because that's the only way you remove all the leverage people have over you."

Both client and manager sat there quietly reflecting for a few moments. Finally, Chelsea turned her attention back to us. "I knew you'd be good. I only took the meeting with you because your reputation preceded you and we wanted a virtual outsider in the industry to give us a fresh take on the situation. The last thing we need is one of the bigger firms with a history of lying to everyone's faces spewing a bunch of B.S.—we've already tried that."

"Then you must realize that we can handle this account. We're going to be opening an office in Los Angeles, and I will personally be handling your account."

Chelsea turned to look at her client. "What do you think?"

"I think trying to deny everything hasn't done fuck except make the media want to hunt me down with more vigor. I like this guy. He's got balls and he hasn't already been corrupted by the L.A. scene."

"Do we have a deal?" Landon asked.

I literally sat on the edge of my seat as we waited for Calder's answer. Landon had done an amazing job handling their objections, but the fact remained that he would be the firm's first entertainment client and it'd be a leap of faith for Calder to sign on. Calder nodded his head 'yes' and I let out a huge sigh of relief.

"It'll be nice having the truth out there and not wondering what dirty deed someone is going to dig up each day."

"Wonderful," Landon said and shook Calder's hand across the table. Pride and excitement shone in his dark eyes.

The waiter approached and Landon leaned in to me, whispering into my ear, "We make a great team."

He pulled back enough that I could look into his eyes. "We sure do." It was then that I realized I meant it—in more ways than one. Question was, did he?

chapter twenty-four

Skye

We stayed at Casa Vega for another drink and to hammer out the details of our next meeting. Afterward, the car drove us back to our hotel and although it was late, we were both on too big of a high to even think about retiring for the night. We'd landed our first L.A. client! This was the beginning of big things for Steele & Associates.

Landon had called ahead and requested for room service to bring champagne to his suite so we could have a celebratory toast. Therefore, I didn't bother going back to my room and went to sit on the couch as he poured each of us a glass. He came to sit beside me, looking utterly delectable. He'd removed his suit jacket and tie, rolled up the sleeves on his dress shirt, and unbuttoned the top two buttons. I wanted to place my lips on the exposed skin where his neck met his chest. I wanted to taste his skin on my tongue, inhale the scent of his cologne...

"Skye?"

Landon's voice brought me out of my thoughts, and I realized he was holding out the champagne glass for me to take. I took it, our fingertips brushing lightly, setting off a lightning bolt that traveled from my hand all the way up my arm. "Thank you."

"A toast. To our success on so many levels here in Los Angeles. I couldn't have done any of it without you. I hope you know that, Skye. So here's to many more successful endeavors together."

My heart was fluttering like I was a schoolgirl again. "I'm not sure the part about not being able to do it without me is quite true, but yes, I'll drink to many more successes." We clinked our glasses together and I took a sip, the bubbles bursting on my tongue as they made their way down my throat.

"I meant what I said. You've been invaluable to me since you started. When I first heard you were the mayor's daughter, I figured you were going to be a spoiled little rich girl with no clue how to get by in the real world. I'm glad I couldn't have been more wrong."

His initial assessment of me stung, but it wasn't something I hadn't had to contend with before. People were always assuming I was some dumb blonde who'd been handed everything in my life.

"I'm sure you're not the first person to think that, nor will you be the last. Yes, my parents are wealthy but I won't apologize for it. They taught me the value of hard work. In fact, my dad is probably one of the hardest working people I know. I grew up watching him work his ass off to get where he wanted. That was my example. My mom never had to work, but she was always involved in one charity or another. I've never thought I was any better than anybody else."

I'd sounded more defensive than I'd intended, and I realized this the moment he began speaking. "I wasn't trying to upset you. I just wanted you to know what an amazing woman I think you are."

I was a little embarrassed at his praise, so I gave him a small smile and looked down to the champagne glass I held in my lap.

"I mean it, Skye." His tone was serious. I looked up to see him gazing at me with admiration and awe. I sensed that our conversation was about to take a turn into more serious territory—Landon's desk and the pool cabana-type territory.

"I've been curious about something."

"Okay..."

"Why did you stay with Vic for so long?" Not the question I was expecting.

"Do we have to talk about him tonight? I thought we were celebrating?"

"I confided in you about the whole fucked-up situation with my dad. I've never spoken to any girl about that before. I did it because I trust you. Do you not feel the same way about me?"

I did trust Landon. Fully. I didn't want him thinking I didn't and I'd known it was a big deal that he told me the story about his father.

"I *do* trust you. You already know the worst part."

"But I can't understand why a phenomenal woman like you would allow him to treat you poorly even before all that."

I put my glass on the table and shifted so I faced him with one leg tucked under the other. "When we first started dating, things between us were fine. After it became more serious and we agreed to only see each other, he started to become more and more jealous. It was small things at first—asking me where I was going, who I'd be with and what we'd be doing. Then it progressed so that he was accusing me of things. If a waiter smiled at me when he was taking our order, he figured we must have a past together. If I went out for drinks with the girls, he was always suspicious of where I *really* was. If I said hello to a guy I was friends with, he wanted to know if we'd ever fooled around before." I grabbed my glass and took a swig of champagne.

Landon seemed to sense there was still more to the story. "I still don't understand."

"The night we broke up, I'd had enough. I couldn't take it

anymore and told him we were done. Up to that point, I'd believed him when he told me he'd change and that things would be different. I've always been someone that sees the best in people. It's what my parents taught me to do. It took me a while to figure out that people need to be judged on how they treat you, not the words they say."

Landon stood from the couch and began pacing, rubbing the back of his neck as he did. "I understand it better now, but I still see red when I think of him hurting you."

I stood too and placed my hand on his shoulder. "Which is precisely why I ended things and haven't looked back since."

That seemed to bring him some level of comfort. He cupped my face in his hands. "If you haven't been looking back, what have you been looking at?" he asked, his voice low and his eyes soft.

Lost in him, I didn't even think before I answered, "You, mostly."

He brought his lips to mine and slowly kissed me, pushing his tongue into my mouth at a languid pace that was the opposite of the energy he'd exuded moments before. It was clear Landon was holding back, trying to control himself. He tasted like champagne and all thoughts of Vic and my past with him fell away. I circled my arms around Landon's waist and pulled him closer until I could feel his hard chest pressed against me. Having him kiss me and hold my face in his hands gave me a feeling of peace that I hadn't had in longer than I could remember. Or perhaps ever.

Landon pulled back and nipped my lower lip, then rested his forehead on mine. We stayed that way, both of our eyes closed, for a few moments before he pulled back and looked at the time on his watch.

Really? He was concerned with our early morning after a kiss like that?

"It's after midnight," he said.

"I guess I should get back to my room."

He chuckled, the sound low in his throat. "That's not what

I meant. Happy birthday." He placed a chaste kiss on my lips. "I suppose it's okay if I give you your present now."

"You got me a present?" I asked softly.

"Of course. I get all the girls in the office a present on their birthday."

"Oh." Disappointment flared within and I lowered my head.

"I'm kidding. Well, I *do* get them something but it's normally a bouquet of flowers for their desk. I put a little more effort into your gift." I looked up to him and he winked at me and then disappeared into the bedroom.

A minute later, he came back holding something in his hand. "Here. Open it." For the first time ever, I saw a nervous Landon standing before me. He bit his bottom lip and shifted his weight from one foot to the other.

He placed the gift in my hands. It wasn't until I started to unwrap the fabric that I realized my gift was surrounded by a vintage handkerchief. I continued to unravel the cloth and when it finally revealed the treasure waiting inside, I let out a gasp. It was a necklace—vintage, by the looks of it. It was an antique silver circle surrounded with diamonds. Two glittery charms hung off the chain. It was gorgeous and just so...*me*. On the white fabric in the center of the circle were the words, *"Don't Let Anyone Ever Dull Your Sparkle"*.

Tears pooled in my eyes as I looked up at the man who I'd grown more than fond of—a man who continued to surprise me by showing me the many sides he possessed. "When did you get this?" I asked past the lump in my throat.

"I saw it at the flea market while you were buying your frame. After you left to meet Ellie for dinner, I went back to get it. I knew I wouldn't be able to wrap it before your birthday so I got the handkerchief, thinking maybe you'd like that, too." Words wouldn't come to my head with all of the emotions coursing through me. "So...how did I do?"

"I love it," I managed to get out. Remembering the handkerchief, I quickly added, "I love them both."

"Good." He brought his hand around to the back of my neck and lightly brushed his thumb up and down. "I knew it was perfect for you when I saw it and that now was the perfect time to give it to you. You light up from the inside, Skye. I told you before...you have this innate sparkle about you that makes others feel better in your presence. Never, ever let anyone take that away from you again."

I remembered Landon's words at his condo that day, and it only made me more overwhelmed by the gift. I nodded my head in agreement.

"I want you to promise me you'll never let another guy steal that part of you away."

"I promise," I said softly. A single tear tracked down my cheek. His hand on my neck moved up to brush it away and his forehead crinkled.

"Why are you crying?"

"It's such a perfect gift and...I didn't expect you to be getting me anything."

"Which is *exactly* why we need to talk about what's going on between us."

"I know." I took a deep breath.

He brought his other hand up to my face so both of his thumbs rested on my cheeks. "I like you. A lot. More than I've liked anyone—ever. At first, I thought it was just the physical attraction between us. Figured it was left over from our first meeting and it would die off over time. But that wasn't it. Don't get me wrong, just seeing you at your desk every morning pretty much gives me blue balls all day, but I didn't expect to become so taken by your intelligence and your grace. I want to get to know you even better and I want to explore this thing we have between us."

Wow. I really wasn't sure what he felt for me or if he felt anything at all, but that speech right there was more than I could have hoped for. And it scared me out of my mind.

"What will people say?" I asked.

"Who cares? What does it matter what anyone else thinks?"

"I can understand why you feel that way but things are different for me. I have a father in politics whose every move will be scrutinized and with his run for Senate, the spotlight is going to extend to his family even more so than before. Never mind the people at work who'll think I'm trying to sleep my way to the top."

He seemed to ponder what I'd said for a minute, never taking his hands from my face. I stood there, looking at him expectantly, knowing that everything I'd said was true but desperately hoping he could find a solution to the problem.

"What if we didn't tell anyone? We keep things between us only for a while until we know where this thing is headed, and then we can revisit it in the future if things change. There's nothing saying we have to let anyone else know what's going on. If we're careful at work, no one will know. Your job already dictates that we have to spend a lot of time together."

"And if it doesn't work out?" I asked.

"I don't know." He seemed a little agitated now. "I can't make any promises. I have no idea what the future holds and I've never been in a monogamous relationship before. And to be clear, that's what this would be. But I'm not going to tell you that everything will work out all right, because I don't know that. Unlike my father, I'm not going to make promises I can't keep. What I *can* tell you is that I want to spend time with you. I want to find out what side of the bed you like to sleep on. I want to know where that little scar on your inner thigh came from. I want to figure out whether you're a morning person or a night owl. I want it to be me you ask what dress you should wear on a night out. I want to know how you take your coffee in the morning and what kind of movies make you cry. I want to know *everything* there is to know about you...and I want you to want all those things, too."

That was the single most romantic thing anyone had ever said to me. I wanted to remember every word, every syllable, and even the cadence with which he spoke, so I could relive this moment in my mind over and over again. Because although I didn't know where this thing with Landon and I would end up, I was positive that this would be one of the most memorable moments of my life.

"A fish hook," I said in almost a whisper. He looked confused. "The scar. A fish hook stuck me when I was ten and my dad was trying to teach me how to fish. I pulled on the line, even though it was caught in my skin—hence the scar."

"Does that mean you want the same thing as I do?"

I nodded my head. "But most of all, what I want right now is you."

chapter twenty-five

Skye

His lips crushed mine as his hands left my face and circled around me. Gone was the tenderness from moments before, replaced by desire so thick it was almost suffocating. I brought my arms around to circle his waist and he pressed closer to me. His hardness pushed into my navel and I wanted so badly for him to take me—to be inside me. My core ached and I moaned into his mouth.

He pulled back to look at me with hungry eyes. "Let's take this into the bedroom."

"Let's," I said.

He took my hand and led me to the bedroom, picking the bottle of champagne up off the table with his free hand. He put the bottle on the nightstand and then turned to face me, taking my gift and placing it beside the champagne.

"I want to undress you," he said. "I've been imagining doing it for weeks."

"Okay," I said quietly. The anticipation of his hands on my body was almost too much to bear. My breathing sped up and I could already feel that my underwear was damp.

He stood in front of me now, not touching but mere inches away. Slowly, he brought his hand to the hem of the light sweater I wore and lifted it over my head. Next, he undid the button of my black cigarette pants and pushed the zipper down. He carefully pulled them down my legs, kneeling when they went below my knees. I placed a hand on his shoulder to steady myself as he lifted one foot after the other out of my pants.

Then he rose to his full height in front of me. I stood before him in only my black lace bra with matching underwear. This would be our first time together. Usually at this point I would be self-conscious about my body, but I felt none of that with Landon. It might have had something to do with the obvious need for me I could see so clearly written all over his face—not to mention the bulging erection in his pants. In that moment, I only felt desired and wanted.

"You. Are. Perfection," he said huskily. I looked up at him to find his coffee-colored eyes raking over my body. He stepped slightly closer to me and without warning, dipped a hand down my underwear and into my slick folds. I let out a moan. "You're so wet for me. I won't be able to go slow once I get inside you."

"I don't want you to." Even I heard the acute need in my voice.

He pulled his hand from me, skimming over my clit as he retreated. What he did next was the single most erotic thing I'd ever seen. He brought his fingers to his nose and inhaled deeply, then put them in his mouth, sucking my juices off them. More wetness pooled at the juncture of my thighs.

"You taste so sweet, Skye. I knew you'd have a sweet little pussy I could feast on for days."

Oh. My.

He took both his hands and plumped up my breasts, which were still encased in the lace bra. The look on his face was pure lust mixed with reverence. He bent down and licked one nipple through the lace before tweaking my other nipple with his fingers. By the time he was done, I was a panting, quivering mess.

With his mouth still torturing my breast, he reached around and undid the clasp of my bra, working the straps down my shoulders. He pulled away as my bra fell to the floor.

"Fuck." He began rubbing his straining erection over the top of his dress pants while I watched. "Get on the bed."

He'd get no argument from me. As I turned to climb up onto the bed, I felt his hands on either side of my lace panties and he pulled them down while I crawled across the bed. I lay there completely naked, ready and willing for him to take me.

He quickly unbuttoned the rest of his shirt and shook it off, then did the same with the rest of his clothes. I'd seen him at the pool but an entirely nude Landon was a different beast altogether. He stood beside the bed in all his naked glory—his lean, muscled body and deep, sculpted 'V' on his lower abdomen looking like something from a Greek statue. His cock jutted up to his belly button, rigid and waiting. He was a beautiful sight to behold. Pure and simple.

He crawled onto the bed beside me and grabbed the champagne off the nightstand. He held it above my stomach and let some of the liquid pour out so that it collected in my navel. I yelped at the cold sensation on my heated skin. My yelp turned to a moan a moment later as he bent his head to lick up the bubbly while his hands played with my breasts.

He made quick work of it and this time, when he lifted the bottle it was over the top of my breasts. He poured the liquid out and my already hard nipples beaded even more to the point that it was almost painful. Champagne ran down the sides of my breasts on to the bed below.

"Landon, the bed," I said in mild protest.

He shrugged.

Fine by me.

His tongue lapped up the liquid, paying extra close attention to my nipples as he played with the underside of my breasts. My hands went into his hair and I writhed beneath him. When he was satisfied he'd gotten it all, he raised the bottle again and with a grin on his face, he poured it over my mound. Cold champagne soaked my curls and dripped down my seam. The sensation had me squirming.

Landon rolled over to return the bottle to the nightstand. Then he kissed his way down my body before finally situating himself between my legs. Gripping both of my knees, he spread them wide so that I was completely bared to him.

"I'm going lick up every last drop of that champagne and then I'm going to lick up every last drop of you as you come on my tongue." With his words alone I was already almost there.

He bent over and spread me with his thumbs, then licked me from bottom to top. When he reached my clit, he sucked it in between his lips. I fisted a handful of his hair, not caring if my grip was too tight. I was so worked up—all I wanted was my release. He pulled back and looked at my core, his fingers running lightly up and down the slit, teasing my entrance but not penetrating it. I was going to go fucking crazy soon if he didn't let me come.

"Please, Landon," I moaned.

"Mmm...I like you begging me. I'll give you what you need, sweetheart. You don't have to ask twice." He pushed two fingers into me slowly and pulled them out, then did it again. I writhed on the bed, fondling my own breasts, looking for any stimulation to take me over the edge. "That's it, baby. Touch yourself."

He bent his head again and while he fingered me, he licked my clit and then made a vibrating motion with his tongue. It was enough to send me spiraling toward the abyss, and the taut cord that had been wrapped around my body snapped. I cried out his name as my insides pulsed around his fingers.

When I finished riding out my orgasm, I was left panting on the bed, my eyes closed, my breathing heavy. Landon pulled his fingers from me. I looked down to him and saw as he rubbed them on the tip of his erection so that it glistened with my juices.

"Lick it off, baby. See how sweet you taste." My limbs felt like Jell-O but I rolled over and crawled to him, as turned on as ever. He was on his knees and I licked the head of him, circling his mushroom tip with my tongue. When I closed my mouth around him, he pushed me away by the shoulders. "Easy. I want to be inside you when I come this time."

I lay back on the bed with a smirk, pleased that I could bring him to the brink so easily.

"Skye, I want to feel you around me without anything else. I'm good. Are you?"

"Yes," I panted.

"Do you trust me?" he asked, his expression hopeful.

I did trust him. After everything that had gone down with Vic, I wouldn't have thought I could trust someone again so quickly, or even trust my own judgement, but somehow I did. I nodded my head and unconsciously licked my bottom lip.

He lay down over me and gave me a punishing kiss that had me wrapping my legs around his waist. He kissed a trail from my mouth to my ear and then down my neck to my collarbone, nipping and licking as he went. I wanted more than anything to feel his hard length inside me so I told him as much.

"I always took you for a patient girl," he said.

"Landon, please..."

My voice trailed off as he pushed up off of me and grabbed his shaft, brushing it up and down my seam. I closed my eyes as a tremor ran through my body.

He arranged his head at my entrance and slowly pushed himself into me, inch by glorious inch. The stretching sensation was exquisite, as was the feeling of him filling me. He didn't move for a minute, squeezing his eyes shut before he began pumping in and out of me. Landon quickly picked up the pace until he was pounding his length into me, wild with lust.

"You are so fucking tight, sweetheart. I can't stop."

"Don't stop," I cried out as I felt another orgasm beginning to overtake me.

"Touch yourself. Finish," he panted out.

It wasn't anything I'd ever done with a man before, but I wasn't embarrassed about it. I felt complete and total freedom to experiment with him. There was no reason to rein in my need for him when we were together.

I brought my fingers to my clit and began massaging it. That coupled with his cock pushing into the deepest parts of my womb was all I needed. I bucked up under him and arched my back, my eyes shut tight as my insides pulsed around him.

Moments later, I felt his cock jerk as he emptied himself into me. A few more short pumps and he fell on top of me, careful to keep some of his weight off of me with one arm pressed into the mattress.

After he'd caught his breath, he nuzzled himself into my neck. "That was phenomenal."

"Mmm...I agree." I was completely sated and didn't want to move an inch.

After a while, Landon excused himself to go clean up. Because I was lying on sheets wet from champagne, I rolled over to the other side of the bed. It was a king-sized mattress so there was still plenty of room.

Once he returned and I was settled in arms with my head on his hard chest and one leg draped over his, I whispered, "I agree that we should keep this quiet. At least until we have a better idea of where this is headed," I said.

"That's what we'll do then. When we're in the office, it'll be business as usual. But outside of office hours, you're all mine." The arm he had slung around me squeezed me into him.

"You realize this means we can't go out in public together."

"I'm sure we could go out to eat together from time to time. It's nothing we haven't already done. I'll just have to grope you under the table instead of above it, that's all." His chest rose and fell as he laughed and he kissed the top of my head.

"Are you going to be okay with that? It could get boring after a while."

"Sweetheart, being stuck in private with you is about the furthest thing from boring that I can think of. Plus, I know all kinds of ways we can pass the time."

I playfully smacked his chest. "I'm sure the press wouldn't make anything out of it if they found out, but I'd rather not take the chance. Why give them any ammunition, right?"

"I understand your reasons for wanting to keep it between ourselves. Let's just enjoy being able to do what we want while we're here in L.A. where no one knows us. We won't have that luxury when we return to Virginia."

"Sounds like a plan." I leaned up to kiss him deeply and pulled back after a minute. "We should probably get some sleep. We're already going to have trouble keeping our eyes open at the seminars tomorrow."

"You're right, although I do it under protest."

"Duly noted."

I returned my head to his chest and fell asleep that way...listening to the thrumming of his heart. I had never fallen asleep to a better lullaby.

chapter twenty-six

Landon

Damn that alarm was loud. Had it been that loud all week? Skye still lay with her head on my chest. I pushed her off me gently and she groaned and rolled over so her back was to me. I swung over to hit the button on the stupid alarm so it would stop its incessant shrieking.

"Mmm...it's too early," she said in a sleep-ladened voice.

"My thoughts exactly," I said as I spooned her naked back from behind. I didn't worry that my cock was basically jabbing her in the ass, looking for some attention. In fact, I hope it gave her some ideas.

I kissed her shoulder and sucked it gently, then trailed kisses up to her neck where I pushed aside her mass of golden hair.

"That feels nice," she murmured.

"Good," I said and continued with my attentions.

"I have to get up and shower. I'm still a little sticky from the champagne."

I nuzzled into her neck. "Yes, the champagne. How could I forget?"

She pushed her ass out, I think in an effort to get me to back off. But if she thought pushing her perfect ass back into my hard cock was going to get me to move off her, someone hadn't explained to her how a man's thoughts work.

"I've got to get up," she said. I bit her shoulder lightly and she yelped. "I'm serious. I've got to go get ready."

I rolled away from her and on to my back. "Fine. But we'll revisit this," I said, pointing to my obvious hard-on under the sheet, "later."

Skye rolled on her side to face me. "Oh, we'll definitely be revisiting that later." She smirked and gave me a chaste kiss on the lips. She rolled off the bed, threw the sheet back, and walked to the bedroom door.

Buck. Ass. Naked.

Jesus, was she trying to kill me?

I ordered us breakfast and some coffee—lots of fresh coffee. The tray had arrived by the time Skye joined me in the suite.

She wore a bright blue skirt that hugged her slim figure and ended above her knee, a white chemise with a matching white blazer and hot-as-hell beige heels. You know, the kind that scream "please fuck me." Her long blond hair was pulled back in a low ponytail. She probably had no clue the ideas her ponytails gave me.

"I ordered breakfast for us," I said and tried to push all thoughts of Skye naked with only her heels on from my mind.

"Terrific. It'll be one thing to be bagged in all the seminars today, but I don't want to be starving, too."

"Or decaffeinated."

As we enjoyed our breakfast, I couldn't help but think about how nice it was to be around her doing normal everyday stuff without the underlying awkwardness of wondering what the hell was going on between us. Everything was out on the table and for once, we could just be. Well, when we were alone, at least.

When we finished eating, Skye went back to her room to grab her bag. As I came out of the bedroom adjusting my tie, I saw her standing beside the couch, obviously waiting for me. I stopped in total awe. The sunlight was streaming in the through the windows and hitting her hair straight on so it shimmered. I swear to God, it fucking shimmered like she was an angel. I was so relieved that she was *my* angel now.

"We'd better hurry if we don't want to be late," she said.

Being late for the damn seminar was my *last* concern at the moment. All I could think about was getting inside of her again now that I had an all-access pass.

I approached her with purpose and she gave me a quizzical look. When I reached her, I grabbed her bag from her hand and placed it on the couch beside us.

"Come here." I put my arms around her and pulled her into a fierce kiss. She immediately acquiesced and opened her mouth to me. She tasted like mint toothpaste. I deepened the kiss and pulled her against my hard-on so she'd know exactly what I was thinking. She moaned into my mouth and that was all the go-ahead I needed.

"I need inside of you," I panted, slipping her blazer off of her shoulders. She responded by palming my cock through my pants. "Fuuuck, Skye. Bend over the couch."

She walked around me and leaned over the back of the couch, her perfect ass on display in her tight skirt like it was begging for me to take her.

I pulled her skirt up so it was around her waist, and although I had great appreciation for the white lace thong she had on, I pulled hard at the crotch, reducing it to mere scraps of lace.

She craned her neck to look at me. "I'm not even pissed that you ruined those but just so you know, they were expensive."

"I'll buy you new ones," I said and lightly smacked her ass.

I spread her legs wide. She was already glistening for me. As if I wasn't already hard enough, seeing how ready she was for me to take her just took hard to a whole new level.

I unbuttoned and unzipped my suit pants, pushing them down enough for my cock to spring free. I grabbed my dick and teased her a bit, running the head up and down her wet folds. When I couldn't wait another second I finally thrust into her tight pussy so hard I was balls deep inside of her, causing her to cry out.

I pulled out slowly, eliciting a moan from her and then immediately thrust in again—hard. Based on the noises she was making, she liked it so I did it a few more times until my control snapped. I grabbed both sides of her waist and jackhammered into her. She was warm and wet and I easily glided in and out of her.

Her cries became more frantic and I could tell she was close. I leaned down so my chest was pressed to her back and reached around with one hand to find her clit. I pressed in a circular motion, causing her to come undone beneath me. She bucked up against me, wildly and almost incoherently moaning out my name.

The base of my spine started to tingle along with my balls, and I knew I was close to my own release. Her pussy continued to milk me from the inside and I felt the cum race up my shaft at lightning speed. I moaned and held myself deep inside her as I released inside of her over and over again until I'd run dry.

The silence in the room was in stark contrast to all the noise we were making moments before. After I could see straight again, I reluctantly slipped out of her.

"I think we're going to be late now. Sorry," I said. But I wasn't—not in the least.

She rose up and turned to face me, pulling her skirt back in place. She wrapped her arms around my neck and gave me a quick kiss. "If we're late because of something like *that*, it's always going to be okay with me."

"I'll have to keep that in mind." I rubbed my hands up and down her sides. I swear it was like I couldn't *not* touch her when she was near me, and I was thankful that I was now free to whenever I wanted.

"I'm going to go clean up. You're, um...running down my legs."

Mother. Fuck.

Just like that, I was ready to have her again. "Right...well. I'll do the same. See you in a few."

She removed her hands from my neck and was about to turn and walk back to her room when I remembered something I'd wanted to address last night. I seemed to have forgotten it, what with the mind-blowing sex and all. I lightly grabbed her wrist before she had turned around completely. "Wait."

She turned to look at me and the radiant and sexually-sated smile that was on her face fell. "What's wrong? You look so serious all of a sudden."

"I wanted to say something last night but didn't get the chance. Although, it should go without saying that if Vic bothers you again...if he calls you or comes near you, I want to know."

"I know. We've already been over that, remember?" she said quietly.

I knew she didn't like to talk about it so I wouldn't press any harder, but I wanted it out there. Especially since I was in her life now on a more official basis. I needed to know if he even came close to sniffing around where she was concerned. If so, he and I would have a come-to-Jesus moment. One where I kicked his ass and showed him what it was like if he took on someone his own size.

"I want you to promise," I said and even I heard that it wasn't a request.

She nodded her head. "I promise." I dropped her wrist and let her go to get ready.

I hated that I'd ended what had just been a very enjoyable lay between us by turning back to the topic of Vic, but it had to be said. I cared for that girl more than I'd cared for any girl in my life, and there was no way I was going to let some motherfucker like Vic hurt her again. I couldn't seem to stop the visions of him putting his hands on Skye. I could see him pushing her up against the door and pictured what the bruises on her arms might have looked like. Thank God she didn't hit her head any harder or things could have turned out much worse.

One thing was for sure—if Vic and I ever found ourselves face to face again, he'd become closely acquainted with my fist. No one hurt what was mine. No one.

chapter twenty-seven

Skye

On Saturday night, Landon and I took a car to Ellie and Mason's place in the Hollywood Hills for some pre-party drinks. I was excited to see where they were living and even more excited for my friend, now that she was permanently shacking up with the man she loved.

I'd never asked Ellie who else might be coming, but I assumed the group would be fairly small. Ellie wasn't really much of a party girl and from what she'd told me, Mason had had to cut his fair share of freeloaders from his life over the years.

The driver pulled into the driveway and we stepped out. Landon took my hand in his and we headed toward the front door of the large bungalow.

"This is amazing, but with Mason's success I expected a mansion in Malibu or something," he commented.

"Whatever you do, don't bring up house-hunting when we're in there. Apparently, the whole process was not a fun one."

"Why not?" he asked with his eyebrows drawn in.

"Mason wanted to give Ellie something grander and she wouldn't have it because she wanted to pull her own weight by paying some of the rent and it just became a whole big thing," I said, waving my hands in front of me.

"Really? And what do you think of that argument?"

"I'm with El on this one. I grew up in a huge house and it's not what I want for myself. I'd like something more homey and comfortable for my own family someday."

Landon let go of my hand and wrapped his arm around my waist as we approached the door. He squeezed me into his side and kissed the top of my head. "Of course you do."

I rang the doorbell and while we waited, Landon asked, "Have I told you what a goddess you look like in that dress?"

I'd gone shopping that morning and found a sleeveless V-neck dress. It was sequined and gold with the beading becoming more concentrated over my chest and along the hemline just above my knees. "Only a few times, but I could listen to it a few more."

I perched up on my tiptoes, no easy feet in four-inch stilettos, and kissed him. Of course, the door swung open at that exact moment.

Ellie stood there with a glass of wine in her hand and a slick grin on her face. I hadn't gotten a chance to tell her about my talk with Landon because she'd been busy all day, but I knew I could rely on my girl to play it cool.

"So nice to see you again, Landon," she said.

He looked a little embarrassed, but he played it off well enough. "Good to see you too, Ellie. Thanks for having us over tonight."

"Our pleasure. Skye, you look amazing."

"That's what I was just telling her," Landon said.

"Mmmhmm. I saw that," Ellie said and laughed.

"Thanks, El. Why aren't you dressed yet?"

"I wanted you to help me choose an outfit."

Laughter came from inside and it was the first opportunity I took to really check the place out. We walked in and I saw an expansive great room with wall-to-wall glass from which you could see the stunning views of the city lights below. I'd see later on our tour that outside those glass walls was an infinity pool, spa, and fireplace. They all looked like they were sitting on the edge of a cliff, which I supposed they kind of were, given that it was the Hollywood Hills.

Mason got up off of the couch to come and greet us. He was looking as fine as ever in a pair of dark denim pants and a cream shirt that hugged his fit body. He enveloped me in a hug when he reached us.

I really liked Mason. He was intense-looking but it couldn't be further from the person he really was. I was so glad he and Ellie had been able to work things out.

"Good to see you again, Skye. Looking as lovely as always."

I laughed. He was nothing if not a charmer. "Alright, save it for your girlfriend," I said and motioned to Landon. "This is Landon. Landon, Mason."

They shook hands, and after a moment of sizing each other up, seemed satisfied that neither posed a threat to the other and they smiled at one another.

"Good to meet you," Landon said.

"Same here. Come on in, guys, I want to introduce you to a few people."

We walked farther into the house, and although I didn't recognize most of the people I saw, Amber Marshall stood out to me immediately. I should've found out who was coming tonight so I could have prepared myself for a fangirl moment. Now I just felt like an idiot as my heart pounded in my chest like it was trying break free and make a run for it. All heads turned in our direction as we made our way into the middle of the room.

"Everyone, this is Skye and Landon," Mason said. Everyone smiled and said 'hello' at the same time. Mason turned to faced us and told us who each person was in turn and how he came to know them. Most I had heard of before from Ellie. Deshawn was the producer who had been at the studio the first time Ellie had visited Mason in Los Angeles. Jas was a make-up artist to many celebrities, including Mason. Of course, I already knew who Amber was. I hadn't heard of the last guy introduced, but apparently he was Amber's manager. His name was Brock Truitt.

"What can I get you guys to drink?" Mason asked. He took our drink orders and once he'd returned with our beverages, Landon and I sat on the couch Amber was on and settled in.

The conversation flowed and I realized that it felt no different than sitting around with anyone else from home. They may work around famous people or be famous themselves, but they were really just regular people when they weren't on the job.

After an hour or so, Ellie asked me to give her a hand picking her outfit out so the two of us retreated to the bedroom. I sucked in a breath when I walked in the room. The master suite had a wall of glass that looked out over the lit pool and the view below.

As soon as we were alone, Ellie cornered me. "So *what's* going on with you two? Spill."

"Okay, but before we talk about that, I want to know why you didn't tell me Amber-freaking-Marshall was going to be here tonight?"

"I wasn't sure she would be. These Hollywood types can't commit to anything. I didn't want to disappoint you if she wasn't."

"I get that, but you know what a fan I am. Some time to mentally prepare would've been appreciated."

"She's like anyone else, Skye."

"*You* might be used to wining and dining with the Hollywood elite by now, but I most definitely am not."

Ellie gave me a half-ass push. "You know I'm not like that."

"I know, but I was just happy I was able to form coherent sentences back there," I said and Ellie laughed. "She's way different than I would have thought."

"How?"

"She's totally sexed up and provocative in the media, and here she seems like this nice, sweet, normal girl our age."

"I thought the same thing when I met her. She was the sweetest little thing. Not at all the man-eater she seems to be in the press. But then we both know how accurate they are most of the time."

I rolled my eyes, remembering some of the shit Ellie and Mason had to deal with last summer, especially the unfounded stories and accusations. "True."

Ellie waved her hand in front of her face wildly. "Enough about that. What is going on with you and the boss man?"

I walked over to the bed to sit on the edge. Ellie joined me. "We had our little talk, which went really well."

"Obviously," she cut in with a smirk.

"But first let me tell you what he got me for my birthday." I told Ellie about everything Landon and I had discussed and all that had happened afterward.

She hugged me close when I was finished. "I'm so happy for you. It's clear he really likes you."

I pulled back to look at her. "Why do you say that?"

"Have you seen how he looks at you? Whenever you're talking, he watches you like he wants to eat you up or something."

"Oh, so you mean the way Mason looks at you then?"

Ellie laughed. "Touché."

"It really is great to be able to hang out like this with you again."

"I know. The only thing better would be if Katie were here, too."

"It sucks that she couldn't come," I lamented.

"I know. Well, I suppose I should get my shit together and figure out what I'm wearing," Ellie said.

"Suppose so." I let out a sigh. As much as I was looking forward to a night out on the town, I missed my girl time with Ellie.

"We'll have to do this more often when Mason isn't touring," Ellie said. "I'm coming to Virginia next time."

I sat up on the bed and then stood up. Grabbing Ellie's wrist to pull her off the bed, I said, "It's a deal."

chapter twenty-eight

Landon

I don't think I'd ever woken from a night at a club with a woman in my bed and not dreaded the awkward morning-after routine. This morning was refreshingly different. Beside me lay a thing of beauty and one in a million—even I could recognize that through the haze of my aching head.

She was currently naked and sprawled out on her stomach, but my mind went back to last night and how fuckable she'd looked in that gold dress she wore. I sported wood almost all night and my balls were aching at the club having to watch her shake her ass to the music and not be able to do anything about it until we'd gotten back here. It'd been well worth the wait though.

Skye slept peacefully beside me and I enjoyed the feeling of contentment that filled me. It wasn't something I was accustomed to. I didn't let girls get close—Skye was the first. But this felt good.

I had a brief moment where I thought that this was probably how my mom felt before it had all come crashing down, but I pushed it to the back of my mind. I was determined not to go there. Skye and I weren't my parents, and I sure as hell wasn't my father.

I reached over and traced my fingers along her lower back, right where her spine dipped in and her ass started to raise. I couldn't help myself.

She rustled and then opened her eyes, blinking several times slowly. Then she gave me a smile that I'll remember until my dying day. Though she still looked sleepy and it was a bit of a lazy smile, she looked content, happy, and serene.

"Good morning. How did you sleep?" she asked in a husky voice. Even though I knew she sounded like that because she'd just woken up, it fired me up anyway.

"Like a stone. Last night really did me in."

"Mmm," she said lazily and rolled over onto her back to stretch her arms above her head.

Fuck. How was I ever going to get anything done at work again now that I knew exactly what lay underneath her clothes?

Work. I'd gotten a few things done since we'd been out here, but the business desperately needed my attention and I really needed to get back. There was a part of me that was dreading it though. Gone would be the days of Skye and I acting like a couple in public, doing what we pleased without worrying who witnessed it.

I understood the need to keep our relationship on the down low, but that didn't mean I had to like it. I looked forward to the day we wouldn't have to worry about what everyone else thought.

"So what did you think of everybody last night? We didn't get a chance to discuss," she asked. She turned to her side and propped herself up on her elbow.

"I thought everyone was great. Mason and Deshawn are cool guys to hang with. We talked quite a bit when you ladies went out to dance on your own."

"I'm glad you got along with them. I'm hoping we'll be seeing a little more of Ellie and Mason now that they have a break from touring. She's going to try to visit more often."

"That's great, sweetheart. I can tell you miss your friend."

"I really like when you do that."

"Do what?"

"Call me 'sweetheart.'"

"Well, believe me, you're deserving of the endearment."

A faint blush formed on her pale face. It was so fucking cute. Who knew cute could be such a turn-on?

"How long until we have to catch our flight home?" she asked.

"We have another hour to relax before we have to get our asses in gear."

She blew a stream of air out from between those perfect lips of hers. "I'm looking forward to getting home, but at the same time I want things between us to stay how they've been while we've been here."

I laughed. "I was just thinking the same thing." We sat there for a few minutes in silent introspection before I asked, "Are you going to tell your parents about us?"

She shook her head. "They have enough on their plates. Besides, if my father knew, he'd want you vetted and I don't want to put you through that."

"Wow, I feel so important. I never thought I'd need to be vetted by the team of a man running for U.S. Senate."

"There's nothing fun about it, Landon. Having strangers dig into your background, unearthing every bad thing you've ever said or done...you know that if you're with me, and even if at some point it is public knowledge that we're a couple, it'll never be like it is for normal people. As long as my dad is in politics, I'm going to have to consider things like my public persona and how what I do affects my father. You sure you're okay with that?"

I rolled over onto my side to face her. "Are you trying to get me to back off?" I said it in jest but a small part of me feared she was having second thoughts.

"No. I just want to be sure you've thought this through."

I placed my hand on her soft cheek and ran my thumb along her lower lip. "Nothing you say to me is going to make me want to back away from us."

Her eyes got a little misty. "I'm glad to hear you say that."

We melted into a kiss and I spent the next hour showing her just how good "us" could be.

Skye

When we returned to Virginia it was business as usual between Landon and me. We did a good job of acting like nothing was any different than it had been before we left. Sure, he copped a feel when no one was looking and we may have had a make-out session or two when we worked late and no one was around, but no one was the wiser.

Our evenings and weekends were spent mostly at Landon's place. His condo was bigger and had better amenities than mine. So far we hadn't gotten bored being confined indoors and alone with each other. We'd discovered plenty of different ways to pass the time.

Christmas came and went, but I didn't get to see much of Landon. It was hard to tell your family you had to leave to go see your boyfriend when said boyfriend was top secret. Besides, my dad had plenty of political appearances he wanted me to tag along on...soup kitchens, children's hospital visits, the local food bank. I was happy to do it. I'd been doing it all my life but I missed Landon.

Finally, New Year's Eve rolled around and we were able to spend the night together. We'd cooked dinner at his place and watched the festivities around the globe unfold on television. Then we engaged in our own festivities until the sun came up.

By mid-January, we'd been spending almost every night at Landon's. I missed my place so we agreed that we'd spend the weekend there. On Saturday afternoon, we'd finally graduated from the bed to the couch, where we were currently cuddled up together.

"I miss the California weather," I lamented. "Can't we go back?"

"As soon as we have those contracts for Calder finalized, we'll head out west to get them signed. How does that sound?" Making a deal and getting a contract signed were two different things, I'd quickly learned. Both our legal teams had been going over and changing the fine print for weeks.

"That's *so* far away. I feel so cooped up."

"Let's go down to the exercise room and jump on the treadmills. You'll probably feel better after a run."

"Good idea. Did you bring any clothes you can work out in?" I asked.

"I did. Boy Scout's motto: always be prepared." He raised his two fingers in the sign of the Boy Scout salute. I laughed.

"You were a Boy Scout when you were young?"

He nodded his head with pride. "Until I was fifteen."

He was so cute but now I was laughing so hard I was bent over and clutching my stomach. "Until you were fifteen? Isn't that kind of...old...to be a Boy Scout?"

"Hey." He looked mock offended and leaned in to tickle my ribs. "Take it back."

"No...way." I gasped for breath as he continued his assault on me. He finally let up and it took me a moment to push the picture out of my mind of a fifteen-year-old Landon dressed in a Boy Scout uniform. Even more difficult was trying to remove the image of a present-day Landon in a Boy Scout uniform. Freaking hilarious.

"I'll have you know that if Armageddon were to happen right now, we could survive just fine because of me."

I got up off the couch and started walking toward my room to go change, still laughing. "I'll take your word for it."

He tossed one of my throw pillows at me as I left the room and got up off the couch to chase me down the hall. We might be stuck inside in the middle of winter, but I didn't see how I'd ever get enough of this.

chapter twenty-nine

Skye

I unlocked the door to my apartment after our workout and we stepped inside. Landon had been right. We'd been spending so much time together that we'd both been a little lax on our regular exercise regimes, so it felt great to work out. I was covered in sweat and needed a shower, but I had renewed energy and had lost the cabin fever.

As soon as I threw my keys down, Landon had me pressed against the back of the door with my hands above my head. He was bent down a bit so his rigid length pressed into me through his gym shorts at just the right spot, but I wanted more. More friction, more of him, more skin on skin. His lips came down on mine and I tasted the salt on them from his workout. He nipped at my lower lip before slowly pushing his tongue inside my mouth. The kiss was slow but thorough, as if he were trying to memorize the feel and shape of my mouth.

I ground my chest up and down against his, the feel of my cotton sports bra providing the much-needed friction on my aching nipples. Landon knew what I wanted and in one fell swoop had my sports bra up and over my head. Then he pushed my breasts together with his hands and thumbed my nipples. It had my underwear wet in seconds.

"We should go get in the shower," he said, his voice raspy, before taking one of my nipples in his mouth. He circled it with his tongue and then pressed it between his teeth, immediately soothing the pain with another swipe of his tongue. He sucked hard as he pulled his mouth off and repeated the process with the other one.

My hands were already in his hair so I gripped tight and pulled him away from my body. "Enough. Shower," I said, panting like a dog on a hot summer day. I'm not sure I'd even huffed and puffed this much through my workout. God, what this man did to me.

"No arguments here." His eyes held the promise that the best was yet to come, and he grabbed my hand to lead me to the bathroom.

Lucky for me, this apartment had been redone shortly before I'd moved in and the landlord had chosen to remove the tub and install one large shower instead. I turned on the water and we undressed quickly before stepping inside. The spray of the hot water hitting my bare skin and aching muscles was always such a relief after a workout.

Landon came up behind me and traced his fingers up my stomach to cup my breasts. In response, I pushed back into his erection. Then when I'd had enough of his teasing, I turned around to face him. I gripped his hair and pulled his head toward me until our lips crashed into each other. His arms circled my back and we stayed that way for a while, just kissing and enjoying our wet, naked bodies pressed into each other while the hot water trickled down us to the shower floor.

I pulled away first and looked him up and down, enjoying the hard male physique in front of me. His muscles were taut from his workout, and the V leading down to his treasure trove was more pronounced than usual. I took a finger from each hand and ran them along the line. When I got to the end of the trail, I gripped his cock in my hand and began stroking him up and down. The water beating down on us provided some good lubrication and Landon was quickly panting. He gripped my head between his hands, threw his head back, and let out a groan.

I'd been determined to have my way with him, but I didn't want him to finish like this. I wanted him inside me. I released him and stepped back. His head whipped up and he pinned me with feral-looking eyes. Before I could say anything, he grabbed both of my thighs, picked me up, and pushed my back against the shower wall. In one swift motion, he was fully seated inside of me. I let out a loud moan as he began thrusting into me.

I couldn't get enough of him when he was like this...out of control with need for me. I dug my fingers into the hard muscles of his back and did the only thing I could do—held on. His lips found my neck and he sucked, tongued, and nipped me until I felt like I was about to combust.

"You feel so fucking good, sweetheart. I have no control when I'm inside you," he grunted. "So. Fucking. Good." He punctuated each word with a hard thrust that left me on the verge of an orgasm.

"I don't want you in control with me." He must have liked what he heard because he groaned and then pushed himself in to the hilt and rotated his hips around so that he pressed against my clit. That final stimulation was all I needed for my inner muscles to contract around him. I moaned as the orgasm sent me spiraling into bliss. My limbs tingled as I rode it out, but it kept coming in waves as I bucked myself against him and arched my back off the wall. Finally, Landon started to move in and out of me again. A minute later, he bit my shoulder and I felt his cock jerk its release inside of me.

We were still for a few minutes, both enjoying the aftershocks of our orgasms. After we'd caught our breath, he lifted me off of his shaft and lowered me to the ground on shaky legs. He held my arms until I was steady then cupped my face in his hands.

"Did I hurt you?" he asked, sounding concerned.

"Of course not."

He kissed me briefly on the lips. "Good. I don't know what came over me."

"Well, obviously I did." He laughed and then kissed the tip of my nose before inching back only enough so that I could see the emotion swimming in his eyes. The way he was looking at me and tenderly holding my face in his hands, I'd never felt as cherished as I did right in that moment.

"I've never been happier, you know. Never," he said and somehow managed to make me feel even more treasured than I did a moment ago.

I felt my eyes misting and worked to control the lump forming in my throat. "Me either."

The weight of those three little unspoken words lay between us, and the magnitude of my feelings for him were suddenly clear to me—I loved Landon. It wasn't as scary as I thought it would be. After Vic, I'd wanted nothing to do with guys, love, or any of it. At the time I'd thought I loved Vic, but I realized now that I hadn't even really known what that meant. When things were good between us at the beginning, I'd just been in a lot of *like* with Vic. I guess it took the right person to come along and show you that a lot of *like* wasn't the same as a lot of love.

I suspected Landon was starting to have similar feelings for me, but I didn't want to ask. He'd tell me if and when he was ready.

When he kissed the top of my head and got out of the shower, I knew he wasn't ready now. I watched as he dried himself off and then wrapped a towel around his waist. That was an image I wanted to sear into my mind.

"Are you hungry? I really worked up an appetite between both of our workouts," he said, wagging his eyebrows at me.

I laughed. "Now that you mention it, I could totally go for some Thai food. Do you want to go order while I finish up in here?"

"Sure thing. You want the usual?"

"Please."

Landon may not have said those three little words, but things between us still felt pretty damn good.

I stayed in the shower for a few more minutes and Landon came back into the room as I was toweling off.

"Need any help with that?" he asked.

I looked up from drying off my legs. He was leaning against the doorframe with his arms crossed casually over his chest. It accentuated his biceps and I already felt my desire for him stirring again.

"I think I can handle it," I joked. "Any problems ordering dinner?"

"They said they'd be here in half an hour."

"Can't wait." I wrapped the towel around me and then used another to wring out my hair. "Are you just going to stand there and watch?"

"Pretty much. I like this show. One of my all-time favorites."

I laughed. "Is that right? What's the name of this show exactly?"

"Picture Perfect, I think." I felt a blush creep from my chest up to my face at his compliment.

"I wish," I said and laughed.

Landon continued to stand there while I went through my routine of applying body lotion and face moisturizer. I was drying my hair with the hairdryer when he said, "I think I just heard the door. I'll go get dinner."

"In that towel?" I asked, laughing.

He shrugged. "It's just the delivery guy. Nothing he hasn't seen before."

I shook my head as he pushed up off the door frame to go retrieve our food. A girl would *never* answer the door like that.

I turned the hair dryer back on and was almost done when

I heard loud voices. I immediately switched it off and listened. Definitely voices—and not the happy kind. I dropped the towel, grabbed my robe from behind the door and scrambled to put it on so I could go see what was going on.

It wasn't until I'd gotten halfway down the hall that I recognized the other person's voice.

Vic.

What the hell was *he* doing here?

chapter thirty

Skye

I turned the corner to see that Landon had Vic pushed up beside the wall, his forearm pinned under Vic's chin. His other hand was clenched in a fist at his side.

"What are you doing here, Vic?"

"This asshole was just leaving. Weren't you?" Landon said between gritted teeth. I heard the venom in his voice. I had no desire to protect Vic, but I didn't want this situation spinning out of control. I remembered Landon's reaction when I'd told him what Vic had done. There was no way I was going to let Landon do something that would result in him ending up with an assault charge.

"Landon, let him go."

His head whipped around and he pinned me with an intense stare. "Are you fucking serious? This guy's lucky I didn't beat him to a pulp on sight for what he did to you."

"What do you know about it, asshole?" Vic unwisely retorted. Landon crushed his arm into him further until he was gasping for air. I ran up and started trying to pull Landon's arm off of Vic, but it was like a vice grip.

"Landon, please. Let him go. He's not worth going to jail over."

"Yeah, Landon. Listen to the lady," Vic barely croaked out.

"Shut up, Vic!" I yelled. God, what the hell had I ever seen in this guy? He was a complete idiot.

I gave Landon a pleading look, and though I could see he struggled with his desire to put Vic through the wall, he finally acquiesced and dropped his arm.

"Thank you," I mouthed to him. I turned to look at Vic, who was rubbing the front of his throat. "Now, you've got one minute to say what the hell you're doing here."

"I wanted to talk to you." He looked over to Landon. "Alone."

"Well, that's not going to happen. Ever," I said.

"I only want to talk, Skye. You know I'm sorry about what happened. I've given you all kinds of space like you asked for, but I'm tired of waiting."

"We're done, Vic, and we have been for a while. Nothing you say is going to change that."

The look on Vic's face was venomous. "Too good for me now that you're fucking your boss, Skye?" I stepped back. It felt like a slap in the face when he put it so crudely. "Yeah, I remember this asshole from the parking lot that day. Guess he was already in your pants at that point. Explains why he swooped in to play Prince Charming."

Landon took a step toward Vic but backed off when I put my hand out. "Who I'm with and how long I've been with them is none of your concern. You gave up that right the night you put your hands on me. Now get out of my place and don't ever come back or next time I *will* call the cops."

"We both know that's a bluff. There's no way you'd risk calling the cops and dragging your dad's name through the press."

"I mean it, Vic. Get out!" I was near tears now because he was right. I wouldn't call the police unless I absolutely had to, and I hated that he knew that.

"Fine." He walked toward the door and opened it, but before he left he turned to Landon and asked, "Enjoying my sloppy seconds?"

I grabbed Landon's arm so he wouldn't race after him. He stood there, breathing heavily, staring at the back of the closed door after it slammed shut behind Vic. "I don't know what you ever saw in that stupid fuck."

"Me either," I said and then my resolve failed. I fell to the floor, sobs wracking my body.

Landon joined me on the floor and surrounded me with his arms, rocking back and forth. "Shhh. It's okay. It'll be okay." He rubbed his hands up and down on my back, attempting to soothe me. After a few minutes, the warmth of his bare chest and the comfort I found in his arms was enough that I was able to stop crying.

"I'm sorry." I rubbed at my tear-stained cheeks.

"Hey." Landon lifted my chin with his finger. "You have nothing to apologize for. That asshole had no right coming here tonight. I'm the one who should apologize."

I sniffed and wiped my nose on the sleeve of my robe. "Why would you have anything to apologize for?"

"First off, after lecturing you about checking your peephole before opening the door, I didn't. I just assumed it was our food being delivered. Second, because I probably scared you with how angry I was. I want you to know that I would never...*ever*...lay a hand on you." He brushed my hair back over my shoulder and ran his thumb up and down the base of my neck.

I shook my head. "I would never think that."

"Still. Seeing me enraged as I was...the thought had to have crossed your mind."

"Not even once." I trusted the man in front of me like no one I'd ever been close to before.

"Seeing him standing there when I opened the door...everything you told me flashed through my head...I wanted to make sure he knew he couldn't hurt you any more."

I cupped his face in my hand. "You don't have to explain."

"You have to promise me that you won't open that door without knowing who it is first. And if he shows up here again, don't open the door—no matter what. You call me if I'm not here."

I had no problem with that. I had no intention of being in the same room with Vic alone ever again. "I promise."

"Good, now let's get out of here. We're going to my place. I don't want to take the chance that that shithead shows back up here tonight. We'll wait until the food arrives and then head out."

I nodded, knowing he was right. I wasn't up for any more turmoil tonight. I only wanted to be safe in Landon's arms, somewhere far away from any reminders of my past mistakes.

I returned home on Sunday afternoon. Landon was hesitant to let me go, but I had laundry I wanted to do and I knew he'd planned to go into the office for a few hours anyway.

I was nervous at first, but when I made it all the way to my apartment without a Vic sighting, I relaxed.

I should have known better.

As soon as I swung the door open and saw the envelope with my name on it that'd been shoved under the door, my stomach dropped. Without even opening it, somehow I knew that envelope would be the end of Landon and me.

chapter thirty-one

Skye

It was after work and I sat in a coffee shop, awaiting Vic's arrival. I'd been jumpy the last few days at work, and although I couldn't tell Landon what was going on, he had started to question if everything was okay. I did my best to reassure him.

It killed me inside that I was lying to him, but the note had been clear that if I cared about my father and Landon, I'd keep my mouth shut about our meeting. I reasoned that it was okay because we were in public so I wouldn't be in any *real* danger, but I knew that was only an excuse to try and make myself feel better about deceiving Landon.

The picture in the envelope was the only reason I was meeting with Vic—that damn picture I'd forgotten even existed. When I'd ripped open the envelope and unfolded the paper inside, a copy of the one and only topless selfie I'd sent Vic sat inside, taunting me. It might as well have been a flashing neon sign saying, *"I'm about to take down everything you care about."*

I'd been nauseous and had a throbbing headache from that moment on. When I thought about the fact that Vic could look at such a private photo of me any time he wanted...there were no words. We'd only been seeing each other for a couple of months and things had been good at the time. He'd had to travel for work for a couple of weeks, I'd been out that night for drinks with the girls, and somehow I'd let him talk me into sending it. I'd trusted him when he said he'd delete it and he'd never brought it up since then. I could have never predicted he'd try to use it against me.

The chime over the door dinged and I looked up from where I sat, nervously spinning my untouched coffee. Vic walked in with a grin. I would have loved nothing more than to slap it off his face.

He took the seat across from me. "You didn't order anything for me?" I just glared at him so he continued, "Seems time away from your parents' house hasn't helped your manners any."

"What do you want?" I demanded, just wanting to get this over with.

"Careful. You might want to be nicer to me now that you know I have the ability to ruin everything for the people you care about most."

"Just get to the point," I said between clenched teeth. I was seething inside, my heart pounding in my chest and I could feel the blood rushing through my neck.

"If that's how you want it. Bottom line, I want you back. I never should've done what I did, but you won't listen to reason and give me another chance. I *know* we were good together and I want that back. If you don't ditch your boss and agree to start seeing me again, I'm going to release the picture to the press. Not only will it be the only thing anyone talks about when your dad's name comes up in the Senate race, but it'll reflect badly on that little empire your soon-to-be-ex-boyfriend is building. Who'd want to hire a PR firm where the right-hand to the owner can't even handle her own PR? I did a little digging and heard that he's expanding into Los Angeles. It'd be a shame for all his hard work to go down the tubes because of you."

My stomach dropped and all the air left my lungs to the point where I felt like I couldn't breathe. He knew exactly where to strike so it hurt the most. Obviously I didn't want to have to deal with the shame and embarrassment of that picture getting out, but having it hurt two of the people I loved most in this world was not acceptable. And I knew it would. If that photo leaked, it would do all of the things that Vic had just spelled out to me.

But in order to save them both from losing much of what they'd worked so hard to achieve in their careers, I'd have to hurt the only man I'd ever really loved. There had to be another way.

"Vic, things were not good between us for the last half of our relationship. Why would you even want to get back together?"

He looked at me like I was crazy for not already knowing the answer. "Because I love you."

I mentally scoffed at his response. He loved me no more than I loved him—he just wanted what he couldn't have. That or he was completely delusional.

"You don't love me. And even if I break up with Landon and agree to start seeing you again, you have to know that I don't want to be with you. Why would you want that?"

"Because I understand that you're angry. I know that once we spend time together again, you'll realize that *we* belong together." So he *is* delusional.

"If you love me, why would you want to hurt me by releasing those pictures? You don't do that to someone you love." I was almost pleading now, hoping he'd see reason.

He pressed his lips together. His anger was back. "I've told you my terms, Skye. I'll give you until the end of the weekend to get rid of Prince Charming. If I don't hear from you, I'll be contacting the press on Monday morning." He pushed his chair from the table and walked out of the coffee shop without a backward glance.

Tears dripped onto the table below. I was so screwed. What was I going to do?

I could live with Vic hurting me, but what I couldn't live with was him hurting the two most important men in my life.

I had no doubt my father would love me all the same, but he was a good man who had worked his whole life to help other people. This run for Senate was the culmination of *decades* of hard work. I would do anything to not put that in jeopardy. And the negative effect a scandal like this would have on Landon's business made me feel physically ill.

It was Saturday morning and I'd managed to avoid staying at Landon's the past two nights, once by saying I had plans with my father and the other by telling him that I wasn't feeling well. I needed some space to figure out what I was going to do. Sleeping in Landon's bed wasn't going to give me the perspective I needed.

Vic hadn't been in contact with me since issuing his ultimatum, but I didn't doubt he'd follow through on his threat if I didn't come willingly back to him.

I'd gone through it all in my head over and over again. I could do as Vic wanted, but I truly couldn't even envision what it would be like trying to let Vic take Landon's place in my life. The idea was abhorrent to me. Not to mention, what happened the next time he got angry at me and lost control? I wasn't stupid enough to think that as sorry as he might be, it couldn't happen again.

If I approached Landon looking for help, there was no guarantee he would want to be with me once the picture came out. What kind of girl would he think I was for sending that to someone? And if that didn't do it, the massive hit his business would take surely would. Whether I did what Vic wanted or not, Landon could fire me either way. It was a real possibility that he wouldn't want to continue to work side-by-side with me every day.

I agonized for days, running every scenario over in my mind. In the end, I was no closer to a decision but I knew I needed to see him. I knew I needed to confess everything going on to him. Landon had contacts and resources; maybe he could help. If he felt about me the way I thought he did, he'd stay by my side even if the picture leaked—wouldn't he?

I knocked on the door to Landon's condo just before lunch. I'd called earlier to see if I could stop by, so I knew he was here waiting for me. He sounded so happy at the news that I was feeling better and able to spend time with him that my heart nearly broke into two and fell out of my chest right then.

I was so nervous about what I had tell him that I couldn't stand in one spot, constantly shifting my weight from one foot to the other. He swung open the door with a big smile on his face and pulled me in for a kiss before I could say a single word. A whimper escaped, knowing that this might be the last time I'd feel his lips against mine.

"I'm glad you're feeling better," he said when we broke apart.

"Thanks." I took a deep breath and walked into the apartment, not bothering to take my coat off.

"Sweetheart, give me your coat. I'll hang it up," he said from behind me.

I didn't have the stomach to turn around and look at him so I just kept walking. "We need to talk."

Landon

This was *not* good. Not only because nothing good ever came from someone saying "we need to talk," but I knew from the tone of her voice that this talk would not be a happy one.

"Why can't you look at me?" I asked her as I walked up behind her, my heart beating fast in my chest, my breathing shallow. She turned to face me as I approached. I searched her face for any indication of what she was about to say, and that's when I saw it. Her eyes held no emotion—no sparkle.

"Something has happened that we need to discuss."

"Okay..." I had no idea where she was going with this.

She looked down at her hands that she was wringing in front of her and then looked up to me. "I'm not sure how you're going to react to what I have to tell you, but I want you to hear me out."

"You're worrying me now. What's going on?" A queasy sensation rolled through my stomach as it dawned on me that I'd only ever seen her like this when it had something to do with Vic. "This is about him, isn't it?"

"Yes. Well, sort of."

"What did he do now?" I asked between gritted teeth.

She let out a deep sigh. "It has to do with—"

The phone broke into Skye's confession with two short rings, alerting me that it was the concierge desk calling. I ignored it and we continued to stare at one another, me waiting for her to continue. "Just get it," she said.

I shoved my hands through my hair in frustration and walked over to pick up the receiver. "What?"

"Mr. Steele, it's Brandon from downstairs. There's an Ingrid Patterson here to see you, Sir."

"I don't know anyone by that name."

"She insists you do, Sir and she said she's not going anywhere until she gets to talk to you. She's been pretty insistent."

"Fine. Send her up." I'd set her straight and send her on her way since she obviously had the wrong person. I did not fucking need this right now.

"Someone's downstairs," I explained as I slammed down the receiver. "Says she knows me. I have no idea who it is."

Her expression turned panicked. "You don't think it's a reporter or something?"

"Why would it be a reporter?" I asked through the slits in my narrowed eyes.

"I don't know. Maybe they found out about us or...something." We'd been careful about where we spent our time together, and no one in the office was the wiser so I didn't understand why she was suddenly concerned that someone had blown the whistle on our relationship.

A knock came from the door. "Hang on a second while I deal with this," I barked, more aggressively than I'd intended.

I swung the door open and the first thought I had was that the girl standing in front of me looked familiar.

The second thing I noticed was her swollen, obviously pregnant belly.

chapter thirty-two

Landon

I knew beyond a shadow of a doubt that this was the topper to an already monumentally shitty day.

Ingrid, or whoever the hell she was, gave me a small, nervous smile. "Remember me?" she said, throwing her arms up to the side.

I tried to figure out where I knew her from and when I finally did remember, my stomach lurched. We'd met last summer. I'd been out with the boys and picked her up and took her home that night. I looked back down to her stomach.

Oh. Fuck.

"I'm kind of in the middle of something right now. What are you doing here?" *Please don't say it. Please don't say it.*

"I'll get right to it then. You're going to be a father."

I swear my heart skipped a few beats—skipped then stuttered in my chest before picking up its regular rythym. When it did, I noticed that Ingrid was focused on something behind me and I turned to see Skye standing at the end of the hallway, all color drained from her face. I didn't doubt I looked the same.

She walked down the hall toward us. "I'm going to go. You obviously have things to figure out here," she said, her voice shaky.

Of all the fucking times for this chick to show up here and hit me with this. Skye brushed past me in an effort to leave, but I grabbed hold of her hand before she could get out of reach.

"I want to finish this conversation."

She pulled her hand from mine and looked over to Ingrid. "I'd say you have more important issues to deal with right now."

I let her leave because what the hell else was I going to do? The situation was completely fucked up. The woman I cared for more than any before her obviously had something big she needed to tell me, and now a woman whose name I hadn't even remembered just told me she was having my baby.

Un. Fucking. Believable.

Skye

I drove my car home, barely able to see through the tears. Landon was going to be a father?

I knew Landon. After what his father had done to his mother, he'd never abandon his own child—not that I would want him to, of course. But this meant he'd be involved in that girl's life forever now.

I couldn't tell him now—I couldn't do that to him. He had enough to deal with and didn't need the added bonus of a girlfriend needing him to help her solve her monumental problem. Particularly one whose past could jeopardize his business, which happened to be his only means of supporting a child.

Maybe this was fate stepping in to lend a hand. That girl showing up had made the decision for me, and I knew what I had to do. I was going to have to walk away from the man who taught me the true meaning of love. And to do so successfully, I was going to have to make him believe I *wanted* to do it, breaking both of our hearts in the process.

I had to pull over as the gut-wrenching anguish of all that I was going to lose hit me. I'd found "the one," and I'd been foolish enough to assume that meant a happy ending for us. Never in my life had I felt pain this intense, so I hunched over the steering wheel and let it all out.

Blackness soon began to settle in my heart like a cancer, growing out of control and rapidly spreading throughout my body. This was the only moment of despair I was going to allow myself. The decision was made and I needed to live by it for both Landon and my dad's sakes. Dad would never know of any of this, but I'd see Landon every day and he needed to believe that I didn't want to be with him. It was for his own good.

Once I'd composed myself enough to safely drive, I merged back into traffic and continued home. When I arrived, I took off the necklace he'd given me for my birthday and placed it in the bottom of my jewelry box. I'd worn it almost every day since he'd given it to me, but I no longer wanted the constant reminder of what an amazing guy he was. Like my emotions, I put it away and locked it up tight.

A knock on my door woke me the next morning. I wish the superintendent would fix that front door so people had to be buzzed in. I had barely slept and was cursing whoever it was as I peeled myself out of bed. I shuffled to the door, running my fingers through my hair in an effort to look somewhat presentable.

I looked through the peephole to see Landon pacing in front of my door. He knocked again. Was I ready to do this?

"Open up, Skye. I know you're behind the door."

I mustered up as much courage as I could by remembering

why I was doing this and with a sigh, I unlocked the door and swung it open. Showtime.

He looked like shit. He was in the same clothes he'd been wearing when I left his place the day before. He was unshaven, and the dark circles under his eyes indicated that he hadn't gotten much sleep last night either.

"You don't look very good," I said.

"I've been out driving all night, trying to wrap my brain around the last twenty-four hours. I got tired of pacing in my apartment, so I finally just drove out of town and kept driving. I haven't slept."

I felt concern for him but I pushed it away. I couldn't afford to feel that right now. "What are you doing here?" I asked, trying to put a hard edge to my voice that I didn't really feel.

"I want to know what you came to tell me yesterday."

Here goes nothing. "Fine. When I saw Vic, I realized that I didn't give him a fair chance after he apologized for what he did. We were together for a while and I should have given him the opportunity to make it up to me. I also realized I miss him."

Fury was etched on every feature of Landon's face. "That's horseshit. What's really going on?"

"I told you. I can't see you anymore. I'm going to try and make it work with Vic."

"So you're saying you just want to give up what we have?"

I squared my shoulders and looked him straight in the eye, hoping that the words I spoke next didn't indicate how torn up I was inside. "It's only sex between us, Landon. That's all it's ever been. Look how things started between us, for God's sake. We fooled around at a club together. And then again in the office. And then in the cabana. It's never been about anything more than the fact that we want to fuck each other. You can't build something to last on that."

"If that's how you felt, then why did you seem so nervous to tell me yesterday? Like you didn't want to?"

"Because the last time I broke up with someone, it didn't go that great, did it?"

He looked like I'd slapped him in the face and a kicked him in the nuts at the same time. "You think I'd hurt you?" he almost whispered.

"Of course not! I just don't want this to be more difficult than it already is."

"Why is it difficult if you *want* to break up with me?"

"You're twisting my words around!" *Ugh. Why wouldn't he just let this go?*

"No. I'm. Not. Now tell me what's really going on."

"I just told you how I feel..." Hurt flashed across his features and I felt horrible inside, but I couldn't let him know how much it affected me. "Besides, seems you have bigger things on your plate to deal with."

He rested his hands on each of my shoulders. "We'll talk about that in a minute. Why are you trying to break up with me?"

"I'm not trying, Landon. It's done. I want to work things out with Vic."

"Why would you want to go back to someone that hurt you like that?" When his voice broke at the end, it was almost my undoing. Then I thought of that photo and the damage Vic could do with it, and I rallied.

"People make mistakes, Landon. Seeing that girl on your doorstep yesterday, I'd say you've made one or two yourself."

"Damn it, Skye!"

"Am I wrong?"

He ran his hands through his hair. "Yes, I was with her last summer. Once. But we used a condom. I don't see how I could be the baby's father."

Hearing him discuss being intimate with another girl was enough to make my stomach roll. Nausea swept through me, and I struggled to swallow the bile at the back of my throat.

"Why would she show up and tell you that you were the father if you weren't?" I crossed my arms in front of my chest.

211

"I don't know. Could be a million reasons. Why would she wait so long to tell me she's pregnant if I was the father?"

"You must have asked her that yourself," I pointed out.

"She said she debated telling me at all since we'd only had a fling, but that as she got further along in the pregnancy, she decided the baby deserved to know its father."

I didn't want to hear about this. I'd daydreamed about us starting a family together someday, and now I was talking to him about this other girl who would end up being the mother of his child. It was all too much.

"Why are we even discussing this? It's none of my business any more."

"I will deal with that situation, but you need to tell me—truthfully this time—what is going on. Why don't you want to be with me?"

"We can't keep going over this. What we had was great, but it was purely physical. I want to be with someone I can be out in public with, someone I can bring to family dinners. I can do that with Vic. He deserves another chance."

Landon was breathing heavy and I could see him trying to rein himself in. He took a moment before he spoke. "I still don't believe you. Something is going on and I'm going to find out what."

"Leave it alone. There's nothing going on. I don't want to be with you—it's as simple as that."

The anguish on his face caused by my heartless words was enough that I had to turn my back on him to hide the tears welling in my eyes.

"If that's really how you want it to be." His voice broke at the end.

"It is," I said, my back still turned to him. I couldn't bear to face him. "If you want me to clear my things out of my desk, I understand."

It was a full minute before he spoke again. "We're both adults. I think we can manage to work side-by-side without it being a problem."

I nodded. "Alright then. I'll see you tomorrow."

I turned and shut the door to my apartment. This was it. It was really over between us. I pulled my cell phone from my purse and texted Vic to tell him I was going along with his demands. I didn't know how I was going to stomach being around him again, but I'd have to figure out a way to protect those I loved.

I crumpled down to the floor. I hadn't thought there were any tears left to cry—I couldn't have been more wrong.

chapter thirty-three

Landon

I begged off work on Monday, leaving a message on Skye's voicemail early that morning before anyone was in. Marci had actually called me at home later that day to see if I was okay because I'd never taken time off for being sick before. She was concerned that something was really wrong with me. I'd told her it was just a stomach bug.

What else was I going to say? There was this girl that I banged forever ago who is now claiming I'm her baby daddy. Oh, and by the way, I foolishly got involved with my assistant and now she's ripped my heart to shreds and I didn't want to face her. Yeah, not happening.

For someone who made his living being quick on his feet and knowing how to handle shit situations for other people, I wasn't dealing with my own very well.

There was just too much to process at once. The thought of being a father with a girl I barely knew was horrible, but the idea of not being involved in the child's life if I *was* the father was abhorrent to me. Before my dad's mistress had lost the baby, he'd had no intention of stepping up and being a father to the child. I couldn't do that. As much as I didn't want to be tied to this woman for the rest of my life, no child deserved to grow up without a father—especially when I was fully capable of providing for him or her.

I spent the day pacing my apartment, working out to relieve the tension, and drowning my sorrows in every form of alcohol I had on hand.

Think, Landon. If this were one of your clients, how would you tell them to handle the situation?

I knew the answer, though I didn't like it. I'd tell them to deal with the baby situation first, to get that sorted and then deal with their love life. Everything inside me screamed that I had to get Skye back and away from Vic, but I knew I wouldn't have any chance to do it if I didn't figure out what the hell this girl's deal was first.

I walked over to the kitchen to find the piece of paper I'd scrawled Ingrid's number on when she left. It still sat there on the granite counter underneath an empty beer bottle. I was usually pretty meticulous about my place, but since Skye had left Saturday morning, I'd let things go to shit.

I dialed the number and waited for the girl to pick up.

"Hello?"

"Ingrid, it's Landon." I tried to change the tone of my voice so that I didn't sound like a total asshole, but I'm not sure I was entirely successful. It was hard to pretend I was happy about her showing up and disrupting my life when I wasn't. What guy would be?

"I was wondering if you were going to call." She may have been wondering, but she sure as shit sounded excited now that I had.

"I said I would."

"I know, but I took you by surprise. I didn't know how you'd handle the news."

I sucked in a big breath. "I'd be lying if I said I was happy about it. We don't even know each other. That said, if I *am* the father, I'll live up to my responsibilities. This child will have a father if I'm it."

"I told you, Landon, you *are* it."

"That's why I called. We need to discuss how to go about determining that."

She paused for a moment. "What do you mean?"

"Well, there has to be something we can do—some test that will tell us with one-hundred percent accuracy if I'm the father."

She was quiet for a moment before she spoke. "There is a test called an amniocentesis."

"Great. Let's get that done right away."

"I'm not doing that test, Landon. Do you have any idea what it involves?"

"I get the feeling you're going to fill me in."

"The doctor puts a needle in your belly and draws fluid out of the amniotic sac. There are all kinds of risks to the baby. I'm not doing it. Besides, I can't afford it anyway."

"I'd pay for it, of course...are the risks to the baby really that great?"

"It's not an option."

I blew out a frustrated sigh. "What *are* our options then?"

"To wait until the baby is born."

"That's months away."

"We don't have a choice." Her tone was firm and final.

"I'd like to come with you on your next doctor's visit. I want to speak to the doctor myself to be sure that those are our only options."

She hesitated for a minute before answering, which gave me hope that perhaps we did have other options. "Okay."

"Great. When is it?"

She gave me the necessary information, and as luck would have it, her appointment was at the end of next week. We made plans to meet at the doctor's office.

I hung up feeling mildly better about *that* situation. At least the wheels were in motion to figure out whether I had any responsibility to Ingrid and her baby. The issues with Skye still gnawed at my gut, but I had to suck it up until I knew what my own life was going to be like moving forward.

Tuesday morning I entered the office with the mantra in my head that it would be business as usual. I'd managed to work beside Skye when I'd wanted her before. Although it had only been a physical yearning then and now it was much more. Whatever. I could do it again. And I believed it until I saw a flower delivery guy dropping off roses at Skye's desk. She looked uncomfortable, almost as if she wanted to refuse the delivery. When she heard me approach, she looked up and guilt flooded her features. She placed the flowers on her desk and grabbed her purse.

I walked over and handed the guy a couple of dollars for a tip. "Here. I've got it."

The delivery guy thanked me and left. "You didn't have to do that," she whispered.

"I know. But we're adults, remember? I made you that promise back in Los Angeles and I intend to live up to it."

Before she could respond, squeals came from behind us as the women of the office descended. Marci made it to us first.

"These are so beautiful, Skye. Who are they from?"

Skye's eyes darted to me and then back to Marci. "Um...they're from my ex. We broke up for a while but we're trying to work things out."

"That is *so* romantic," one of the other women said.

It was too much for me. I couldn't stand around here while all these women mooned over what a great guy Vic was when I knew the truth. And so did Skye—apparently, she just didn't care.

I retreated to the solace of my office and didn't come out until lunch.

Skye

I'd felt awful when Landon showed up while the flower shop was delivering. Leave it to Vic to try to make a point to him under the guise of doing something nice for me.

Tomorrow night was going to be our first "date." I'd managed to persuade Vic that we couldn't just pick back up where we'd left off, that I needed him to prove to me he'd changed and I could trust him. I was buying time and I knew it. Until when exactly, I wasn't sure, but I couldn't imagine letting him put his hands on me in an intimate way so I knew we needed to be out in public whenever possible.

Landon didn't buzz me at my desk or make an appearance outside his office until he came out to grab some lunch.

"I just talked to Chelsea. Their legal team is almost done with the contracts for Calder Fox. Can you follow-up with her tomorrow if we haven't seen anything and make sure they get to me ASAP?"

"No problem." He started to walk away but I stopped him. "Mr. Steele?"

He stopped walking but didn't turn to face me. "What is it, Skye?" His tone was abrupt.

"I'm sorry about this morning. I had no idea those flowers were coming."

He spun and walked closer to my desk, his voice low so that only I could hear him. "You don't need to apologize. You've made your wishes clear, and although I don't understand them and it's not what *I* want, I will respect them if that's what you think will make you happy. But let's be clear—I don't think it will. I think *I'm* the man to do that. He'll only end up hurting you again or worse. I'll stay out of your business, Skye, but if you show up here looking like he's used you as a punching bag, all bets are off."

Before I could respond, he turned and walked away.

I knew how much he despised Vic, and the fact that he wasn't going to make my life difficult at work after how I'd hurt him was just another example of why I'd fallen in love with Landon in the first place.

chapter thirty-four

Skye

I walked into the movie theater to see Vic waiting for me—popcorn and drink in hand. The smile on his face probably looked charming to anyone else, but I knew the snake that existed under the faux exterior and to me he looked like a cobra waiting to strike.

"Hi, Vic," I said when I reached him.

"Is that any way to greet your boyfriend?" he asked and leaned forward to kiss me. I backed away instinctively.

"I told you I need to start from scratch," I said, trying to cover for myself. "I'm pretty sure you didn't kiss me on our first date."

"Fair enough. How about a hug then?" He took a step forward and wrapped his arms around me, popcorn in one hand, a drink in the other.

My body was screaming at me to move back, but I forced myself to lean into the hug. When he backed away, a shiver of revulsion ran down my spine.

"How did you like the flowers? I was surprised I didn't get a call or a text from you about them."

Seriously? This guy really was living in his own universe if he thought I'd appreciate anything from him. But I kept up the charade saying, "They're lovely. I meant to call but work was crazy today. Plus, I knew I'd get to see you tonight to thank you in person."

"What did Prince Charming think of them?" Ah, the snake wasn't even trying to hide his fangs.

"I didn't ask but let's be clear, Vic...I'm not going to discuss him with you. At all. Ever. So just drop it."

He ignored my comment—it was like I hadn't even spoken. "Let's go get our seats before it gets too busy."

"Fine."

We walked side-by-side down the hall that led to our theater. He placed the hand holding the drink on my lower back as we walked. Six months ago, I would have liked the intimate gesture. But now it felt wrong—dirty.

Once we'd settled in our seats, Vic placed the popcorn on my lap and I feigned interest in the pre-show quizzes on the screen.

"You always were really good at these," he said.

"I watch too many movies, I guess."

"I think it's because you're so brilliant."

Oh God, he was laying it on thick. If I still cared for him, I'd probably be happy he was trying so hard. Unfortunately, I'd spent every second since I arrived wishing it was a different man entirely who sat beside me.

The theater darkened as the previews began. Vic put his arm behind the back of the seat. What was I to say? It wasn't like I wouldn't have let him do it if we'd been on the kind of date I actually wanted to be on.

I sat ramrod straight throughout the entire movie, refusing to fully relax against Vic's arm. The lights came up at the end of the movie and I immediately stood and grabbed my jacket and purse from the chair beside me, where I'd set them when we'd arrived.

"That was pretty good. Did you enjoy it?" Vic asked.

"It was okay." Truth was, I'd barely paid any attention to the movie—I'd been too preoccupied with my thoughts.

Vic walked me to my car like the perfect gentleman that he *wasn't*. "I had a great time tonight, Skye. I'm glad we did this."

"Thanks for asking me to come. Well, I'd better get going. I've got a busy day at work tomorrow." I didn't mean any of it—except the work part—but I hoped he was buying it anyway.

"Before you go..." He leaned in to kiss me and I panicked, giving him my cheek instead. He didn't look happy when he pulled away, his eyebrows drawn and his lips pressed into a thin line.

"First date, remember?" I said, purposely keeping my voice light.

That seemed to appease him. He rubbed his hand along my upper arm. "Drive home safe. I'm busy tomorrow night with a client, but maybe we could get together on Friday."

"I have to help my dad with some stuff for his campaign. I'll call you though and we'll definitely do something over the weekend."

"Okay. Sounds good," he said and I breathed a sigh of relief that he'd accepted my obvious brush-off. He leaned in and gave me another kiss on the cheek. I gave him my best fake smile, and when he turned to walk away, I quickly got into my car and rubbed at my cheek furiously.

When I was satisfied that all remnants of Vic had been removed, I leaned my head against the headrest. How was I ever going to pull this off?

The week seemed to drag on and by the time Friday afternoon came around, I couldn't wait to get away from all things Steele and Associates—specifically all things Steele.

He hadn't been terrible to me. Just the opposite, actually, which was somehow worse. He treated me as if he barely knew me. Like we were just co-workers, and had only ever *been* co-workers. I wish he would've just lashed out at me and treated me as poorly as I'd treated him. Any show of emotion from him would've been easier to deal with than having to pretend I was working with a complete stranger.

It was close to the end of the day when I looked up from my desk to see the pregnant girl that had been at Landon's condo walking toward my desk. I hated to admit it but she was cute, and I could see why Landon had been attracted to her.

"Hi, is Landon in?"

My mouth went dry and it was all I could do to get the words out. "Is he expecting you?"

She smiled wide. "No, I thought I'd drop in and surprise him."

I stood from my chair. "Let me see if he's available."

"You're the girl who was at his apartment, right?"

I was hoping she wouldn't recognize me so this wouldn't be any more awkward than it already was for me. "Yes. I'm his assistant. We were just wrapping up a large project when you arrived."

"Really? Well, sorry to just barge in on you guys like that, but I think you'll be seeing a lot more of me. I'm Ingrid."

Alright, now she was really pissing me off. She stuck her hand out to shake mine. I took it, though I didn't want to. "I'm Skye. Let me go see what Mr. Steele is up to."

"Oooh, Mr. Steele. I like the sound of that. So all this is his?"

"He's the founder of the company, if that's what you mean." I didn't like her line of questioning. I'd give her the benefit of the doubt and assume she was just happy to know that the father of her child wasn't a complete deadbeat. "I'll be right back."

I knocked on Landon's office door before entering and closed it behind me.

"There's an Ingrid here to see you."

He looked up from his computer screen, his eyes wide. "Ingrid? Christ, what is she doing here?"

"I didn't ask." I was impressed with how even I was able to keep my voice when all I wanted to do was scream at being put in the position of having to see the two of them together. Romantic or not, they were still having a child together.

"Skye, I'm sorry. I had no idea she was going to show up here."

"I've moved on with my life, you've done the same. There's no need to apologize."

His expression turned to stone. God, I hated myself when I had to play the part, but it was for his own good in the long run.

"Show her in."

I left his office and then did as he asked—my heart breaking as I escorted the woman who was carrying the child of the man whom I still loved...and always would.

chapter thirty-five

Landon

Ingrid walked into my office with a smile on her face like I'd been expecting her and should be skipping through fucking daisies at the fact that she was here. Was she kidding me? She shows up unannounced at my company, flaunting her pregnant belly, and I'm supposed to be *happy* to see her? The last thing I needed these days was to be fielding questions from my staff as to who she was. Happy was about the furthest fucking emotion away from what I was feeling at the moment.

I gestured to one of the chairs in front of my desk for her to sit. "What are you doing here, Ingrid?"

"I came by to see if maybe you wanted to grab some dinner. I thought it might be a good idea if we got to know each other a little better. We *are* going to be spending a lot of time together, after all."

I took a deep breath in an attempt to rein in my agitation. "You can't just show up at my work unannounced. People are going to ask questions."

Tears pooled in the corner of her eyes. *Way to upset the*

pregnant lady, asshole. "I didn't realize I was the dirty little secret."

"I didn't mean it that way. I'm sorry. But you have to look at this from my perspective. I was with you one time, and then months later you show up at my door to tell me that you're pregnant and I'm the father. Until we confirm that fact, I don't need people sniffing around my business."

"Fine. Sorry. Did you want to get dinner or not?" She sniffed a bit and wiped at a tear in the corner of her eye.

Damn it. "Sure. I've got to eat anyway before I come back to do some more work so why not."

"Great." She looked pleased now and popped up out of her chair. That was a quick turnaround.

I grabbed my jacket from where it was hanging on the back of the door and put it on. Ingrid waited for me and when we exited my office, it didn't escape my notice that Skye didn't even glance in our direction.

"I'm going out for a bit. Can you finish up those reports and leave them on my desk so I can take a look at them when I get back?"

"Yes, Sir." She didn't look away from her computer screen.

I let out a sigh and turned to Ingrid. "Let's go."

"It was nice to meet you, Skye. I'm sure we'll be seeing much more of each other in the future."

"I'm sure we will," Skye muttered as we made our way to the elevators.

Somebody. Fucking. Shoot. Me.

Chicks were all kinds. of crazy. Skye said she didn't want to be with me, but she seemed pissed that Ingrid was here. All I wanted was for this situation with Ingrid to be settled. Then I could figure out what the hell was going on with Skye.

When I saw Skye sitting at her desk on Monday morning, I was filled with a mixture of relief and longing. I'd pined away all weekend like a damn teenage girl, wishing I could see her gorgeous self and hear her beautiful laugh again. But now that I'd seen her, I found it pained me, knowing that she was sharing that part of herself with someone else. I still didn't understand how she could go back to a guy like Vic. I knew they had history but still...

My meal with Ingrid went well. Even though she tried, we didn't talk much about the pregnancy. I wasn't willing to involve myself in that any further until I spoke with the doctor this week. She was a nice enough girl, but there was only one girl I wanted sitting across the table from me.

Late morning, Skye buzzed through to my office.

"Mr. Steele?" She sounded hesitant.

"Yes?"

"Your father is out here to see you."

Why the hell did everyone think it was okay to just show up at my work without warning all of a sudden?

I walked out of my office to see that my father was in fact standing there chatting with Skye. He looked the same as the last time I'd seen him, which had been months ago. Maybe there was a little more gray in his hair, but besides that he looked unchanged. When Skye turned toward me, she looked at me with sympathy, knowing full well where I stood when it came to my dad. I didn't want or need her sympathetic looks. What I needed was for her to look at me the same way she did when we were together.

"Dad, what are you doing here?"

"Well, since you seem to be too busy to call your old man back, I thought the only way I'd get to talk to you would be to show up here."

I flashed a look over to Skye. "Hold my calls."

My dad followed me into my office and took a seat.

"I don't appreciate you just showing up here unannounced. I'm very busy."

"I know how busy you are, son. I couldn't be prouder of how successful you've become."

"Great. I can die a happy man. Let's get to why you're really here."

He bit the inside of his cheek before speaking. "You know why I'm here, Landon. I can't stand how strained our relationship is." He ran his hand through his hair, a habit borne out of frustration that I recognized in myself.

"Do I have to remind you that was all your own doing?"

"I realize that, son. I messed up. No one is sorrier for the pain I inflicted on you and your mother than I am, but how long are you going to continue punishing me?"

I smacked my hands down on my desk, the frustration of the past week finally spilling over. "Do you have any idea what it was like to have my entire life uprooted in high school? To find that everything I knew growing up was a lie?"

"It wasn't a lie. I lost myself when my job went to shit. My identity was so wrapped up in that job that once it was gone, I didn't know who I was. I felt like such a failure and disappointment...I was scared to tell you and your mother what happened."

"So you just decided to ignore it? And what? Magically, everything would work out?"

"I realize now that I was in a depression and made choices that I wouldn't have made otherwise." He held his hand up to stop me from speaking when he saw I had a retort on the tip of my tongue. "It's not an excuse. I did those things and I have to live with the consequences, I know that. I just hoped that maybe we could get to a place where we could start to rebuild our relationship. I miss my son and I'm not getting any younger. I really want to be a part of your life, Landon." He had tears in his eyes and a small portion of me felt horrible for being the cause of that. But my mind was immediately assaulted with visions of my mother sobbing on the couch, not eating or showering for days, and immediately any sympathy I had for him dried up.

"You have no idea how much mom suffered because of what you did. She was a mess. You want to talk about depression? I know all about it because I had to watch her go through it after you completely devastated her. *I* was left to pick up the pieces—not you. I shouldn't have had to but I did."

"I don't deserve your forgiveness, son. I know that. And I don't expect you to ever be okay with all the bad choices I made. But I'd really like it if we could find a way to be in each other's lives again. Haven't you ever found yourself in a situation you didn't know how to deal with? Have you never made a mistake you wish more than anything you could take back?"

Fuck. Those two statements right there were the only reason I allowed the door to my heart to crack open for him. Because I did know what it was like to wish you could take back something you did. If I could go back, I would have never taken Ingrid home with me that night. The two situations were entirely different, of course. I didn't have a wife and kid at home, but I could empathize with the gnawing feeling in your gut when you wished you could go back and rewrite history.

My dad looked at me with a hopeful look on his face as I wrestled with my emotions. Recalling my mom's words when she said that having some kind of relationship with my father *wasn't* a betrayal, I struggled to let go of the anger I had toward him. It was the only feeling I'd allowed myself to feel for him for so long that anything else felt foreign.

"I'm not going to get into it with you, but let's just say that I *can* understand what that's like." I paused and took a deep breath, almost unable to believe what I was about to say. "I can't give you the kumbaya moment you're looking for dad, but I will make an effort to try. I'll see if I can put the resentment aside enough so that we can at least maintain some sort of relationship."

He smiled bigger than I'd seen since I was a teenager. "That's all I'm asking, son."

"I can't make any promises."

"I know. I'm just happy you're willing to try. Maybe next

week we could go for a beer and catch a game somewhere?"

"Give me a call mid-week." He gave me a look that I remembered from my childhood, the one that said he didn't believe a word coming out of my mouth. "I'll answer."

He stood from the chair and I came around to show him to the door. He clamped a hand on my shoulder. "Thanks for seeing me today."

"No problem." I could tell he wanted to hug me, but we just weren't there yet. I turned to open the door and he made his exit, saying goodbye to Skye as he left.

I sat back down at my desk but couldn't get my mind on work yet. I had to admit that it felt a little like some of the emotional weight I'd been carrying around had been lifted. We hadn't taken a big step, but I suppose it was a small shuffle in the right direction. Although I didn't think we'd ever get back the relationship we once had, it would be nice if I could think of my father at some point without the burning anger that had been there for years.

"Are you okay?" I spun my chair around to see Skye standing in the doorway, looking all kinds of concerned. My immediate reaction was to tell her everything I'd just been thinking, but I caught myself in time. She'd made it perfectly clear she didn't have any feelings for me—that what we'd shared had been purely physical—and whether I thought there was more to it or not, her actions indicated that everything she'd said was true.

"I'm fine. Why?" I asked in a clipped tone.

"I know how difficult things are between you and your father...I just thought...well, I wanted to see if you're okay."

"That's really not your concern anymore, is it?"

She looked like I'd slapped her. "I'm sorry, I—"

"I spoke with Chelsea this morning," I interrupted her, not wanting to hear what she had to say at this point. "Calder is prepared to sign the contract next week when he gets back to Los Angeles. He's traveling right now. I need you to book me a flight out on Monday morning. I'll be staying two nights. Make the arrangements please."

Originally, we'd planned for her to go with me to L.A. when the actual contracts were being signed, but things were different now. Her lips pursed into a thin line, so I knew she'd caught the drift of what I was implying.

"Yes, Sir." She turned to leave.

"Oh, and book me a different hotel than the last time. I have no desire to revisit the past." She paused momentarily and then continued on to her desk.

I don't know why I said that—it was unnecessarily cruel. But after telling me how there was nothing but sex between us and then coming in here looking concerned for my emotional well-being, I hadn't been able to hold back. It didn't make me feel any better though because hurting Skye was the last thing I wanted to do—no matter how much she'd hurt me.

chapter thirty-six

Landon

Friday couldn't come soon enough, and I looked forward to it with both dread and anticipation. I had every hope that the doctor was going to tell me we had some other option to discover the paternity of the baby besides an amnio or waiting for the kid to be born. I'd googled 'amniocentesis' myself, and it seemed that Ingrid was right about the risks involved. If it *was* my child in her belly, I didn't want to take those risks either.

But having my life on hold for the next two months until the baby was born seemed like slow torture to me. Not knowing if Ingrid was telling the truth, I didn't know if I should try to get closer to her and the child growing inside her.

Ingrid looked anxious as we sat in the waiting room. Her foot hadn't stopped tapping since we'd arrived, and she was more fidgety than usual.

"Ms. Patterson," the nurse finally called.

We both rose and followed her down the hall until we reached one of the exam rooms. When we got settled, Ingrid on the exam table and me in the chair beside it, the nurse went through what I assumed must be the usual round of questions. How are you feeling? Is the baby moving? Any concerns? She took Ingrid's weight and blood pressure and measured her belly.

When she finished, she shoved Ingrid's file in the holder on the back of the door, advising us that the doctor would only be a minute.

Sure enough, a moment later a middle-aged man with a receding hair line walked in, grabbed the file from the back of the door, and began to look through it.

"Dr. Lee, this is Landon Steele," Ingrid said to get his attention.

I shook hands with the doctor. "Pleasure to meet you," he said. "Well, it looks like everything is going well here, Ingrid. I don't have any concerns, but we should probably move your visits up to every week now. Is there anything you'd like to discuss with me?"

"Actually, there is something we'd like to discuss, doctor," I said.

"What can I help you with?"

"There seems to be some question as to the paternity of the baby," I said and was impressed that his face remained passive at this news. Guess it wasn't the first time he'd heard situations like this. "I've looked up amniocentesis and I agree that the risks aren't worth taking. What I'd like to know is if we have any other options to figure out the paternity, rather than waiting until the baby is born?"

I looked over to Ingrid. She was looking down at the floor, probably embarrassed.

"I see. I have to agree that an amnio poses certain risks that aren't worth taking at this late stage in the pregnancy. At this point, I'm afraid your only option is to wait for the child to be born and then do a DNA test."

"Thank you, Dr. Lee," Ingrid said quickly.

"I'm sorry I don't have anything better to tell you. I'm sure the waiting is difficult."

"I appreciate your time today," I said as I shook his hand again.

"It was good to meet you, Landon."

He placed the file back in the holder and left us alone.

"I told you we'd have to wait," Ingrid said.

"I know you did, and I wasn't trying to call you a liar. I'd just like to know one way or another which way my life is headed."

"I guess I understand." I helped her into her jacket and opened the door, letting her lead the way. "Did you want to go get something to eat? Maybe we could pick something up and go back to your place?"

It was getting harder and harder to politely deny Ingrid's advances to *get to know one another*. She was a nice enough girl, but if we weren't having a child together, I wouldn't be spending any time with her. The girl I wanted to be with was spending her time with some douchebag.

"There's a new place over on Main Street I wouldn't mind checking out. Maybe we could just go there?" I suggested. At least then she wouldn't be at my place.

She shrugged. "Alright, I guess."

We made it to the end of the hall when I realized that I'd forgotten my jacket back in the exam room. "Shit, I left my jacket in there. You wait here. I'll only be a minute."

I made my way back down to the exam room we'd just left and knocked softly on the door. I guess they hadn't filled the room yet because no one answered, so I opened the door and peeked in. Empty. I grabbed my jacket off the chair. When I turned to leave, I noticed Ingrid's file still in the holder on the back of the door.

I knew I shouldn't look at it, but something about the whole situation didn't sit right with me. In my gut, I knew that file would give me the answer.

I grabbed the file from the holder and quickly rifled

through the paperwork. Most of it didn't mean anything to me. Results for blood tests, ultrasounds, and other scribble-scrabble obviously written by the good doctor. It wasn't until I looked at the paper stapled to the left-hand side of the folder that I found what I was looking for.

It was a patient information card with Ingrid's name, date of birth, allergies, etc. What I was interested in was the part that read:

Due Date: February 24

She'd told me she was due at the end of March. I knew when we were together, because it'd been the Fourth of July holiday weekend. I did the math in my head and realized that there was no way I could have fathered her baby. If she was due in February, it mean she'd gotten pregnant at the beginning of June.

She was already pregnant by the time we'd spent the night together! Sweet relief mixed with anger. I wasn't ready to be a father yet, and I certainly didn't want to have a child with someone I didn't even know.

I quickly replaced the file, put my jacket on, and made my way back down the hall to the waiting room. Ingrid and I were going to have a *serious* conversation.

She must have been able to tell when she spotted me that something was wrong, because it was written all over her face. "Is everything okay?" she asked nervously.

"Just peachy. Let's get out of here." We didn't say a word again until we exited the elevator. "Did you drive here?"

She shook her head. "No, I took the bus."

"Good. Follow me to my car. We need to talk." By the time we'd reached my Audi, she had tears in her eyes. "Get in." She did as I said without argument.

I started the car to get the heat going but didn't pull away. I sat for a moment, taking deep breaths in an attempt to control the anger that simmered below the surface.

"Landon—"

"What I don't understand is how you thought you'd pull it off? You had to know I'd want a DNA test."

She hunched over and started crying uncontrollably. I was pissed but I wasn't a complete asshole. I didn't take any pleasure in seeing this pregnant girl sobbing beside me—even if she did try to deceive me. "I didn't know what else to do."

"Maybe tell the *real* father that you're pregnant?"

She composed herself a little and wiped the tears from her face with her sleeve. "He knows. He doesn't care anymore."

"How can a guy who knows he's having a baby not care?"

"We were together for a couple of years. We broke up and I went on a bit of a tear afterward. That's when you and I met. He and I got back together, but he found out that while we were broken up, I'd been with a few other guys and he threw me out. Called me a slut and asked how I could possibly know he was the father."

The tears started again and she was near hysterics, so I leaned toward her and wrapped an arm around her shoulder. "He'll come around. I'm sure he was only angry."

She shook her head back and forth frantically. "It's been a couple of months and he still won't take my calls."

"Where are you staying now?"

"At my sister's. But I can't stay there after the baby is born, and I don't make enough to get my own place and support a baby."

I pulled away from her. "That doesn't give you the right to lie to me and try to rope me into something that isn't my responsibility. What if I had helped raise this child and the truth came out years later?"

"I was desperate," she cried, "I didn't know what else to do. You were the only one of the other guys that I was able to track down. When I saw how well you were doing, I told myself that it didn't matter since you had lots of money to spare. And you seemed nice that night we met."

I ground my back teeth. I was furious with this girl, but

she was pregnant and had enough to deal with in her life at the moment. I didn't think I'd get any satisfaction by coming down on her with a sledgehammer, even though it was my impulse to do so.

"And the DNA test?"

"I wasn't sure. I thought maybe if we spent some time together before the baby was born, you might like me and want to stick around anyway."

This girl was delusional, but I wasn't going to tell her that. "Look, you have to try to work this out with the father. I'm sorry that he's being an ass of epic proportions, but what you did was in no way okay. Did you give any thought about what would happen if the real father did come back into the picture down the road?"

"No." She sniffled a bit. "I couldn't think of anything except how my baby and I were going to survive."

My heart went out to her. She was in a shitty spot, but there really wasn't anything I could do to fix it for her.

"Look, I'm sorry there's nothing I can do to help." She nodded and looked out the passenger window. "I'll drop you off at your sister's, if you want."

"That'd be good. Thanks."

She gave me the address and we drove in silence. It didn't take too long. When she opened the door to get out of the car, I exited and went around the other side to help her out. Navigating that belly in and out of cars didn't look like an easy thing to do.

"Thanks for the ride," she said quietly.

"Ingrid, after you have the baby...if you need a job or something, give me a call. I know a lot of different business owners in town—they're clients of mine. Maybe I can put in a good word for you with one of them."

Her eyes welled with tears. "Thanks, Landon. I really wish this baby was yours. You'll make a great father someday," she said and walked toward the house, leaving me stunned and speechless.

chapter thirty-seven

Skye

A Friday night date with Vic. I was completely dreading this. During our last couple of dates, Vic had become increasingly impatient with my unwillingness to forge ahead with our physical relationship. No matter how I framed it in my mind, I couldn't stand the thought of Vic kissing me—let alone the idea of being intimate with him. Landon and I may not be together anymore, but he still held my heart and it felt traitorous to even entertain the thought.

Vic had planned an evening in at his place tonight—a homemade dinner and a movie. I knew tonight he was going to be expecting our "take-two" relationship to move forward. My excuses were only going to take me so far, and that was what scared the hell out of me.

We'd just finished a chicken stir-fry dinner, which wasn't actually half bad. I could barely eat anything though because my stomach was in such turmoil with the knowledge of what was sure to come next.

I'd just finished putting my dishes in the sink when on cue, Vic suggested we head to the living room with a bottle of wine to "relax." Maybe wine would be good to calm my nerves.

"I'll open the bottle and pour us a glass. Why don't you go chill? I'll be there in a second."

"Okay." I tried to keep my voice even, which was a difficult feat at the moment.

I purposely took a seat in the armchair so Vic wouldn't be able to sit beside me. As I waited, I looked around. Vic's place was in direct contrast to Landon's. It was urban, cold, and sterile with ice gray walls and sleek contemporary furniture. It struck me what each man's environment said about the real man underneath the façade. Vic, upon first glance, appeared to be warm, respectful, and every bit the gentleman. Landon initially seemed aloof, intense, and intimidating. Turns out the opposite was true of both.

"Here you are." Vic pulled me from my thoughts by holding the wine glass in front of me.

"Thanks." I took a bigger swig than was probably ladylike, but I wasn't trying to impress him. On the contrary, I'd been secretly hoping that by this point he would've been over his competitive need to win me back. No such luck.

Instead of going to sit on the couch across from me, he perched himself on the edge of the coffee table, sitting just inches away.

"Cheers," he said and clinked his glass with mine. "I'd like to make a toast to new beginnings. To leaving the past where it belongs and starting fresh." I smiled and took another sip from my glass.

After he took a sip from his glass, he continued,"You must've had a long day at work. You're really tense tonight."

"I guess, yeah."

"Come here," he said, taking my glass to set it on the table and then reaching for my hand to lift me to my feet. He placed his hands on my shoulders and turned me so that my back faced him. The minute I felt his hands on my shoulders, I knew I was in trouble. "Let me massage some of this tension out of you, baby."

I couldn't speak, my tongue suddenly feeling like it had grown five times larger than normal. Alarm bells rang in my head at the same time my mind flashed back to when Landon had given me similar treatment at his place, and I recalled how it had elicited a completely different reaction in me.

Instead of relaxing me, Vic's hands made me even more tense and I had to fight the urge to squirm out of arm's reach. I took a couple of deep breaths, hoping to fight off my body's natural reaction. My heart was pounding in my chest and the blood rushing through my body was whooshing in my ears.

I sensed Vic inch closer to me. His hands moved from my shoulders further down my back, his fingers massaging into my skin through my t-shirt. His lips met my neck and his hands moved under my arms to grope my breasts.

I immediately stiffened and cringed, fighting back tears. If I couldn't do this, everything my dad and Landon had worked for would suffer. I tried to keep this in mind, but when Vic started feathering open-mouth kisses up my neck, my mind flashed to what he might do next, where he might put his hands. The idea and the images it brought to mind were abhorrent to me.

I wrenched from his grasp and spun around to face him, hot tears running down my cheeks now. "I can't do this! I can't do this!" I buried my face in my hands.

When I lifted my head to look at him, I saw the menacing look on his face. "What do you mean?" he said between gritted teeth.

"I don't want to be with you! I don't love you! I don't even like you. And I can't stand to have your hands on me." I raced over to the kitchen to grab my purse, fearful of what reaction my words might provoke in him.

"You know what's at stake here, Skye. You sure you want to do this?"

I had a split second where I reconsidered what I was doing, but I knew it wouldn't make a difference. In the end, I'd still end up in the same place—unable to be with him because I was in love with a different man.

"I don't want to see you. Don't call me, don't text me, don't come to my work. I want you out of my life for good!"

I bolted for the door and raced down the hall, not stopping to look back and see if Vic was following. When I reached the elevator, I heard Vic's voice ring out behind me, "You'll be sorry when your tits are plastered across every tabloid in this country, you little bitch!"

The elevator dinged and when the doors opened, I stepped in and stabbed at the ground floor button. I couldn't think about that right now, I just had to get out of here.

I walked through the large oak doors of my parents' house, the dread a heavy stone in my stomach. Between telling my parents and Landon, the conversation with my dad was the one I dreaded the most. He still looked at me like I was his little girl. I knew he'd be disappointed, and I hated letting him down. I just hope his campaign could recover from the scandal.

"Mom...Dad," I called through the house, my voice shaky. My dad emerged from the den with his arms out at his sides.

"What a wonderful surprise. I didn't know you were coming by tonight," he said.

I approached and he embraced me in a hug. I felt so safe and protected here in his arms, almost as if everything else wasn't really happening—but it was. And it was time for me to face it head on, no matter how badly I wanted to run and hide.

I pulled away and looked up at my dad. "Honey, what is it? What's wrong?"

Unshed tears were already clouding my vision. "Where's mom?"

"She's out at a charity dinner. Are you going to tell me

what's wrong?" he asked and the concern in his voice was already breaking my heart.

I sniffled. "Yes, this can't wait."

I walked into the den. I'd always thought this was the coziest room in our house with its oversized wood-burning fireplace and bookshelves lining many of the wood-paneled walls. I took a seat in one of the old-fashioned armchairs where I used to curl up at all hours of the day and night.

"I have something to tell you. A few things, actually, but you're not going to like any of them."

My dad grabbed a tissue off his desk and passed it to me before sitting in the chair opposite mine. "Okay. Start at the beginning."

I went through everything with him—and I mean, *everything*. The deterioration of my relationship with Vic, the scene of our breakup, the way I'd fallen for Landon, and Vic's subsequent blackmail. He sat, not saying a word, not interrupting. Ever the politician, I couldn't read his face one way or the other as to how angry and disappointed he was with me.

When I finished speaking, he stood from the chair and walked over to me. He motioned for me to stand and when I did, he enveloped me in a crushing hug.

"Oh sweetie, why didn't you tell us what was going on with Vic? You've been dealing with all of this on your own this whole time?"

I broke out into the ugly cry, sobbing for what I'd forced my dad to deal with and for not believing in him to stand by me and offer his support.

"I'm sorry, daddy. I should never have taken the picture. I don't know what I was thinking. I'm so embarrassed."

He ended our embrace and held me away from him by the shoulders. "Sweetie, you're only twenty-two. You're going to make mistakes and have errors in judgment. It happens. I've always expected you to do your best, but I never expected perfection. I hope you know that."

I broke down again. When I'd wiped my tears away with tissue and composed myself once again, my father's tone changed from comforting to confrontational.

"I could kill that little shit for putting his hands on you. You should have told your mother and me about it when it happened."

"I was embarrassed and you had enough on your plate. I didn't want to be a bother."

He cupped my face in his hands. "You are *never* a bother my dear. Ever. Heaven forbid, but if anything like that were to happen again, I want you to promise me that you'll come to me."

"I promise, daddy."

"And I want you to leave Vic to me. He and I are going to have a little chat and see if we can't come to an understanding."

"I don't want you to get yourself in any trouble. You'll put the Senate race at risk."

"Honey, if those pictures come out, it's already at risk. I don't say that to upset you but it's the truth. I need to try and get him to change his mind."

"I'm sorry for all the trouble I've caused."

He took a deep breath and exhaled on a sigh. "I'm disappointed you took the picture, okay? But I can't change it and right now I need to do damage control." I nodded. "You go home and get some rest, honey. You look like you could use it."

"I have to go home and figure out how I'm going to break the news to Landon. This will affect him, too."

"This Landon, is he a good man?"

"The best, daddy. But it doesn't matter. He'll want nothing to do with me after all this comes out anyway."

My dad gave me a small smile. "Not if he's the man you think he is, sweetie."

243

My dad called later that night to tell me that no amount of reasoning would change Vic's mind. There wasn't even any way to hold the fact that he hurt me over his head—too much time had passed and it was his word against mine. My dad had even gone so far as to call Vic's father about the situation and even *he* couldn't reason with his son. I'd held out little hope that my dad's talk would make a difference—I'd seen what a vindictive person Vic was.

I apologized again to my dad. It was late but he was on his way to meet with his campaign manager to figure out a plan of action to deal with the shitstorm that was surely coming his way.

chapter thirty-eight

Skye

At least I hadn't had to beg Landon to agree to let me come over the next morning. When I called him, he'd said that there was something he wanted to talk to me about as well. I had no idea what it could be, but that didn't matter. I had to get out what I needed to say before I lost my nerve.

He opened the door and the fragile shell that was my heart cracked a little more, knowing what I'd have to tell him and the negative effect it was bound to have on his business.

"Come on in, Skye."

I still loved hearing him say my name. "Thanks."

I stepped inside and walked down the corridor to the living room. Being back in his apartment was bittersweet and surprisingly, everything looked the same as the last time I was here. I didn't know why, but I expected it to look different somehow—maybe because things between us were so different than how they'd been then.

"Can I take your coat?"

I turned to face him. "I think I'll leave it on. You're

probably not going to want me to stay very long once I tell you what I have to say."

He let out a sigh and ran a hand through his hair. "It can't be any worse than the last time you were here. Have a seat."

I sat down on one end of the sofa. He sat at the other. It didn't escape me that our seating arrangements were a perfect example of the emotional divide between us.

"So, what's going on?" He looked at my face and, like a switch had been flicked, his contorted into one of rage. "It doesn't have to do with Vic, does it? Did he hurt you again?"

"Yes and no."

Landon sprung up off of the couch. "That son of a bitch! I'll fucking kill him."

"It's not what you think. Sit down."

"If he laid a finger on you, Skye..."

A warm feeling invaded my chest, because on some level he must still care if he was that angry at the thought of Vic hurting me. "Vic and I aren't together anymore. I ended things with him, and I never should have gotten back together with him."

He took his seat back on the couch, a little closer to me this time. "Pretty sure that's what I've been saying all along."

"Let me finish, please, before you say anything." He nodded tersely. "Back when Vic and I first started dating, he went away on a business trip. While he was away, he convinced me to send him a picture of me...topless. Things were good between us at the time and I had no reason not to trust him, so I sent it. I hadn't thought anything of it until after Vic showed up at my place that afternoon you were there. He left me a note later saying I needed to contact him and inside the note was a copy of *that* picture.

"He told me that if I didn't want the picture to become public, I'd break up with you and give him another chance. I couldn't let him do that, and not because of how embarrassing it would be for me. I wouldn't like it but I'd deal. What I couldn't deal with was that a stupid, hasty decision *I'd* made would hurt two people I care so much for."

I wasn't sure how Landon was reacting to my news, since the mask he used for business was firmly in place. "You didn't want to hurt your parents," he stated.

"No. Well, yes, but that's not what I meant. If that picture got out, I knew it would be devastating to my father's campaign. But the other person I was referring to was you. When the assistant to the owner of a PR firm has a PR nightmare of her own, it isn't exactly good advertising for the business. Especially when you're so close to setting up shop in L.A. Celebrities aren't going to want to be tied to someone with as many issues in the press as they have."

"Why are you telling me this now?" The mask was slipping, and he seemed angry.

"Because I couldn't do it. I couldn't be with Vic. I tried, Landon, I really did for your sake and my dad's, but I can't stand him. My skin crawled every time he touched me."

Panic flashed across his face. "Did you and he...?"

"No! Absolutely not. Lying to you and making you believe there was nothing between the two of us but sex was the hardest thing I've ever had to do. You meant so much to me...hurting you was—"

"I meant so much to you, yet you made this monumental decision on your own? You didn't even tell me he'd gotten in contact with you after promising me that you would!" Definitely angry. My mind couldn't help but draw comparisons between him and Vic. I cut that train of thought off immediately though. He had every right to be angry with me, and someone being angry didn't mean they were capable of hurting me the way Vic did.

"That day I came over to your place I had planned on telling you, but then Ingrid showed up and everything got messed up. I didn't want to add another complication to your life. I also knew there would be no chance for us anyway with you finding out you were going to be a father. You probably would have tried to help me, sacrificing yourself and your business in the process, because that's the type of guy you are."

"So now you're judge, jury, and executioner? Is that how it is? You didn't even give me the choice, Skye! You had no right to make that decision for me," he said sounding more hurt than angry. "We were a couple! I might not have had a lot of experience with that sort of thing, but I do know that real couples talk about the problems they come up against. And real couples keep their promises when they make them. *Real* couples don't make decisions that hurt the other person without giving them a say."

I had nothing. What could I say? It was all true. Every word. But I *hadn't* thought of it that way. I thought I'd done the right thing by trying to protect him. "I'm so sorry I hurt you, Landon." My eyes welled with tears and I willed myself to stop them—I was forever crying in front of this man. I swallowed past the lump in my throat and the pain in my chest.

"So, how did your little plan work out for you? I assume you're here because the minute you ditched shithead, he said he's going to the press with the picture."

I nodded my affirmation. "I wanted to tell you before you saw it."

"Gee, thanks for that. Now you decide to tell me when it's too late for me to do anything to help you. I thought we trusted each other—"

"I did trust you," I said and then quickly amended, "I do."

He shook his head vehemently. "No. If you trusted me, you would have called me the minute you saw that note from Vic."

I couldn't hold back the tears now. "But I did it for you, Landon. *Because* of my feelings for you. Can't you see that?"

"What I see is a girl who said she trusted me but didn't. A girl who acted out of fear in an effort to protect people she cared about, but instead ended up destroying something that could have been really wonderful—something that never even got a chance to get off the ground."

I wiped the tears from my face. "I don't know what else to say."

"There isn't anything else to say. We'll need to issue a statement as soon as possible. If we can get it out before the picture is released, maybe we can minimize some of the collateral damage."

"What do you want me to do?"

"Just get me the name and number of your dad's campaign manager. They're going to want to see our statement before we release it, and we should make sure whatever we say is going to jive with whatever statement they're going to release."

I nodded. "I can do that. What are you going to say?"

He ran a hand through his hair. "I need to give it some thought. I'll probably spin it into what a douchebag Vic is, which shouldn't be hard to do. I'll say you were in a committed relationship with someone you trusted and never imagined that he would release it because he was angry you'd moved on with your life."

"Please don't mention anything about him hurting me. It's his word against mine, and something like that will just get dragged through the press for months."

He put a hand on my shoulder and squeezed it reassuringly. "That's your private business. I'm not going to say anything about it."

I put my face in my hands. "Everyone is going to see. It's so embarrassing."

Landon reached over and pulled my hands away. "Well, it's a good thing you have a fabulous rack then," he said with the first humor I'd heard in his voice in what seemed like forever.

I smacked him across the arm. "I'm serious."

He shrugged. "I know. Just trying to lighten the mood."

"Thanks for that. It's the first time I've smiled in a while."

We sat there in silence looking at each other. I'd royally fucked up. I'd hurt the man I loved, and I didn't know if he'd have it in him to forgive me. It hit me then that, in a way, I'd done the same thing that his father had so many years ago by not trusting him to be able to handle what I had to tell him.

"What about us?" I almost whispered.

He broke eye contact. "There is no us. That was your doing. I don't know if we can go back to where we were."

Keep it together. Keep it together. Inside it felt like my heart had splintered into a million pieces of glass, cutting me from the inside out. And I had no one to blame but myself.

"I understand." I rose from the couch to leave. I couldn't be near him anymore—not when he felt so far emotionally.

"I'm going to get something together and send it over to your dad's people before I issue the press release," he said as he stood. "Do you want to see it before it goes out?"

"I'm sure whatever you guys come up with will be fine. I'm going to go hide in my apartment for the foreseeable future."

"Well, I still expect you to be at your desk on Monday morning."

"Are you sure?" I figured he'd want to distance himself from me, and at the very least suspend me for a while, if not fire me altogether.

"We don't even know the effect this is going to have on our clients. Let's take it day by day, okay?"

"Okay. Thanks for not hating me."

He just gazed at me for a moment, searching my face. "I could never hate you, Skye. I'm just not sure what we can be right now."

Without a word, I showed myself out of his condo, the feeling of complete and utter loss gaining traction with each step I took that led away from him.

chapter thirty-nine

Landon

I grabbed a beer from the fridge and went to sit on the couch. I didn't give a shit if it was before noon—it was noon somewhere. I was still reeling from Skye's confession that had sent my entire plan into a fiery nosedive.

I'd planned to tell her about the doctor's visit with Ingrid and how I wasn't the father and then basically beg her to leave Vic. I knew I wasn't delusional and that what we had between us wasn't just about sex. It was more—way more. And come hell or high water, I had planned on getting her to admit it.

Damn it! How could she have kept this from me? She knew what my father had done to my family, how much pain and anguish his lies and deceit had caused in my life, and now she'd done the same thing. I understood that Ingrid showing up threw her for a loop, but she had every opportunity to tell me the next morning when I'd shown up at her house.

I was so conflicted. I knew her heart was in the right place, but how could I get past the fact that she'd kept it from me and hadn't trusted me to be able to handle it? She didn't have the right to decide that for me. And she broke her promise.

She'd *promised* to tell me if he contacted her again and she didn't. How could I ever believe a word she said again?

I brought the beer to my lips and downed the last of it. The old adage 'be careful what you wish' for was true. For weeks, all I'd wanted was to find out that I wasn't going to be the father of Ingrid's child and for Skye to be free of Vic. Well, I'd gotten my wish alright, but I couldn't imagine the distance between us being greater than it was right now and I didn't know if there could ever be an us again.

I set the empty bottle on the table and got up to head to my home office—I had a press release to prepare. I may not have been able to let Skye into my life and into my heart again, but I'd still do my best to help minimize the fallout from the impending scandal. Not to mention, I stood to lose a lot, too.

Skye

By Sunday afternoon, my naked selfie was splashed across almost every gossip magazine and reputable newspaper's website. Most had the black bar across my chest, but there were a few—the not-so-reputable sources—that decided to forego it.

Between my friends and the nosy reporters, my phone had been ringing off the hook since the moment the photo was revealed. Eventually, I just turned it off.

Landon and my dad's staff managed to beat the release of the picture and put out a statement calling Vic out on the piece of shit that he was. Judging by the comments, the consensus seemed to be that most agreed Vic was an ass for releasing the picture, but everyone seemed to agree that it was shameful that the daughter of a would-be Senator would behave so poorly and with such disregard for her father's career.

I stood in front of my mirror, dabbing concealer under my

eyes in an effort to reduce their red, puffy appearance but it was no use. I might as well just give up. I looked like a mess. I *was* a mess. There was no hiding it. I gathered my things and braced myself for dealing with the stalkarazzi downstairs.

Coat on, purse and lunch in hand, I went to grab my phone from the charger. I had it turned off all day yesterday and was afraid to see how many missed calls and texts I had. I hit the power button and without scrolling through my unread texts, pulled up Ellie's number and called her. I'd been avoiding both her and Katie's calls all day yesterday, but I needed to talk to a friend who would understand before I faced the world. Between the YouTube video and her life in the spotlight with Mason I knew Ellie would be able to relate. Thank God Katie had been out of town for the weekend or she'd be breaking down my door right now.

I thought perhaps she wasn't going to answer since she'd likely be sleeping because of the time difference but she picked up on the fourth ring. "It's about time! I called you a thousand times yesterday!"

"Sorry. I just didn't feel like talking to anyone."

"What's going on? Are you okay?" she asked with genuine concern in her voice.

"Not really." By sheer will alone, I held my tears back. "I'm sure you saw the picture."

"I did," she said quietly.

"Things with Landon have gone to shit, too."

"Oh, honey. What happened?" I quickly told her everything that had happened with Vic and Ingrid—the whole mess. When I finished she asked, "Do you think he'll forgive you?"

Unshed tears threatened to spill over. "No, I don't think so. It's a long story, but trust and lying is a big deal to him because of his past." I paused for a moment. "How am I going to face everyone at work today, Ellie?"

"You're going to do it with your head held high. Everyone makes mistakes, Skye, but you have nothing to be ashamed of."

I scoffed audibly. "I called Landon yesterday trying to beg off."

"What did he say?" she asked.

"He insisted that for outward appearances, it needed to be business as usual."

"As much as you don't want to hear it, he's probably right."

"I'm thankful Landon let me keep my job but I can't imagine walking in there this morning, knowing everyone has seen the picture. Now I have an idea how you felt."

Ellie laughed but there was a bitter edge to it. "There's no way around it, and I know how bad it sucks. But it doesn't matter what anyone else thinks of you. You know you're a good person. Whatever portrait the press decides to paint of you is out of your control. To everyone that knows and loves you, that won't matter. And to those that it does...well, they don't matter."

"I know you're right, but it still doesn't make it any easier. I'm sure there are a throng of reporters waiting for me downstairs."

"How did Landon tell you to handle it?"

"He gave me orders not to say a word to them, just make my way to the car and go to work like I normally would on a Monday morning. I'm supposed to show them that this was not that big a deal and I won't crumble and fall apart. He thinks the press will move on to the next juicy story once they see they aren't going to get a rise out of me."

"Then that's what you do. It's no different than when the press prints some bullshit story about Mason and me. Don't add any fuel to the fire. They'll catch the scent of some other wounded animal soon enough and move on."

"Thanks for the pep talk, El," I said, glad I'd decided to call her. Then, remembering the time difference, I added, "Sorry to call you so early."

"Please. If you hadn't called me by lunch, I was hopping on a plane to Virginia."

"I could use a friendly face. Maybe I shouldn't have called."

That got a small laugh out of her. "I know better than anyone how hard it is to be under the microscope but you just have to tune it out and go about living your life. I know you can do it, Skye."

We said our good-byes a few minutes later and I made my way down to the lobby. As expected, a mass of reporters were waiting for me outside my building. There was another mob were in the parking lot at work. I pushed through them without saying a word. Facing them seemed like easy work compared to having to look my co-workers in the eye this morning.

I stepped out of the elevator onto the floor that housed Steele and Associates, and all conversations immediately halted.

I took a deep breath. Here goes nothing...

chapter forty

Landon

I'd called an early morning meeting sans Skye to explain the situation to the rest of the staff. My directive went like this...no one was to make any comments to the media, all calls that made it through to Skye's desk had to be vetted first to ensure they weren't reporters, and no one was to mention the photo to her unless she brought it up first.

Skye was well-liked in the office and the sentiment had pretty much been what I'd expected—Vic was a complete douche for releasing the picture. My only hope now was that the media would see it the same way and run with that opinion in order to get some of the heat off Skye, my company, and her father's campaign. The only thing to do now was to wait and see how the world would react.

I noticed the usual murmur in the office died down suddenly, so I got up from my desk and walked into the main office area. Skye had just gotten off the elevator and was standing there, looking like a little lost puppy.

"Back to work, everyone." Skye's gaze turned to mine and she gave me a small smile, but it didn't reach her eyes. No sparkle whatsoever. She'd obviously been crying at some point this morning, or maybe she hadn't stopped since she'd left my place on Saturday. A pang of guilt went through me that I hadn't been there to offer her any comfort when she'd needed it the most.

She walked toward me with her head down, all of the confidence that usually radiated off of her now gone. My instinct was to wrap her in my arms, but I still didn't know if I could get past the fact that she had knowingly deceived me. I didn't want to offer her false hope either—somehow that seemed crueler to me than not offering comfort in the first place.

"How are you this morning?" I asked, for lack of anything better to say.

"Mortified, embarrassed, depressed...should I go on?"

"I think you covered it. Let's go talk in my office for a second." She nodded and when we reached my office, she immediately moved to sit on the couch. I closed the door behind me, hit the privacy switch, and joined her there.

"Shouldn't you be on a plane right now?" she asked.

"I postponed my meeting with Calder until later this week. This took precedence. I spoke with Chelsea this morning and she was very understanding."

That was a complete fabrication. I'd gotten an e-mail from Chelsea late last night stating that Calder had seen everything that was going on and was hesitant to sign on with the firm for the very reason I'd feared. I understood why he felt that way; he had enough scandal of his own and didn't need any more. I still hadn't figured out how I was going to put out that fire—but somehow I would.

"Landon, you can't cancel that meeting. This is what you've been working so hard to achieve. Go. I'll be fine."

I put her small hand in mine. "I know you'll be fine. You're made of stronger stuff than letting one picture bring you down."

"Have you seen what they're saying online? Have you

looked at the picture?" She was near tears again.

I hadn't been able to bring myself to look at the picture. Just knowing she'd sent it to Vic in an intimate moment between the two of them had my stomach in knots. I'd keep an eye on whatever slant the media was going to put on the situation, but I would *not* look at that picture.

"You need to stay away from any coverage, Skye. I'm serious. Let me handle it, and if there's anything you need to know about—I'll tell you." She didn't respond. "Looking at that shit is only going to make you feel worse." I gave her hand a small squeeze and then let it go.

"Fine. But what about the reporters? They were outside my apartment this morning when I left, and they're camped out in the parking lot downstairs."

"You know the drill. Ignore them, and whatever you do, don't react to any of the bullshit they yell at you. The last thing we need is a video loop of you telling a reporter to stuff it on the evening news."

"Okay." She sounded so defeated. I wished there were something more I could do to help her.

"Good. Now head over to your desk and get to work. I'm not paying you to sit around, you know," I said, clearly conveying with my tone that I was kidding.

I received a genuine half-smile as she got off the couch. "Thanks for the pep talk."

"Anytime."

She stopped and turned around to face me before she left. "I'm sorry for ruining everything."

"I told you, I'll work out the situation with Calder Fox."

She shook her head side to side as her eyes welled with tears. "No, I mean between us. I really did think I was doing the right thing." She shut the door behind her before I could say a word.

What would I have said anyway? I'm pissed at you for ruining us, too? Why didn't you think I could handle it? How could you betray me like my father did?

I pushed all of that to the back of my mind. I had some phone calls to make, and I needed to figure out how I was going to convince Calder Fox to sign with the firm. The easy answer was to get rid of the problem—the problem being Skye. But I knew getting her out of my office building wasn't going to get her out of my heart...or my head.

chapter forty-one

Skye

I watched from my desk as Landon left to grab some lunch. My heart broke a little every time I saw him, knowing he felt betrayed and would most likely be unable to forgive me. At the same time, his genuine concern for me and his attempts to help the situation where he could caused my heart to swell. I stopped myself before I traveled too far down that road though. Even if my current photo scandal was not an issue, Landon, becoming a father with another woman was.

I'd managed to get through the morning without having to discuss the situation with anyone, but it didn't escape my notice that everyone avoided my desk. I dreaded having to walk through the maze of desks to get to the kitchen to prepare my lunch, but the people here were too nice to be outwardly rude to me. At least, I hoped that was the case.

I grabbed some reports I'd prepared for Landon this morning so I could leave them in his office. I dropped them on his desk and as I went to leave, a name on the computer screen caught my eye. I wasn't snooping but he had a giant iMac screen on his desk—it wasn't hard to miss. I guess his computer hadn't shut itself down and gone into sleep mode yet.

I glanced nervously at the doorway, and when I was satisfied no one was around, I sat in Landon's chair and moved the cursor so I could see the entirety of the e-mail. It was from Chelsea...*Calder doesn't feel he can move forward...given the situation you're dealing with on your end...it's unnecessary to continue with our previously scheduled meeting...if she's still in your employment, we think it's best...*

Oh my God. Landon had lied to me. He hadn't postponed the meeting with Calder, they'd told him they were no longer willing to sign the contract because of the mess *I* was in.

Why? Why would he do that? He'd been working toward this for years and here it was within his grasp and he was throwing it all away because of me. I couldn't let him do this. I may not be able to do anything to save my father's campaign, but I sure as hell wasn't going to let Landon sacrifice his L.A. office dreams for me.

Landon

I returned from lunch to find that Skye wasn't at her desk. I sure as hell hoped she hadn't ventured out to grab something to eat—those fucking reporters were still down in the parking lot. If I'd been any kind of gentleman, I would've asked if she wanted me to pick her up something, but I'd been too preoccupied after receiving Chelsea's e-mail. I had needed to clear my head so I could figure out some kind of strategy to ensure I would keep Calder's business. I'd just sat down at my desk when Marci came flying into my office.

"Is the building on fire?" I asked.

"No, Sir. I just thought you'd want to know...Skye left here about forty-five minutes ago. I don't know what happened but she was visibly upset. I tried to calm her down and get her to stay, but she kept saying something about making things right. She wouldn't listen to me."

"Did she say where she was going?" What the hell could have happened in less than an hour?

"No. She just ran out of here in a hurry."

"Okay, thanks for letting me know, Marci."

"I'm worried about her." She stood, wringing her hands in front of her.

"I know. Me, too. I'll find her and see if I can figure out what's going on."

She nodded and left my office. Damn it! What made her bolt like that and where could she have gone? I sat there pondering before it came to me, and I knew exactly how I'd find out where she'd gone.

I moved some reports out of the way, hit the mouse to bring my computer back to life, and entered my password. Chelsea's e-mail still sat on the screen. Realization dawned on me when I looked down at the reports I'd just moved.

Fuck. Skye must have seen the e-mail. DAMN IT! I had a hunch where she might have gone, but I wanted to be sure. I went to Twitter and searched for her name. Sure as shit, a few media outlets had tweeted that she'd just been seen arriving at the airport.

I loved her for wanting to do what was best for the company, but I didn't want her to do this. Wait—I loved her? Did I? I *did* love her, I realized. If she was anyone else, I probably would have fired her to protect the company I'd worked so hard to build, but she *wasn't* just anyone.

She was the first girl I'd given my heart to, and I realized that just because she hurt me and I wanted to take my heart back, it didn't mean I could. She still held it in her delicate hands. Deep down, the truth was that I didn't want it back.

My father had made a mistake and I'd been carrying

around the resentment and anger about it for years. Skye had made a mistake, too, and I didn't want that to be our fate as well.

I had to tell her how I felt. Maybe together we could figure out how to put the puzzle of *us* back together.

chapter forty-two

Skye

The cab pulled up in front of Sur restaurant in Beverly Hills. I grabbed the last of my cash from my wallet and almost threw it at the driver in irritation. How could he have gotten lost trying to find this place? Wasn't it his job to know where all the hot spots in town were? I'd have to use my credit card to pay for my cab back to the airport since I'd come wholly unprepared, having only the clothes on my back and my purse when I left Virginia on the first flight to L.A.

As soon as I'd hopped off the flight, I'd called Chelsea's assistant. We'd spoken a few times before to set up the meeting that was supposed to take place today, and I'd convinced her to tell me where Chelsea was lunching so I could meet up with her. I managed to make her believe it was going to be a friendly surprise visit from Landon. I felt terrible for lying to her and I hoped that she wouldn't get in too much trouble for telling me, but it was the only way I could think of to track Chelsea down.

I walked inside and had I been there for any other reason, I probably would have stopped to admire the elegant, comfortable atmosphere and one of my favorite songs playing throughout the restaurant. But my only concern at this moment was to find Chelsea and set things right.

"Can I help you?"

I was definitely in Beverly Hills. The hostess looked like she could be walking the runway in a Calvin Klein show. "I'm looking for someone." I craned my neck to look around when I spotted her. Bingo. And she was dining with Calder. Perfect. "I found them. Thank you."

I quickly approached the table, feeling anxious and jittery. Calder was the first to spot me. He said something to Chelsea that made her look in my direction.

"Ms. Summers. This is quite the surprise. I thought we'd canceled our meeting for today?" Chelsea said.

"I'm sorry to interrupt your lunch. I really am, but I had to talk to you."

Calder pulled out a chair on the other side of the table. "Why don't you sit down?"

"I'm not staying, I just wanted to meet with you both face-to-face so I could tell you myself. I'm quitting Steele and Associates. I know you decided against signing with Landon because of my stupid mistake and all the heat I'm taking for it. I'm quitting and Landon can tell the press he fired me or whatever you prefer, but please don't back out of the deal because of me."

"This is really something we should discuss with Mr. Steele," Chelsea said, disapproval clear in her voice.

"Please. He'll do an amazing job for you. He cares about his clients and he works his ass off for them. He's full of inventive and fresh ideas and if anyone can turn your image around, it's him."

"Does he know that you're here?" Calder asked.

"No. Why?"

"Because he's coming up behind you and he doesn't look too stoked."

I whipped around to see that Calder wasn't lying. Landon

was here and most definitely was not...stoked.

"What are you doing, Skye?" he asked with barely restrained fury.

"I'm making things right. How did you get here?"

"After you ditched us at the office, I figured out where you'd gone so I followed you out here before you did something stupid. Looks like I'm too late."

"I just told Calder and Chelsea that I'm quitting. They can still sign with you and you can still have your dream of opening up shop in L.A."

"I didn't ask you to do that." He seemed a little calmer now—maybe. He pressed his fingers to the bridge of his nose.

"I know you didn't. You never would because that's the kind of guy you are, but I can't let you fall on the sword for me. Our relationship is already the collateral damage of my stupid decisions. I'm not going to let your business suffer, too."

"That's what I came to tell you." To my utter amazement, he framed my face with his hands. God, it felt so good to have his hands on me again. In true Mr. Mercurial fashion, he'd gone from hot-tempered to tender in about a millisecond. "These guys are expendable. If Calder doesn't want to sign, then I'll find someone else after the dust settles. But I could never replace you in my life. Never. You're like those one-of-a-kind vintage pieces you're always searching for. Rare, precious, and if I don't snatch you up while I have the chance, you can bet someone else will."

"Does this mean you forgive me from keeping the truth from you?" I near whispered.

"This means that I love you, Skye. It means I understand why you did what you did. It's the same reason I was trying to protect you from knowing what Chelsea's e-mail said. I've finally figured out that sometimes the people we love make mistakes, but if the intentions were good, we have to be willing to forgive—or at least try. And I do forgive you. I *choose* to forgive you because I still want you in my life. I know now that forgiveness is a choice." He rubbed my cheek with his thumb and I leaned into his touch.

"I love you too, Landon. So much. I couldn't stand being away from you—you're all I've thought about." He brought me into a crushing embrace and kissed the top of my head.

This was where I belonged. I was a fool to ever think I could deny myself of him. "Wait," I said, pushing away as I remembered something that could still stand in our way. "What about that girl...?"

He smiled jubilantly. "Not mine."

"Really?"

He nodded and then brought his lips to mine. I'd been starved of him for too long and my body reacted instantly. I pressed myself into him and dug my hands into his hair as our tongues tangled. His arms weaved around my back and one hand came to rest at the base of my neck, the other on my lower back.

Applause broke out around us and I quickly became aware of our surroundings...and the fact that we were in the middle of a crowded restaurant making out. I knew my face was the color of the setting sun, but I was surprised to see Landon give a small nod to the restaurant, even though he looked a little embarrassed, too. Which looked charming on him, of course.

He turned to Calder and Chelsea. "I didn't mean any disrespect when I said you were expendable. My apologies."

Calder was the first to speak up. "No problem, man. In fact, I'm rethinking things and maybe I spoke too soon when I said I wouldn't be signing with you."

"We should talk about this privately, Calder," Chelsea said, her voice stern.

"Nah. After that display there, I know all I need to about the people that'll be handling my PR. They're loyal—that's hard to come by in this town."

"Are you sure you want to do this?" Chelsea asked him.

"Are you kidding me, Chels? That was sick. I mean, come on. They're both basically tripping over each other to do the right thing for one another. That's what I want in the people working for me—that kind of commitment and loyalty to do what's right." He turned his attention back to Landon and me. "Do you happen to have the contract with you?"

The excitement was oozing out of Landon now. "No, but I'll need to check in at a hotel somewhere anyway, so I could get them printed in the business center."

"Perfect, man. You do that and then call me and we can meet up in a few hours to get it all put to bed."

Landon stuck his hand out to shake Calder's. "Thank you so much for the opportunity. We won't disappoint you."

"Be sure that you don't," Chelsea warned.

Landon put an arm across my shoulders. "Ready to go?" he asked me.

"Absolutely. Let's go check in somewhere." I had one thing on my mind and one thing only. I wanted to make love to this man. My man.

"Hey, dude," Calder said before we could go. "Make it this evening. You guys obviously have some making up to do." He winked at Landon.

"Great idea," Landon said. "I'll talk to you guys soon."

The next thing I knew, Landon had hoisted me up over his shoulder and was carrying me out of the restaurant. I giggled and squirmed and he smacked me on the ass.

"Come on, sweetheart. You heard the man. We have some making up to do."

He'd get no argument from me. This man had practically swept me off my feet when we'd met with only a gaze from across the bar. It was only appropriate that as we moved into the world as an official couple, he'd be doing the same—literally.

epilogue

Skye

"You're sure you can handle it?" Landon asked.

"Would you relax? It's not like it's my first time doing this."

"Sweetheart, you've never had this much power underneath you before."

"I beg to differ. It was only a couple of hours ago." I giggled.

"Don't remind me or we won't even get out of this parking lot."

"Behave, Landon."

"I'm nervous. No one has ever had control of her except me."

I rolled my eyes at him. "It's just a car. Why did you agree to let me drive it if you were going to act like this?"

He gave me *the look*—the smoldering one that could reduce me to ashes. "I was under duress at the time."

"Hmm...that's not how I remember it." I laughed and turned the key in the ignition. Mmm...the purr of the 454 horsepower under the hood of Landon's Chevelle made me smile wide.

"I wasn't exactly negotiating from a position of power when you had your hands and mouth all over my cock, now was I? I'm lucky I could form a coherent sentence, let alone be capable of making important decisions like this one." He reached over and squeezed my leg.

"Stop being such a baby. It's a beautiful day out. Just sit back and relax." I checked my mirrors and when it was all clear, I pulled out into traffic.

We were headed to the Virginia countryside to hit up some antique fairs in search of a couple of decorative pieces for my apartment.

The last few months together had been everything I'd imagined they'd be when Landon and I had first started dating.

As it turned out, someone in the restaurant at Sur the day that Landon and I rekindled our romance had filmed the entire scene. Once that video got out, it created such a splash that my topless selfie quickly faded into the background. Suddenly, the public and the media were rooting for Landon and I and our relationship, instead of trying to bring me down. Public sentiment turned nasty toward Vic, which was more than fine with me. Everyone thought Landon was the consummate romantic and we became America's sweetheart couple for a while there. Then some pop star was caught drag-racing in Miami under the influence and nobody paid attention to us anymore, which was even *more* fine with me.

My dad's campaign took a hit at first, but over the past few months he'd managed to claw his way back up in the polls and his chances of being elected to Senate were still looking good.

Landon and I drove in comfortable silence, tunes blaring. After a while, I turned down the music and looked at Landon.

"Where did you say this flea market was?"

"Just stay on this road for a bit. I'll tell you when to turn off."

"Are you sure? If we keep going, we're going to end up in North Carolina."

"Trust me, sweetheart." He leaned forward and turned the music back up—apparently our conversation was done.

We kept driving and Landon navigated until he finally directed me onto a small oceanfront road that wound through sand dunes and oceanfront properties.

"Landon, what's going on?"

He pointed to a blue house on the right. "That one, right there. Pull in the driveway."

I did as he asked and when the car stopped, Landon got out, came around to my side, and opened the door. I stepped out and gazed up at the huge house, which was set apart from all of the neighbors on the edge of the Atlantic. Landon took the keys from my hand and moved toward the trunk. He opened it and grabbed a pair of suitcases out of it, neither of which I packed or even knew we had with us.

I smiled. "Are you going to tell me what's going on now?"

"You and I are taking an extra-long weekend together. I've rented this place out so I can have you all to myself without any interruptions."

"Are you serious?" I ran and threw myself at him, straddling his waist. He dropped the suitcases to the ground to catch me and held me there.

"We've been so busy lately, and with all the travel back and forth to L.A., I felt like we needed it, so I recruited your mom to help me pull it off."

"Mmm. That explains things. She is the founding member of the I-Love-Landon fan club." I kissed him deeply. As our tongues tangled, I felt him grow hard underneath me. "Why don't we go check this place out? I want to show you what a fan I am, too."

"You don't have to ask me twice." He gripped me tighter

and walked toward the house with me still wrapped around his waist.

"Wait! What about the bags?"

"Later. I need inside you. Now."

I understood exactly what he meant. Our path to love hadn't been picture perfect, but the journey had been worth if it had meant we ultimately ended up here, in this moment—together.

– THE END –

a note to readers

I know that sometimes when I read a book I often wonder where an author gets their ideas from. It's with this in mind that I figured I'd share with you where a couple of ideas for Picture Perfect came from...

In the scene where Landon and Skye first meet and the guy vomits on her in the middle of the bar...yep, that happened to me! And I did exactly what Skye did—ran to the bathroom, stripped, and washed all my clothes off in the sink. The only difference being that I live in Canada and it was winter, so as soon as I stepped outside my entire outfit froze—completely! I was twenty and it wasn't "cool" to wear your coat into the club so, needless to say, I was pretty much a Popsicle. I can remember vividly to this day the feeling of warm liquid running down my exposed stomach and wondering what it was. Ewww!

Also, the penis in the shoe thing—real! Happened to a good friend of mine. LOL Why some random guy would send a stranger a picture of his penis in a shoe I'll never know, but stranger shit has happened, I suppose.

And finally, Landon's Chevelle. My dream car but also the car Wooderson drives in the movie *Dazed & Confused* (although a different color). So yep...a little bit of vicarious living there for me when Skye drives it in the epilogue.

I hope you enjoyed this latest installment of the Limelight series. There is more to come but keep turning the pages to get a glimpse at what I'm working on next!

XOXO
El

— Coming Fall 2014 —

MOMENT OF IMPACT

A Standalone Novel

They told me the driver of the semi had been drinking when he barreled into my car at sixty miles an hour, leaving only a mass of twisted and gnarled metal in its wake. It'd been a beautiful July day. I remembered that. One of those days when you left the house in the morning and you felt it in your bones that it was going to be a wonderful day.

I hadn't known anything was wrong until seconds before impact when I saw my friend's face twist in horror where she sat next to me.

I couldn't have predicted that by day's end, my loving husband and precocious two-year-old daughter would effectively be left a widower and a motherless child.

Who knew when fate was going to step up and show just what a cruel and sick bitch she could be?

I didn't know then but I now I do. Because six years later when I woke up from a coma, my husband had a new wife to love and my daughter had a new mommy.

My name is Annie, and this is my story...

— Coming Winter 2014 —

COLLATERAL DAMAGE

Limelight #3

Now trending

Hollywood It Girl, Francesca Leon, has just landed the biggest role of her career...one that could clinch an Oscar nomination and open doors. If she's going to move her career to the next level and work with top directors, she has to nail this part—and keep her sexy, but unreliable leading man from screwing everything up.

Team Calder

Bad boy Calder Fox is the son of Hollywood royalty and fresh out of rehab after his best friend's death sent him on a downward spiral of drugs and alcohol. While his fans still love him and the paparazzi continue to stalk him, he's never taken life, or anything about his career, seriously. He may be charming and drop-dead gorgeous, but if he doesn't stay sober, he could ruin Frankie's future and expose her long-hidden family secret to the voracious media.

Behind the scenes

During filming, Calder breaks through Frankie's defenses and their on-set romance soon develops into something hotter, deeper, and much more real. But when Calder is forced to choose between salvaging his last chance at a movie career or revealing Frankie's secret to the world, Frankie fears her days in Hollywood are numbered.

Elisabeth has a soft spot for happily ever-afters and a hot spot for alpha males. If she's not curled up somewhere with a romance novel in one hand and chocolate in the other you can probably find her typing madly on her keyboard creating her next story. She currently lives outside Toronto, Canada with her husband, two small children, and a killer cat.

One of the best ways to support an author is by leaving a review! If you enjoyed Landon and Skye's story I'd appreciate it if you'd consider leaving a review, whether short or long, on the retailer's site where you purchased the book. Alternatively if you prefer to leave your reviews on Goodreads you can click

Questions? Comments?

I love to hear from readers! Feel free to connect with me via e-mail at authorelisabethgrace@gmail.com at any one of the social media platforms listed below. I love talking books—even if they aren't my own! Also, if you enjoyed what you read and think you may want to join my Street Team, please drop me a line!

Website: Elisabeth-Grace.com
Facebook Profile: facebook.com/Elisabeth.Grace.790
Facebook Author Page: on.fb.me/1a5Ts4a
Twitter: @1elisabethgrace

Want to know when my next book comes out? Sign up for my newsletter by visiting my website. I take your privacy seriously. I will not sell your e-mail address. I will only contact you with important news like cover reveals, special giveaways for newsletter subscribers, and to tell you when a new book is available. I won't be spamming your inbox every week!

acknowledgments

To say that the warm reception readers gave the first book in the Limelight series, *Rumor Has It*, was surprising and overwhelming would be an understatement. So many of you took a chance on an unknown author and I couldn't be more grateful.

Someone asked me in an interview what the best part of being an author is and without hesitation I answered that it is connecting with other people who love to read. I've been beyond blessed to become friends with some amazing women—from readers to bloggers to fellow authors. The indie community is one of the most inclusive and supportive that I've ever been a part of, and I count myself lucky to be a part of it.

To the people that reached out to me to let me know that they enjoyed *Rumor Has It*—THANK YOU from the bottom of my heart!! It's scary to put your work out there and knowing that so many of you enjoyed it and even found yourself a book boyfriend in Mason couldn't make me happier!

They say it takes a village to raise a child...well, let me tell you, the same can be said for publishing a book. A huge thanks goes out to all the people below for helping me get *Picture Perfect* in top form...

To Regina Wamba from *Mae I Design* for her amazing talent in putting my covers together!

To my developmental editor Laura Shin who always has a great big picture view of the story.

To my fabulous line editor, Sheri Thomas...you are a talented writer, a kick-ass line editor, and a fabulous friend! I look forward to more projects together and hope I don't drive you too crazy (though I know you'll insist I don't).

To Angela Marshall Smith—your suggestions greatly improved my story! Thank you for investing time out of your busy life to help me. It's great to meet another girl who can make anything into something dirty!

To the beta readers that had a first look at a very rough version of the book...Shawna Donner-Gavas, Jessica Goldstein, Tracey Brewer, and Alexandria Erin. Thanks for taking the time out of your busy lives to help improve my story!

To Jennifer Wolfel who proofread the story and let me know all of her story pet peeves. LOL

Thanks to Amy Atwell from Author E.M.S. for holding my hand through the formatting for my first book. Your patience was appreciated!

To my brother, Kyle, who assigns everyone in my stories with his vehicle of choice by questioning me on character traits, jobs, and how they dress. I wouldn't know where to start so thanks for being my go-to.

I've been blessed to have a wonderful set of friends in my life...many of whom have been around for 20+ years. Thank you for all your enthusiasm as I pursue my dream! Your support and encouragement mean so much!

To all the bloggers who were early champions of my work...thank you for taking on an unknown author and being so generous with your time and spirit! It's my sincerest hope that I'll be able to continue creating stories that you'll want to share with the world.

Last, but by no means least, to my husband, Terry. It would not be possible to get these stories written and ready for publication without the support of this man. He very rarely grumbles when I'm engrossed in all think bookish and feigns interest when I rattle on and on about characters and storylines. He picks up the slack—and there is lots to pick up—when I'm writing and never makes me feel guilty for pursuing my dream. Babe, the note you sent me when you finished reading *Rumor Has It* in a San Diego airport that day are probably my favorite words *you've* ever written to me. Thank you. You are as much a part of this process as I am.